COVER STORY

COVER STORY

STILL DEADLY AFTER ALL THESE YEARS

RONNIE COHEN

BOOKLOGIX
Alpharetta, Georgia

This is a work of fiction. Names, characters, businesses, places, and events are either the products of the author's imagination or are used in a fictitious manner. All historical persons and events are written in the interpretation and understanding of the author and do not claim to be absolute truth.

ISBN: 978-1-6653-0322-4 - Paperback
ISBN: 978-1-6653-0728-4 - Hardcover
eISBN: 978-1-6653-0323-1 - ePub

These ISBNs are the property of BookLogix for the express purpose of sales and distribution of this title. The content of this book is the property of the copyright holder only. BookLogix does not hold any ownership of the content of this book and is not liable in any way for the materials contained within. The views and opinions expressed in this book are the property of the Author/Copyright holder, and do not necessarily reflect those of BookLogix.

Library of Congress Control Number: 2023910255

⊚This paper meets the requirements of ANSI/NISO Z39.48-1992 (Permanence of Paper)

070523

PART ONE

"Passing the baton while running
as fast as humanly possible,
is not as easy as it looks."

—Berta Rosenzweig

aron Spencer loves where he lives. He loves his small Tudor cottage at the edge of Hancock Park, his manicured, albeit postage-stamp yard, the smell of hibiscus near his front door. *"Hey Charlie,"* he calls out to the poodle next door and as he fumbles for his key, a Ralph's bag wedged against his hip.

Aaron tosses the bag onto the table in the hall and runs for the bathroom, not noticing there's someone standing in the dining room, waiting for his return.

That was close, he thinks. *Okay, chop the onions then . . .*

A hardball that turns out to be a fist throws him to the ground — he lays there panting, head spinning, and tries to work himself up to a seated position.

"PAY!!!" is what he thinks he hears.

"Don't . . . keep . . . cash . . ." he croaks.

Peripherally Aaron sees the guy getting ready to hit him again — he closes his eyes, he can't help but — and hears his mother's antique hall table get smashed to smithereens. He works to unhook his watch while trying to catch his breath —

"Here, take this, it's . . ."

"MONEY! You owe!"

He's going to get hit again, he sees the wind-up.

"Wait!"

But there's really no reason to wait. The hardball-fist connects squarely with Aaron's nose and the unmistakable sound of bone crunching echoes down through the Tudor hallway.

There's a momentary whiff of onion before he blacks out, blood rushing from where he lands.

CHAPTER ONE

On the far west side of LA, away from the hustle and bustle of the city, there's an old stone castle that sits five miles inland from the Pacific, hidden inside several acres overlooking the ocean. It's a setting not found on any map.

Like in a fairy tale, you reach it by driving a long, winding mountain road that ends at a gated sentry. Having said the magic words, the gate will open and you continue passed manicured lawns and gardens full of colorful, exotic flowers—each arranged in a complementary color palate—until you arrive at a circular drive with a fountain in its center. An imposing, Tuscan-like castle is nestled behind.

And if you're one of the lucky few to have come thus far, you could be excused for mistaking the castle for the home of royalty—it was clearly built for someone with extraordinary wealth, taste, and power.

Yes, this is where George Baxter lives.

And the cherry on top? Beyond the castle, with its turrets and balconies and lawns that go on forever, there are three mini-castles that dot the property, ones that are only seen from atop the main house steps, each magical, each with its own view cascading down the canyon to a sparkling blue Pacific.

It's in one of these that George has installed his brother Ira, insisting he lives there while he puts his life in order. Which is exactly what Ira's been trying to do—spending long days and even some nights toiling over his next screenplay.

But it's not going well.

———

"So, you're sure, Ira? You're positive?"

He's been trying to convince his cowriter, Phoebe, to take a different strategy.

"You keep whining about our deadline, so here it is, Phoebe, a fully realized character that checks all the boxes. We gotta go for it."

"I don't whine," she whines.

"We take what we get and we make it our own. That's what we do."

"But . . . another person? It's hard enough with just the two of us."

"Whattya mean? I'm the easiest person in the world to work with," Ira says.

"I was speaking of me," she says, picking up the paper plates left on an eighteenth-century ottoman. "Let me see that again."

"C'mon, Phebes, we're an award-winning team. This'll be our best one yet."

"Nominated—award-*nominated* team. Waiting and waiting to hear our names called."

"The call that never comes," he laughs, hoping she will too.

She does. "That dress cost a fortune!"

"What, the purple thingy?"

"What, you told me you liked it!"

"No. I said it, um . . . made a statement."

"Which was?"

"Pick me, please. Please," he uses his whiny Phoebe voice.

They laugh again.

"George will buy the rights to the whole thing. Just to keep it kosher. I don't want her coming back for points or god knows what else."

"So, Mr. Hollywood's back in town?"

"Not yet, but he lent me his Lamborghini while he's gone. That's some machine!"

"Oh. I didn't realize Miss Wyoming took your car as well as your house," she teases.

"Miss Utah—and you know she took everything."

"Oh spare me, Ira. This place? He throws in a sportscar? I should be so lucky." She makes her way to the blackboard through a pile of rejected ideas.

"So this says he's a small guy, under-nourished, thin greasy hair, creepy smile." She erases all their chalk marks. "Jewish. So that's something."

"With a strong Chicago accent," he says, trying for a Chicago accent, "that could be fun."

"And he's gay—well, possibly gay," she says jotting a note. "Yes, gay—that would change it up."

He stoops to kiss her on the forehead. "This is it, I can feel it."

Phoebe walks into the kitchen and returns with refreshments. "Let's hope so." Ira's beer looks tempting, but no way is she risking one, not even to celebrate. She pops open her Coke and contemplates the other hurdles that come next. Professional and personal.

"Okay, so let's get this Ross-lady signed up and we can start afresh Monday morning."

"You got it chief," he says.

"And we take it one day at a time," she says paraphrasing her AA mantra.

"Fine. And take your purple thingy to the cleaners."

CHAPTER TWO

Joan Ross has a headache and this day is for shit.

The latest rejection letter arrived this morning from a *highly placed* intern who has a *very important* position at a well-established New York publisher with *decades of credentials . . .* blah blah blah.

And she needs to deal with her creative director.

And Aaron isn't answering his phone.

Shit.

Jeff, the creative director, is pacing around her office, waiting for her to approve his layout.

"So—yes?"

"I wanted to shake them up," she complains.

"Yeah, I get it, but Grace thinks . . ."

"I know how Grace thinks. But this is crisis-time and we need to treat it like a crisis, not like a new attraction at Disneyland."

"This means you don't agree?" Grace saunters in after listening in at the door.

"Look; the sea is rising and nothing is being done about it. Nothing. It'll destroy us, wipe us off the map," Joan stands, headache pounding, "this must FRIGHTEN THE BEEJUS out of us!!!"

"How about I take another crack?" Jeff asks, backing out with the layout draped over his arm.

"You do that," Joan calls after him.

———

August 19, 2015, the day Joan's life changed forever—the day Grace Yuen's designer pumps crossed her threshold and nothing's ever been right at the magazine since.

Grace's preconceived notions about how the magazine should look, what readers want to read, nearly everything she believes runs counter to *Relevant's* long-standing tradition and Joan's own vision. Meetings end in conflict, sometimes screams, once in tears—Jeff's—and once with Joan's door slammed so hard that a pane of glass popped out and shattered on the floor. Joan swept up the shards but never bothered to replace the glass—it reminds her how much she despises the woman.

"I know you're new to the business," Joan is trying to be civil, "but we are not *Arch Digest* with banal content and pretty pictures. Trailer parks can be destroyed by global warming, not just bloody estates in bloody Brentwood."

"Well, I prefer looking at Brentwood and so does everyone else on the planet. Let's just see what *he* comes up with," Grace says, signaling the end to their little editorial discussion.

Grace may be a novice, but she's got balls. And dresses like a million bucks. The private equity firm she works for assigned her to watchdog *Relevant* once they made their investment in the magazine. It's why she's always hovering over Joan's shoulder.

"So, good news for a change," Grace says, "newsstand's up." She flips through some pages in a document until she lands on a chart.

"See that, covers sell!"

"Yes, I know," Joan nods, trying to stay cool and making a mental note to change her clothes before going to Aaron's for dinner.

"But subs—they're still in the toilet," Grace tsks-tsks. "Let's just see if my editorial suggestions don't improve those numbers as well." She smiles her Brentwood smile and gets ready to leave.

"Hold on," Joan says. "Look, you know how I feel about this story. The world doesn't need more pretty pictures, it needs us to tell it like it is!"

"Says who?" Grace snorts, brandishing the report, "Not subscribers! They want to hear about that new restaurant opening, that hot play, where to take their kids for the weekend . . ."

"Yeah, yeah, we got all that, but that's not the—"

"This is about them," Grace points out Joan's window, "Not about us. Wake up, will you! The South Bay Nissan Dealers canceled their ad this month, said we're not reaching the 'lucrative millennials'— the guy's threatening to pull the whole account!"

"Fuck 'em."

"I'm stuck taking him out for drinks tonight to change his mind. *Me.* That's what YOU should be doing!"

The two ladies glare at each other.

"You're only still in business because of *me*," Grace continues. "You don't listen to *ME*, you don't follow *MY* direction, you'll be out on the street. Mark my words!" She storms out.

Joan leans back in her chair and takes in several deep breaths. She focuses on the magazine covers that hang on her wall, some of her best stories are captured on those covers: Cesar Chavez, Mayor Tom Bradley, a renovated Union Station, the Beach Boys reunion at the Troubadour—she remembers paying a small fortune for that photo.

Her old buddies, friends from better days.

Look, she knows some things have to change. She's not an idiot. And she's been trying to do that, to accommodate Grace and the investors—she needs their dollars to stay afloat. But the soul of

Relevant? No, that's not for sale. She has no intention of bargaining that away. It's perfect the way it is.

Just like when she took over from Aunt Berta.

She thinks about Berta reviewing her first issue, telling her how relieved she was to be leaving it in such good hands. A frail Berta, no longer the vibrant, strapping lady from her childhood.

And she's stayed true to Berta's vision, she's made it her own. No way anyone is wrestling that away from her now.

She phones Aaron again—she's got to get the hell out of the office, have a nice meal, a pleasant conversation—anything, something—put this day behind her.

But his phone just rings and rings.

"So, okay then, I'll take a rain check," Joan says when his answering machine finally kicks in. "I'm beat, anyway."

In his dreams, Aaron's father lifts a nine-year-old Aaron, still in pajamas, still skinny with hairless, swinging legs, and kisses the top of his head.

"Raining cats and dogs, buddy."

His father tosses a rain-soaked slicker onto the upholstered chair in Aaron's childhood bedroom. His yellow slicker. His one-hundred-watt smile. Aaron's dad knew how to make a muddy track pay.

"Mom's gonna holler," little Aaron mumbles, thinking about the slicker.

Aaron's father passed along many talents to his son. He taught him how to count, ride a bike, make scrambled eggs, then dirty gin martinis, for which young Aaron became a local legend. But it's his handicapping prowess that made its most lasting contribution. Consolidating syndicated racing forms into one master spreadsheet and then weighing the averages based on the reputation of the handicapper and his success rate at the track—well, it's a work of art.

It becomes Aaron's signature dish.

Even better than his martinis.

He dreams on.

CHAPTER THREE

In late afternoon, Joan's many windows—one of the few redeeming features of her office—becomes a curse. The angle of the sun forces her to pull down all her shades and she ends up sitting in the dark. Although today, it's something of a blessing, helping to take the edge off her throbbing headache.

The magazine is allotted several reserved spots in the parking lot—a godsend in this crowded neighborhood—and Grace has parked her late-model BMW right next to Joan's own crummy station wagon—a high point among the sorry collection of cars and vans that most *Relevant* staffers drive.

She tries to compute what it will take to buy Grace and the private equity firm out of its investment in the magazine. The numbers haven't changed much since the last time Joan ran this calculation, she's still looking at nearly ten years to pay back the losses. Ten years *if* the business continues to perform at this level. Ten years before she can get rid of this menace.

She's sick just thinking about it.

She's on her way out when she notices a tall, young, handsome man standing in the lobby. It takes her a minute to place him.

"Ira? Whatever brought you to this neck of the woods?"

"Came to talk to you about your book," Ira says, smiling broadly.

"My book! Wow. Come in, come, tell me more." Joan leads him back to her office and closes the door.

"It's just the craziest of coincidences. George gave me a couple of pages of a manuscript about the Kennedy assassination, I really liked it and then I saw that *you* wrote it."

"Wow. Wonderful. Who's George?"

"My brother, George Baxter. Surely you've heard of him?" Ira teases.

"'Mr. Hollywood'? Oh, I didn't know—that's your brother?"

"From the beginning," he laughs.

"And so, George, or you, are thinking of developing my story for—what—a film maybe?" she asks, ever hopeful.

"Not *exactly*. Hey, why don't we get out of here—I'll buy you a drink and we can catch up on life."

"Thanks, Ira, but it's been a crazy day. I'm beat. Let's just talk here, okay?"

Ira and Joan met when they were both working to save an old, historic Pasadena building from demolition. They spent weeks arguing with the zoning commission and bonded when they realized each was capable of delivering a persuasive argument—others on the committee were less gifted. And while ultimately they lost their fight, a steel and glass monstrosity stands testimony to that failure, their respect for one another lives on.

"Here's the thing," Ira says. "I'm writing a film about a big jewelry heist, it's fiction, and there's this one guy who is central to the story, a lot revolves around him, but he's under-developed. We can't seem to get him—my cowriter and me—outside of that ubiquitous tough-guy mode. You know? We've been at it for weeks. And then I read your manuscript where you describe Jack Ruby and I think 'hey!—this could be him, that guy, what we're looking for!'"

"He's not your typical gangster," she nods.

"Right. And we're getting killed by a deadline—Phoebe and

me, my cowriter, just struggling to nail this son-of-a-bitch while the clock keeps ticking away. He keeps turning out like Joe Pesci in, um . . ."

"*Goodfellas . . . Cousin Vinny . . .*"

"Yeah, like in everything. And the pressure's mounting 'cause George set this up for me in the first place. And Phoebe—that's my cowriter—"

"So you said."

"—is freaking out because of the deadline and we refuse to settle for some run-of-the-mill Mafia character. I mean, that's the whole point, that's why they hired us to begin with, we need a different—"

"I get it Ira," Joan walks to her file cabinet. "And you've come to the right place. Jack Ruby—he's not like those other guys—he's a fish out of water. Never 'made it' 'though he sure tried. Tried and tried. Had a few sleazy nightclubs and some second-rate operations but it amounted to bupkas. Hold on a sec, got something you can watch."

She pops a DVD into an ancient video console, and up comes:

DALLAS COURT HOUSE, June 7, 1964

And there is Jack Ruby, in a prison uniform, fighting a nervous tic, addressing four visitors from the Warren Commission:

> **"The world will never know the true facts of what occurred or my motive. The people that had so much to gain for putting me in the position I'm in will never let the true facts come above board to the world. Gentlemen, I want to tell you the truth, but I cannot tell it here. I tell you that a whole new form of government is going to take over the country and I know I won't live to see you another time."**

"Yikes! How come I never heard that before?"

"There's a lot that never got out about him or the assassination.

And here's the best part—I have it, it's all in here," she pats her cabinet. "A ton of material you can use if you want."

"But what about your manuscript?"

"I sent it to over a dozen publishers," she shakes her head. "They all passed. Ten years of pulling it together—weekends, holidays—whatever time I could steal away from the magazine. Ten years. Well, I guess someone thought enough of it to give it to your brother, right?"

"So, why not just run it in the magazine?"

Joan's face turns dark. She thinks about her last knock-down fight with Grace over this very subject.

"*Relevant's* not doing well, Ira. Financially. You know, the publishing business has taken a lot of hits these past years and we're no exception. I had to go outside to raise money just to keep us afloat. So I took on a partner, an investor, to help guide us to profitability. Problem is, her idea of what we should be doing doesn't always jibe with mine. Particularly in the area she calls 'old news.'"

"Oh," Ira says.

"So as long as this investor is around, it won't see the light of day."

"Got it. Okay—in the movie business we typically write a back story on each major character, their bio, you know. You happen to do that for Ruby?"

"No, no. But like I said, there's a ton of information in these drawers, take whatever you want."

"It's actually too much for us, Joan, digging through all these files, we don't have the time, we'd be overwhelmed. The deadline. But I have an idea—how about you helping us? Would you consider being part of the team? You could feed us Ruby information, character insights, interesting traits—not the normal tough-guy bullshit. We'll use that to sculpt our character."

"You sure could build an iconic character off Ruby."

"So? We'll work around your schedule and I'll get George to handle compensation. You know he'll be more than fair."

"Don't worry about the money, Ira. I'd be more interested in getting the story out there."

"So is that a yes?"

"Let me think about it."

"Okay. Did you think about it? Are you in?"

They laugh.

"I forgot that about you," she says. "You can be very convincing."

"Not in Pasadena I'm not."

They laugh again.

"Can't wait for you to meet Phoebe. She's the real brains of the operation."

"Oh I see, you're just the salesman." They walk back to the lobby, still chuckling.

"I've got to tell you, I'm really feeling this. And wouldn't it be a blast to work together again?!" He's all smiles.

Joan hands him her business card and they hug.

"Call me in the morning. If it's a yes, we can figure out a schedule and the rest of it."

She walks back to her office on cloud nine. Of course she's going to help Ira and his partner. Of course she'll do this. She can't wait to get started. She hasn't felt this hopeful in a long, long time.

CHAPTER FOUR

Ira drives back to his cottage thinking he's turned the corner on his career.

After a string of bad luck, the normally charming, unflappable guy has been missing from action, replaced by a lost, wandering soul. Now he may finally reclaim his rightful place in the world.

The business world. His personal life is still in the toilet.

Some on-again/off-again relationships persuaded him to marry a beautiful, talented woman that he had only dated for a short time. She was the kind of woman his brother would go for: statuesque, well-spoken, a beauty. Actually the whole family approved of her, not only because she was a knock-out, but she had a very sweet nature—genuinely sweet—plus she understood the business, she was a dancer. And a Catholic to boot! Non-practicing, still . . .

But it didn't take long before Ira realized their marriage was a mistake. They had very little in common. She liked to socialize with her dancer friends; he thought they were shallow and boring. He liked going to sporting events, she had no interest in that at all. She worried her clock was ticking but he knew he wasn't ready for kids. But the biggest problem of all turned out to be her sense of humor. Or lack of it. He still can't figure how he missed that.

By the time they decided to call it quits, three years had slipped by. These were important years for her, critical years, with lost opportunities for dancing and pageants that she could never get back, especially since she was nearing an age when those opportunities came fewer and farther apart.

She took him for all he had.

And that was only half of it.

The other piece of bad luck had to do with *Bridges Down.* It had been a coup for Ira to score in the first place, a serious foray into drama after years of writing comedies, but it ended up being a turkey. A disaster. And with so much advanced publicity and hype—and, let's face it, the fact that he was, is, George Baxter's little brother, well—it got skewered by the press:

Bridges all the way *DOWN*—

BRIDGES DOWN to the bottom—etc., etc.

It replaced *Ishtar* as one of the biggest flops of all time. Dustin Hoffman even sent him a thank you note.

So without George's help, Ira might never have gotten another chance to write another script. He's under a ton of pressure to knock this one out of the park.

———

Ira's nursing a coffee, waiting for Phoebe to arrive this morning so they can both welcome Joan officially, get this off on the right foot—but when the doorbell rings he knows that's not to be, Phoebe doesn't ring.

"Got a little turned around finding the place," Joan says by way of greeting.

"Please don't tell me the guard hassled you, I left your name."

"Oh no, no. Just don't know this part of Malibu. My GPS was no help. Hey, nice joint," she says sizing up the cottage.

"It's just temporary."

"Must be really challenging having George Baxter for a brother," she muses. "I mean, not that you're not successful in your own right, clearly you have an incredible reputation." She worries she's insulted him.

"Hey, it's okay, I get it," he smiles.

"I mean, I rented *Bridges Down* but the DVD kept skipping," she says. "I sent it back."

"Consider it a blessing."

"Huh?"

"A joke, Joan. A bad one. Like the film."

"Oh, you!" She laughs and ventures on. "Saw *The Problem with Mimi* last year at the Roxy. That was very funny Ira, the audience loved it. They were howling."

"Yeah, thanks. I've had good luck with comedies. But *Bridges Down* . . . now, that was different. That was supposed to be a thriller," he says as Phoebe walks in. "The critics were howling."

"Sorry—late meeting last night. So pleased to meet you," Phoebe says turning to Joan. "Can't wait to get going on this."

"My name is Phoebe, and I'm a substance abuser. It's three years since I'm sober."

She's leaning against a wooden podium.

"You go girl!" someone yells and everyone chuckles.

Phoebe takes a mock bow, "One day at a time, right?"

The same guy yells, "That's right, darlin'."

And it all comes barreling out.

"I made a lot of changes to get here, but I'm in a pretty good place now. Not my love life, that's non-existent, but just about everything else. I'm even out of debt—well almost. It's amazing how far a dollar will go when it's not going up your nose."

A good audience, encouraging her on.

"I've been an abuser since, well . . . it started innocently, you know—of course you know—a little weed, a couple beers. Then pills . . ." She makes a face. "We had a thing. Coke when I started making money. So, a couple of crazy years there." She gets quiet. "Actually, some terrible years, I put my family through hell. But look, that's all behind me, in the past."

Phoebe knows she lacks a filter—it's on or off, no middle ground. And while she's extremely self-aware, it doesn't seem to matter. She can watch herself spin out of control and be powerless to do anything about it.

"But there's a problem now, why I'm here, it's my problem but I share it with my partner—my writing partner. We're doing this really big project and it's not going well. Getting nowhere. And this is important for me, but it's like an even bigger deal for him. It's like the most important gig of his life!"

Phoebe pictures Ira wincing that she's saying this out loud.

"Look, I know we're not supposed to talk about other people, but he and I, we're in this together and it's eating him up. And that's seriously affecting me. And I know my signs, what to look for," she's getting all worked up now. "Not sleeping, not eating right, losing focus. And after all this hard work, all I did to get here, I just can't throw it away."

"You're tough!"

"Stay strong!"

"Yes, you're right, you keep reminding me how tough I am. I will get through this like I did before. I will. Thanks."

The chair calls for a break and walks over to where Phoebe stands.

"Some people like us—we tend to take on other people's problems. Something about the way we're wired I guess. But it's important to remember your limits. Keep your boundaries— protect yourself. And don't worry, you'll have enough problems of your own to deal with."

Phoebe sees she's smiling.

"Look, you're here, doing the hard work. I see that and you're doing great keeping it together. So I'm not saying don't care, don't empathize, but remember: *who owns the problem?* If it's not you, then ultimately you let it go. Remember this, Phoebe, remember to protect yourself."

———

They give Joan a quick tour of the cottage and walk her into the kitchen to show her the ropes. Joan, who claims to be a cook, oohs and aahs over gleaming commercial-grade appliances, custom cabinetry, and a giant marble peninsula.

"Now, that's something I could use," Joan remarks on the pot filler installed above a six-burner range. "And it all looks brand new."

"Well, of course it does, no one's ever used it," Ira says.

"You have a built-in food processor!" she exclaims.

"Is that what that is?" Phoebe asks.

"Here, let me make you a coffee," Ira motions to his espresso machine.

"No thanks, Ira, no coffee for me. Naturally caffeinated," Joan says.

Phoebe takes a Coke from the fridge and they walk back to the great room to get started.

Joan has brought along some background material and heads out to her car to retrieve it. She returns with several binders, some large reference books, and a stack of folders balancing on top.

"I told the office I'm taking a small sabbatical. There's someone who can cover for me when I'm gone. You said we're on a tight deadline so I told her it won't be very long."

"Killer deadline," Phoebe clarifies.

Joan goes back out to retrieve more books, binders, and folders, which are now piling up on the floor.

"How about a hand?" she asks Ira.

He too makes several trips, including one to lug in her metal filing cabinet.

"Please tell me this is it," he groans.

"'Til tomorrow," she says.

Then she'll bring a corkboard and a portable whiteboard with multicolored markers and two spray-erasers that are made especially for the board.

"Sell that station wagon!" Ira kids.

Joan's corkboard soon is overrun with photos: a young Jack Ruby aside his idol, Al Capone; the official mug shot of Santos Trafficante, full-on and in-profile; another gangster, Whitey Bulger, flanked by two tough guys in a photo credited to the Boston Globe; and an older Jack Ruby, nearly bald, standing in front of a dimly lit night club.

Not to be outdone, Phoebe squeezes on a visual she's chosen for inspiration: Miami in its heyday—men in pinstriped suits, fedoras and cigars, and women dressed in modest one-piece swimsuits and high heels—all posing around an Olympic-size hotel pool.

The cottage is filling up with all of Joan's materials, there's very little unclaimed territory. The great room looks like it's been ambushed by some overactive kindergartners.

Over lunch of tuna sandwiches, they discuss how best to organize the mess.

"I've got a few more things," Joan says, chewing noisily, crumbs falling everywhere. "Can I drop them off tomorrow before I go to the office? Say, seven a.m., okay?"

"Oh sure," Ira says. "Peachy."

Phoebe looks to see if Ira has noticed Joan's table etiquette.

"You know, Joan," he says. "Phoebe and I been meaning to check out George's film library. I'd like to go now but you can keep on here if you've still got the energy."

"Great idea, guys, you go, I'll stay," Joan says, expelling tuna breath.

———————

Two days later, Joan is back with three more cartons and many more visuals to squeeze onto the corkboard: Ruby in his nightclub; JFK in his presidential office; Lee Harvey Oswald in his backyard with a rifle. Phoebe is about to blow her top, but Joan promises it's the last of it—she crosses her heart—and they finally, FINALLY, are ready to begin.

Now, a full three weeks behind schedule.

Joan places a straight-back chair squarely before them, classroom-style, while Ira and Phoebe sit casually on the sofa; she begins her data dump on Jack Ruby.

"This is the infamous Warren report," she says, handing Ira a large tome. "Actually, it's just the summary. The full report is twenty-six volumes."

"Wow, who'd read all that?" Phoebe asks.

"Nobody," Joan smirks. "Which was exactly the intent. It's mainly horseshit anyway."

Ira and Phoebe learned about the Warren report in school, it was taught as the undisputed authority on the Kennedy assassination.

"Seriously," Joan says reading their looks. "Here's *The House Select Committee on Assassinations* if you don't believe me," she passes Ira another big book. "You'll see what I mean."

"See what exactly?" Phoebe asks.

Joan's eyes narrow. "That JFK's murder was a conspiracy. Not the act of one lone-nut gunman. Not what it says in the Warren report. That's horseshit."

"The House, um . . . what?" Ira asks.

"*The House Select Committee on Assassinations*. The HSCA." Joan hands over another book, this time to Phoebe. "Or this, this is from the Church Commission. That one or this gets you much closer to the truth."

"The Church Commission?" Ira asks, never hearing of this either.

"How come I never . . . ?" Phoebe says.

"People got tired of it. The reports, the newscasts, the half-baked theories. There was a new theory every day, it was total media overload. People just settled for the Warren report—LBJ signed off on it, the major media outlets endorsed it, it became gospel overnight."

"And it's horseshit," Phoebe repeats, still not fully believing.

"Yes! Okay class, Assassination 101. You up for this?"

"Will this get us to Ruby?" Phoebe asks.

"Of course," Joan says. "So, John Fitzgerald Kennedy, the thirty-fifth president of the United States, gets gunned down in Dallas on November 22, 1963, his third year in office. Lyndon Baines Johnson, his vice president, gets sworn in as president on Air Force One flying back to Washington with his wife, Lady Bird, and Jackie Kennedy, and the whole world watching. Johnson immediately convenes a commission to determine what happened. It was led by Earl Warren, Chief Justice of the Supreme Court, thus the Warren Commission."

She takes a breath and nods to Phoebe.

"Two decades earlier, on the south side of Chicago, Jack Ruby nee Rubenstein is trying to impress the local mobsters that he's someone to watch. Al Capone tries him out on a couple of jobs: a bagman, a numbers runner. He's working hard to show the big guys he's got what it takes."

"Rubenstein, Jewish right?" Ira asks.

"Yup," Joan says.

"We're definitely using that!" Phoebe says to Ira.

"Meanwhile, Kennedy authorizes Operation Mongoose, something he inherited from the Eisenhower administration that authorizes the CIA to eliminate Castro—this is at the height of the Cold War, remember. But after about a year of botched attempts, Kennedy decides to call it off. Unfortunately, it's too late so—"

"What do you mean 'too late'? He's the president," Ira says.

"Okay, yes, but let me explain. You guys remember the Bay of Pigs, right?"

They nod somewhat unconvincingly. Joan pushes on anyway.

"Well, so that puts Kennedy and the military at odds. The Joint Chiefs of Staff think he's a novice and a coward, he wouldn't send in the Air Force when their operation started falling apart, so they start doing stuff behind his back. And the CIA is already running its own ops in Cuba, they've been using the Mob for enforcement. You know the Mafia used to be all over Cuba with their nightclubs and drugs and prostitution, but when Castro took over, he threw them out. That's why they're willing to help out the CIA, they both want Castro gone."

"I'm lost—what about Ruby?" Phoebe asks.

"Wait a sec," Joan holds up her hand, committed to her story.

"So the thing is," Joan says looking at Phoebe, "Ruby had been involved in one of those early unsuccessful Mongoose missions *and* he owes the IRS forty grand in back taxes, so they coerce him into taking part in another mission, this one in Dallas. He'll be their advance man, scope out the parade route, do things like that, and later he'll silence the fall guy, Oswald, once the deed is done."

"Oswald's a fall guy?" Ira asks tentatively.

"A patsy," Joan says.

"What's the IRS got to do with it?" Phoebe asks.

"It was part of the treasury—the CIA was too back then. It was all decentralized, everyone operated independently, ran their own show. There was no central compositor for information, that's why the CIA was created in the first place, that's supposed to be its role. They're not authorized to have an enforcement arm or do anything domestically. So they use the Mafia when they need to get something done. Or don't want to leave their fingerprints."

Phoebe shoots Ira a look—*help!* Joan sees her do it.

"I know it's a lot to take in, that's how most people felt back then. That's why they defaulted to the Warren report," Joan says dismissively.

"And that report says that Oswald acted alone, right?" Ira asks.

"Right. And that Ruby acted alone. And that there was only one gunman and only one bullet . . ."

"Got it," Ira says.

"No, Ira, not *'got it'*—it's horseshit, remember? Turns out some of those Warren commissioners weren't the most persnickety."

Persnickety? Ira and Phoebe trade looks.

"The feds played fast and loose with the facts. The Warren report, the Rockefeller Commission, the Freedom of Information Act—they're all just smoke screens."

Phoebe shoots Ira a look of despair. "Joan, what's this got to do with—"

"Ruby? Yeah, yeah. Look, they were supposed to release the Kennedy files last year, but they keep moving the date, now they say 2029 or 2048! You don't need to be a conspiracy nut to wonder what's hiding in those files. Anyway, we can use this," she waves another document at Phoebe. "It's all about Ruby."

"Great!" Phoebe says. "What's in it?"

"Confirmations of phone calls between Ruby and the top guns in the Giancana family leading up to the assassination."

Phoebe elbows Ira.

"Joan," Ira says after a long pause, "you know we really need to lean on you for background material."

"Of course, that's why I'm here."

"Right. And you need to serve us enough so we can create our character, an unusual but believable Mafia guy," Ira says.

"But not so much we get lost in the sauce," Phoebe interjects.

Joan nods. "We've discussed this."

"He's a fictional character based off your factual information," Ira says, reminding her, and Phoebe, and himself as well. "And we'll be focusing on the early years when he's being groomed by the Mob, working his way up, proving his mettle, just like you were saying before."

"We've got a pretty solid plot line, we just need to weave him into it," Phoebe adds.

"But it makes no sense to leave out what happens next. What he did to Oswald, how the mob families manipulated him, that's the best part of the story!"

"Joan, we agreed—*remember*—we're not going anywhere near the assassination. This has nothing to do with that," Ira says with a forced smile.

"The studio approved our approach—we need to stay focused," Phoebe says.

"But we're including the botched Castro thing?" Joan asks.

"Maybe. Maybe that's where it will end, you know, in Cuba," Ira says.

"Hmmm," Phoebe says. She gets up and walks behind Ira, resting her hands on his shoulders. "You know what I'm thinking?"

"We could set the whole thing in Cuba."

"It's better than Miami—less expected, more exotic."

"Yeah, maybe," he says. "But no pink flamingos. This Cuba's gotta be dark and scary, rain-soaked cobblestone, smoke-filled alleys, danger on every corner."

"Yeah," Phoebe says, unconsciously kneading his shoulders. "So here we have this small-time Jewish thug, this little guy from the wrong side of town. Been trying his whole life to break into the big leagues, to get noticed. He's a wanna-be who'll finally get a chance."

"Yeah. The boss tells him to go down to Cuba and open up a nightclub. Make it big, beautiful, extravagant. Make it the best club in town!"

"So he finds a choice location and spends all the cash they gave him. More than they gave him. He's over his head, this could be trouble and he's very nervous, but then the club opens and it just takes off!"

"It's an amazing place! Where you go to be seen, to gamble, the best restaurants, the best entertainment," Ira starts pacing. "THE place. No one cares he spent so much, they're beside themselves with how great this place is, how they've outdone all the other families. They were late to the party but now they're on top!"

"So, now Ruby's thinking he's made it, he showed them he got what it takes. Everyone knows who he is, everyone knows his name. He gets seduced by the money, the power," Phoebe starts acting it out. "Strutting around, beautiful women on his arm, acting like a kingpin. He's got the magic touch, see? What else can he do down here?"

"Maybe he opens a temple?" Joan suggests.

It breaks the mood. Phoebe whoops with laughter, Ira laughs so hard he cries. Then Joan laughs too.

"No, no, Joan, something bad has to happen," Ira says, drying his eyes.

"Well, I can see him getting sloppy," Phoebe says. "Maybe he's spending too much on the ladies? Skimming off the tables?"

Ira is delighted, they high-five each other.

"Of course, Chicago finds out and of course, they can't let it go. They had planned to use him on the heist—that burglary part we still need to figure out—but now? No way—he can't be trusted, no one *ever* takes advantage of them," Phoebe says.

"So he gets caught with his hand in the cookie jar and . . ." Ira makes the motion of a throat being cut.

"Or maybe they set him up to take the rap on the heist?" Phoebe grins.

"Yeah, that might work."

"Maybe he should die down there—you know, alone, all alone. A little man, an unmarked grave," Phoebe is still grinning.

"I can see the Chicago bosses arguing over who to send to take him out," Ira says.

"And that's where it ends. In Cuba. Fade to black," she says as she walks to the corkboard and pulls off all the Miami visuals.

"Okay. So, maybe we got something here, Pheebes," he says.

They take a moment to let it sink in.

"So besides this Ruby stuff," Ira says to Joan, "we'd like anything you might have on Cuba back then."

"But don't go overboard, we've still got to make up lost time, the—"

"Deadline. I remember, Phoebe," Joan says nodding.

"Man, I'm feeling it," Ira says.

"How about this for a working title: *A Long Road to Havana*," Phoebe says.

"Sure."

They sit back, feet up, relieved they're finally on the right path.

———

Joan heads for home, not sure how she feels. On the one hand, it's what they wanted, why they asked her for help. And yes, a partial victory for her too, a chance to shine some light on Ruby, expose him for who he was.

But it still burns, Ruby's real role in the assassination.

And who is to blame for all that happened.

And why they killed her president.

She has the truth, it's there in those files. Waiting for some damn publisher with the guts to open the drawer and let it out to the world.

Okay, she says to herself as she pulls into her driveway, just don't push it. You've waited this long, be patient, maybe you can turn them around.

CHAPTER FIVE

Aaron's liquor store sits on a big corner in an old neighborhood. The sidewalks are a jumble of bicycles, skateboards, and kids; the park has a couple of swings, two basketball hoops that have seen better days, and an overflowing dumpster. Whatever gentrification has happened in Los Feliz, it has yet to reach this part of town.

From the outside, the store looks run-down; his display windows are a hodge-podge of promotions accompanied by a thick layer of dust. Aaron leaves it purposefully so as not to attract undue attention.

Inside it's a totally different story.

Designer vodkas, exotic tequilas, and small-batch bourbons pack the shelves—Aaron's kept up with the changing tastes of his clientele. His wine section is particularly well stocked, full of low-priced favorites as well as some elegant, vintage selections that rarely anyone seriously shops.

Except for today.

Joe Capano, a short, friendly-looking customer, is fondling a Chateauneuf de Pape; he's been combing the aisles, placing several choice bottles on the counter, asking for the details on its vintage and vintner.

Aaron, who knows a lot about wine, is impressed.

Joe eyes a rare Shafer Cabernet. "Hey, Aaron," he calls out, "did you know this guy Shafer just kicked the bucket? You should put this away for a couple of months and you can double the price."

Aaron nods respectfully, allowing Joe to do his thing despite the fact he's feeling awful—there's a bandage over his nose and his right eye hasn't stopped tearing.

"Revolutionized the business this guy, the first to go solar, and talk about organic! Schafer was light years ahead. Hey, that's funny. Solar, light years, get it?" Joe keeps rambling and Aaron keeps praying for this to end.

"You really do look terrible," Joe says as he finally comes close to where Aaron has been standing.

"I'm doing the best I can here, Joe, you can't get blood from a stone."

Joe puts a 2009 Meursault on the counter next to the others.

This is one of Aaron's most expensive bottles, he never expected anyone to buy it—he was saving it for himself. For a special occasion. Like a date with a starlet.

"My boys get blood from a lot of places pal, some of which I'd rather not mention." Joe points at Aaron's face, "just a taste."

"What can I do, I don't got it."

"Yeah, I figured, so I put a little plan together for you. A workout plan. It's easy. Basically, all you got to do is help us with some banking through the business. We bring you cash. You deposit it. Then you wire it back to us. Stuff like that. Simple. Oh yeah, and we use your basement to store stuff, just once in a while, it's no big deal. See?"

Aaron is starting to feel better.

"Oh," Joe says like he just remembered, "and you'll need to come up with the cash, what you owe us. That's way overdue."

"WHAT!!! I just told you, I don't got that!"

"So you take out a mortgage on that cute little cottage. That's gotta be worth a pretty penny," Joe smiles, having solved the dilemma.

"No, there's not, I'm . . ."

"So a loan against the store, you know, like a line of credit. Look, Aaron," he says sternly but still smiling, "they're tired of waiting. That's our money. Capiche?"

Aaron puts his head in his hands. "You're killing me, you'll put me out of business!"

Joe puts his arm around Aaron's shoulder. "Look pal, you should be down on your knees kissing my feet. This is a much better plan than my boss had in mind, believe you me."

"You got a boss?" Aaron asks just as his cell phone rings.

"Of course I got a boss. Who doesn't have a boss? We're a professional operation, we got hierarchy like everybody else."

He motions for Aaron to get rid of the call.

"I can't talk now . . . yes, better. That's nice . . . no just the soup. NO. You're not listening, I can't hear about Jack Ruby now, OKAY?!!" He ends the call. "Sorry, that's just my crazy friend . . ."

"Jack Ruby?" Joe scrunches up his nose in delight.

"She's a writer, working on a screenplay about the '60s," Aaron explains, happy to change the subject.

"Oh yeah? I love the '60s—the cars, the clothes."

Aaron laughs, kid's seen too many movies.

"Hey, you know, Uncle Donny knew Jack Ruby back in the day, I think maybe he was even a distant relation!"

"Really," Aaron says just to be polite.

"Yeah, so he says. But he's old Uncle Donny, you know? So anyway, the plan goes into effect starting now. Got a couple boxes I want to put down in the basement. And you need to make me a key."

"A KEY!?!" Aaron explodes again without meaning to.

"What, you think I'm gonna rob the place?" Joe says darkly. "Like I'm some two-bit punk? That's what you think of me, Aaron? I went to UCLA you little prick."

"Sorry, my dad left—UCLA? Me too. Play any sports?" Aaron starts to feel his blood pressure returning to normal.

"On the winning swim team. What'd you play?"

"Hooky," Aaron answers truthfully. "All-star."

"Division champs, got trophies and everything."

Aaron works his face into a smile, "Oh yeah, what'd you swim?"

"Breast-stroke, held the school record for an entire year!"

"Wow. So you're a breast guy, huh?"

Joe laughs and nods, "Sure am."

"I was in the 'dramatic arts' program, training to be a thespian," Aaron says theatrically.

"Engineering," Joe counters raising an eyebrow, "Five-year program. Talk about grueling."

"And yet here you are, working in the family business," Aaron says before thinking it through.

"Yeah. So? Think we both are."

"Yeah. You know," Aaron waves Joe to a back door, "it'll be easier if you come 'round that way. I'll get the door for you."

Joe holds up a finger, pulls himself to full height, and speed dials a call.

"Hey, Uncle D, it's Joey. So good news, our gentleman will happily accommodate us," he nods over to Aaron. "And remind me to tell you about one of his closest friends, yeah, very interesting, he's got a writer friend making a movie about Jack Ruby . . ."

CHAPTER SIX

Ira and Phoebe are in the den watching Joan's tape of Ruby shooting Oswald in the basement of the Dallas police station for the third time. This time, they're paying special attention to how he shifts his weight when he draws his gun, how he tilts his head as he pulls it from his pocket—physical characteristics and quirky mannerisms that will inform the character they are developing.

"Look at that—his finger is twitching, he can barely keep the gun steady," Ira says.

"Wish we had a better angle—I think he closes his eyes when he pulls the trigger," Phoebe says.

"Some hit man!"

"Guy's a neurotic mess."

"Let's use this in the heist—how the gun shakes, how he steadies it with his other hand."

"Definitely!"

Joan is in the great room working on the blackboard, she's been at it for hours, drawing circles and arrows and scribbling notations. In the top left corner, she's drawn what looks like a solar system with Ruby as the sun and a dozen smaller circles surrounding him like planets—she's busy filling in with captions when the writers return.

"Should help with Ruby's relationships—keep them straight," she says.

"Wish my relationships were like that," Phoebe smiles, "well-defined, me in the center."

"Keep dreaming," Ira says. He knows all about Phoebe's relationships.

Phoebe and Ira met on a film—she was a script editor, new to Hollywood, and he was the head writer and, not uncoincidentally, the producer's younger brother. They were both somewhat underqualified and overwhelmed by the experience—it led to an immediate connection.

Their friendship blossomed when the project moved out of the studio and on to location. With the heavy lifting behind them, and when not making revisions on the fly, there wasn't much to do in Waco, Texas. They ended up spending a lot of time together "hanging out"—lots of time with nothing to do and nowhere to go.

They ended up going to bed.

To Phoebe's dismay, the relationship cooled once they were back in California. Ira was happy to hear from her when she finally did reach out—but grabbing a coffee seemed so anticlimactic after their intense weeks on location. The experience left her dazed and confused. And embarrassed—she finally had to face the fact she had been used solely as a distraction.

Many months later, after she had almost forgotten the episode, George reached out to see if she was free to work on his next film, *The Problem with Mimi*. It was being billed as a romantic comedy and going to feature a star-studded cast. Phoebe jumped at it. George didn't mention that Ira would also be on the project.

They reconnected on day one in the writers' room, found out they were natural writing partners, and even incorporated some of what happened to them in Texas into the script.

Ira admitted that while he enjoyed being with her in Waco, he wasn't ready to settle down—and sensed she was—so he backed off not wanting to lead her on any more than he might already have.

Phoebe didn't buy it—she thought the real story was that Ira needed 'more' from a woman—that she needed to be gorgeous or famous or wealthy or something . . . something she obviously lacked.

But one thing they did agree on, they made an excellent team. *Mimi* was a big hit, Ira cemented his reputation as a "go-to" comedy writer and Phoebe made her first real money in Hollywood. After a few more solid films to their credit, they agreed to stay together as writing partners—and not take it further.

———

"So these circles are siblings," Joan says. "Ruby came from a very large family—eight kids—going to try and locate some of them." She opens a binder. "And I dug up this testimony from an ex-employee of Ruby's nightclub. There's an interesting point here, he said he didn't drink."

"Who didn't drink?" Phoebe asks. "Ruby or the employee?"

"Ruby. He was a teetotaler. Imagine, he's in the nightclub business," Joan shakes her head.

"Maybe a reformed alcoholic?" Ira asks not looking at Phoebe.

"Not according to this guy. Said it was Jack's bragging right. Ruby's father had been a notorious drunk and Jack swore not to follow in his footsteps." She writes *LHO* in one of the circles on the blackboard.

"Hey, Joan, take Oswald off the board," Ira says. "We're not going there, you know that."

"I know, I know, but just hear me out. He's got ties to the CIA. His stint in the military puts him in Russia. That connects to Cuba and maybe to Ruby," she says. "Get it—Cuba!"

"Yeah. We get it, but we're not going anywhere near Oswald. Just take him off the board."

"Look, Ruby knew about Oswald's Cuban ties, the 'Fair Play' committee he started, Ruby even knew the name of that—no one else had even heard of it."

"Read my lips—NO!" Ira says.

Joan's face gets red. "That assassination rocked the world, nothing has ever come close. Nothing!"

"Oh yeah—what about 9/11?!" Ira yells back, now furious.

"This country went from Camelot to crap in a blink of an eye," Joan is digging in her heels. "Jack, Bobby, Martin Luther King, they were out to change the world!"

Ira moves close so they are almost nose to nose. "Look, Joan, you lived it, we didn't, but that said—we're doing this *our* way. That means the story ends with Cuba. There is no Oswald, there is no assassination. Don't make this any harder than it has to be," he erases the LHO circle from the board.

"You know—the deadline," Phoebe says.

"If you can't work under this scenario then you don't stay," Ira says, still fuming. He turns to Phoebe, "I'm not risking it—I got everything riding on it, you know that. Everything!"

"Okay, okay, let's all calm down," Joan puts her hands up in submission. "I get it. No Oswald. Let's get back to work."

"Yes, why don't you?!" Phoebe says, deciding she has had enough. "The magazine must be wondering where you are."

"It's under control Phoebe, thanks for your concern," Joan answers snidely.

"Let's call it a day—we'll pick this up tomorrow," Ira says wearily but Joan is already out the door.

Phoebe types *Joan Ross* into her Google search bar and starts scrolling through hundreds of hits; she adds *reporter* and tries again.

"Add a birth year," Ira suggests.

"Like what?"

"I don't know. Old."

"Like 1960s?"

"Well, before '63, right? That's the year of the assassination. She was a kid then so, I dunno, maybe 1950s?"

"Bingo!"

Ira peers over Phoebe's shoulder. "Wow! Look at this—it's an Iran-Contra story . . ."

Joan Ross, investigative reporter for the *Chicago Sun-Times*, was relieved of her White House reporting responsibilities . . .

He's reading aloud as George, Ira's famous, gorgeous, extremely wealthy, and quite nice older brother saunters in, followed by his bodyguard Tom, who positions himself by the door.

"Didn't know you were back bro!!!" Ira hugs him hard.

"Literally, just now, straight from LAX. Thought I'd pop by to see my favorite writing team and hear how it's going."

George is smiling at Phoebe while taking in the whiteboards, the corkboard, the blackboard, the piles on the floor. "Like what you've done with the place." They laugh. "So, how's it going?"

"It's going good," Ira says.

"Very good," Phoebe echoes.

"Think we're closing in," Ira adds. Phoebe nods.

"Great," George says as he turns back to face them. "Joan working out okay?" He asks like he knows something.

"Sure," Ira says.

Phoebe nods. "That's all her stuff," she says, referring to the boards and the piles. "We're really making good headway," she says somewhat awkwardly.

George, who has an abundance of terrific traits, also has an uncanny knack of putting people at ease—he doesn't take himself seriously and comes off as a nice guy—just a regular guy. For some reason, it never works on Phoebe.

"How about a drink, bro?" Ira heads to the kitchen. George plops down on the couch, puts his feet up in an identical manner to Ira, and helps himself to some grapes. He's all relaxed and comfy, acting like he owns the place. Which, of course, he does. Phoebe remains somewhat at attention.

"George," she says, sounding rehearsed, "I've been meaning to tell you how much we appreciate your support on this project. It's really very important to Ira and me."

"I'm expecting great things, Pho," George smiles genuinely.

"Us too," Phoebe says albeit less sure.

"Maybe kick-start the conversation this country should have been having for the last fifty years," he adds.

"Which is?"

"What really happened in Dallas."

Oh shit. There's a long, somewhat awkward, moment as Phoebe mentally decides how to broach this.

"I hear you," she says finally, "but you know our script won't deal with Dallas. We're using Ruby just for the character build— him as a kid, then messing up in Cuba later on, but not . . ." She's sounding apologetic and doesn't mean to.

George interrupts. "I know, I read the treatment, it's what the studio ordered. But we own this now so maybe down the road, you know, down the road we do something else with it. Something that gets people talking again—who was that Ruby? How did that happen? A guy strolls into a police station and shoots the alleged assassin of the president of the United States in front of everyone— just like that? Maybe we can be a spark that lights the fire."

"Well, do you think we should rethink it now, George? I mean, try to find a way to include Dallas, his role in the whole assassination thing? That's what Joan keeps pushing for," Phoebe asks with a shaky voice.

"Heck no. The studio isn't paying for that," George says, patting her hand. "Sounds to me like you're doing the exact right thing here," he adds as Ira walks back, balancing a bottle of champagne, two flutes, and Phoebe's Coke Zero on top of a bucket of ice. He pops open the champagne just as George motions he'll pass.

"Sorry can't stay. Wonderful to see you as always, my dear," he says as Tom opens the door. "Ike, it's been real," he calls back as Tom leads him to his car.

"Your brother," Phoebe smiles broadly, "what a guy."

"Da best," Ira says.

"*Ike*, huh?"

"Off limits, just for family. My dad left it to George in his will."

"Oh yeah? Miss Idaho didn't get that too?"

———————

Flying into *Relevant*, Joan attacks her computer like it's on fire and starts pounding away. From the corner of her eye, she sees Jeff leaving the lobby and rushes out to stop him.

"Wait a sec!"

He follows her back to her office with his antenna way up.

"I decided about the book. I'm gonna serialize it. A major series, multi-issues. JFK dies in November so we kick off with the November issue and him on the cover."

"Um, how many installments you thinking?" Jeff asks, pretending this is a normal conversation.

"Don't know, not sure yet, why do you ask? Three, four, I need to finish the outline." She stops to collect herself. "Here's what I need you to do," she says after taking a breath. "Develop a kind of graphic treatment, something that's ownable to the series. And to us. You know what I mean? You read this right?" she points to her manuscript on the table.

"Yes, I told you I did. So . . . something bold but with legs. Give me a day or two, I'll come back with a couple of ideas," he nods while keeping an eye out for Grace.

"Here's what I got so far. November: who planned it? December: who executed it? January: who covered it up? First three installs. Maybe there's a fourth, maybe we add a retrospective, you know, like it's fifty years later—where are we now?"

Grace's perfume wafts in, sucking up oxygen. "The same question I keep asking myself, where are we now?"

Jeff sidles to the door. "Got it." And he's gone.

"We're doing a series on the Kennedy assassinations, Grace," Joan says bracing for a fight, "three or four installments. Maybe five. I'm thinking we'll need to launch it before the end of the year."

"You can think about it as long as you want, but we're not doing it. Not now. Not while we're still digging ourselves out of a hole. A hole, may I add, made by you and some of your other poorly thought-out ideas for the magazine."

"Don't tell me what's running in my magazine," Joan's voice rises despite herself, "I'm the publisher here and don't you forget it!"

"And I hold the purse strings. The board put them in my hands for good reason Joan, they want a return on their investment. It's clear that won't happen if these decisions are left to you." Grace states this with no emotion, simply as fact.

Which makes Joan even angrier.

"We'll see about that. I'm going to plan it out and I'm going to present it to the board at the next meeting. We'll see what happens then!" she's yelling and there's a tear in her eye.

"Fine. Meanwhile, I'll just stop Jeff from spinning his wheels."

She slams the door on her way out, popping out another pane of glass.

Tom is driving along the Pacific Coast Highway as the sun slowly dips into the ocean. He pulls into a scenic lookout area and reaches toward the back seat with a clipboard and pen, a move he's perfected over time.

"You need to sign this," he says. "It says you will never, *ever*, discuss this evening with anyone. No one. Not your best friend. Not your agent. Not your shrink. Not even your mother. No one."

"Okay," says a quiet voice in the back.

"And you'll need to come up with a story about tonight because—and here's where it gets really serious—if you mention where you've been to anyone, I promise you, you will never work in Hollywood again. We will drum you out of the business. This is George Baxter we are talking about."

He lets this sink in.

"Okay," the voice says again.

"I can tell you that George is very excited about this evening. About spending time with you. He's been talking about it all day. But if I have to disappoint him . . ."

Tom doesn't get to finish this speech, he seldom does. The clipboard and pen are on their way back. He drives into the compound through the winding path that's even more impressive when lit at night. The car careens past Ira's cottage and stops at the front door of the main house.

George is dressed casually for dinner and holds two wine glasses. His handsome head tilts to see inside the Escalade's rear window, his charming smile and playful eyes are twinkling. The perfect host.

"Terry," George says sincerely. "I'm so happy you could make it."

Phoebe is wrung dry from another stressful day. Tonight's AA meeting is circled on her calendar but she's too damn tired to go.

She finds her favorite sweats and pads into the kitchen to order a pizza and it reminds her of an old family memory—the epic sausage/pepperoni wars.

Her brothers always wanted to order pepperoni but her dad insisted on sausage—they'd arm wrestled until dad finally won. Her mother wouldn't touch pizza anyway . . .

She's been on my mind lately.

It started with an epiphany: *Joan reminds me of my mother!*

Phoebe was in her car and nearly drove off the road. Certain aspects of Joan's personality—her condescending way of speaking to Phoebe and how she unleashes fury with little or no provocation—that was Phoebe's mother to a tee. Just being in Joan's presence when she's pontificating, pulling them away from their deadline, makes Phoebe apoplectic.

An AA meeting is exactly what she needs tonight.

So, that's it? Joan reminds you of Mom. C'mon Phoebe, put all those years of analysis to good use why don't you?

Phoebe's older brother Sam, Mr. Pepperoni, teased her constantly growing up, claimed she was adopted and made-up funny stories about driving with his parents to pick her up at the orphanage.

The "kiddie pound," he called it.

Sam and her younger brother Rick were both sports-crazy and loud, overflowing with energy. Their voices echoed through the house and Phoebe tried to squeeze into whatever free corner of quiet she could find, envious of the warmth and comradery they shared.

She, the blond skinny nerd—the runt of the litter. From the lost kiddie pound.

"Come home for a visit," Sam would beg when he phoned. "Come see your nieces and nephews before they're all grown up!"

She'd like to but it never seems like the right time to go.

Her dad, the sausage king, was a fun, easy-going guy, but her mom was another story. The boys called her *"Your Highness"* and bowed and scraped. Phoebe never found it funny. She once confided in Phoebe that she had married the wrong man and was living the wrong life—and she wasn't joking!

Worst of all, she expected Phoebe to agree with her.

Phoebe had to put hundreds of miles between them before she could find herself—become herself. Make a life for herself.

It wasn't easy.

She resists the urge to see if there's wine in the house.

The doorbell snaps her back to the present, and distracted, she over-tips the delivery boy then devours three slices at a dizzying pace. She's still working through her feelings when she realizes she was right all along—the connection to all this angst is Joan.

She's making her crazy.

She glances over to the empty, greased-stained pizza box.

"You take charge *now*. You can't let her get to you," Phoebe says out loud. "Take charge!"

She thinks back to an AA meeting.

Who owns the problem? she was asked then.

Okay. She knows the answer and is pretty sure she knows what to do about it. But this time it's not Phoebe who will be leaving, putting thousands of miles between her and her problems. This time, she's not the one who doesn't fit in. This time, it's Joan.

She'll ask Ira to let Joan go.

Not ask, *tell*. At the first possible moment. Maybe tomorrow.

Yes. She's feeling better already.

———

Phoebe gets to the cottage early the next morning but Joan's already there, making phone calls in the kitchen. She tells Ira she needs to speak to him privately, his look suggests he can read her mind.

"I know—you're tired of butting heads. Me too. But I thought a lot about it, Pheebes, and I don't think now is the right time," he says. "We're talking about Joan, right?"

"Yes, Ira. She's driving me crazy and I think we should just move on without her. We've got her manuscript, we don't need *her*."

"I came to the same conclusion, but . . . look, we're not as far along as we need to be with the Cuba connection. I mean, if we have to start digging into that from other sources . . ."

"Ugggh."

". . . and she's still feeding us nuggets about Ruby, helping to make him the unique, authentic bad guy we need, right?"

"Okay, okay. But just one more week, Ira, please. It's all I can take. I mean that."

"Deal. One week. And look, hit me here whenever she makes you crazy," Ira says half-joking, pointing to his shoulder.

"As long as you don't hit me back."

"So . . . lunch?" he asks, moving on to the next pressing problem of the day. Phoebe suggests they go out instead of ordering in—leave Joan to continue making calls from the kitchen. Ira wants to try a new sushi restaurant, "It got a great review."

"Nah, let's go back to Donburo Kai," she suggests.

They're debating the finer points of shumai when Joan rushes in, jumping up and down.

"Got something?" Phoebe asks.

Joan writes *EK* in one of the circles on the blackboard. "Eileen Kaminsky!"

"That's nice," Ira smiles and Phoebe nods and they go back to debating dumplings.

"It's his sister! I found a sister! I just spoke to her, I just spoke to Jack Ruby's sister!"

"Wow," Phoebe says, trying for more enthusiasm.

"Good for you," Ira says.

"She lives here! In California! She's agreed to meet me!"

"Nice," they both say.

"I'm in shock. I just spoke to Jack Ruby's sister!!!"

"It's amazing she'd talk to you," Ira says, playing to Joan's enthusiasm.

"Oh, you don't give up, Ira. You call and call and call and call and eventually something gives."

"Of course, that's you in a nutshell—the pit bull!" he says referring to their time on the landmark committee.

Phoebe playfully gives Ira a tap on his shoulder.

"The only way I know how to do it," Joan says.

"She must be getting on," Phoebe says. "I mean she must be pretty old."

"Well, of course she is, that's part of it, she needs to tell her story before it's too late."

Ira and Phoebe trade smiles, they'd been thinking the same thing about Joan.

"Oh, she was resistant at first," Joan's talking mainly to herself now, "but I have a very good feeling about this lady."

"From your lips," Phoebe smiles.

"I've got to see where she lives."

Joan runs out to her car for a map and Phoebe taps Ira again, this time not so lightly.

"Listen, if it gets me off the shit list and onto the A list."

"Not again," she groans.

"They wrote me off after that turkey!"

"Can you please, please, stop feeling sorry for yourself."

"It kills me to live here."

"You ingrate, this is a palace."

"It sure is!" Joan says running back in. "You should see where I live." She lays her map over their sushi menus. "So where is this place—McCloud? do you see it? I need to get there right away, she mentioned something about assisted living, who knows what that'll be like?"

Phoebe winks at Ira, she thinks Joan will find out before long.

"What town?" he asks.

"McCloud. Oh, here," she points to a small dot north of Sacramento, near the Oregon border. "That's it. That's where Ruby's sister lives. Not that far! Wow, what a day. I found Jack Ruby's sister!"

It's been an auspicious day for Joan, even more than she realizes.

Ira proposes a toast with his coffee.

"Here's to Joan Ross—the reporter with the chops to find anyone."

"You should go celebrate, go, I award you the rest of the day off," Phoebe kids.

"I think I will. Aaron and I are driving to Reno tomorrow and I've got a couple of errands to run." She slips her backpack on.

"Aaron—again? Who is this Aaron?" Phoebe teases.

"I've told you about him, he's a friend."

Ira makes a silly gesture, "Nooo . . . ?"

"No, no. We're just friends. Gambling buddies, really."

"Gambling?" Phoebe asks.

"What kind of gambling?" Ira asks.

"Poker mainly," Joan says with one hand on the door.

"Texas hold'em?" Ira can't let go of this just yet.

Joan turns back with an eyebrow raised. "Seven-card stud. Five-card draw. You know, *real* poker. Aaron's the master, taught me everything I know."

"Oh, I stand corrected," Ira smiles.

"In a million years, never would I peg you for a poker player," Phoebe says, shaking her head.

"Just one of the many reasons I'm so good at it."

They have to laugh as she walks out the door.

"A poker player. Who'd a thunk," Phoebe says.

"So she gets a reprieve?" Ira asks.

"I guess. Well, for now," Phoebe reluctantly agrees.

CHAPTER SEVEN

A vintage, baby-blue Mercedes two-seater whips into the *Atlantis* parking lot and Joan and Aaron alight.

"Wash it, will you," Aaron tosses the keys to the casino's valet.

Inside, the *Atlantis* is bright and noisy. Joan slows her pace to adjust to the clanging slot machines, the back-beat disco, and the overhead lights that are blinding. She side-steps a waitress carrying cocktails and mentions to Aaron she smells peppermint.

"Aromatherapy, they pipe it in to keep you awake."

Aaron fishes an old subway token out of his pocket, rubs it ceremoniously, and makes a beeline to a roped-off area where he signals for chips. A stocky pit boss appears from nowhere, blocking his way. An argument ensues against the clanging insistent sounds of the casino, a dispute that regulars know will end in a call to someone "upstairs" to settle.

And so it goes.

The pit boss steps aside and Aaron takes his rightful seat beside a neatly stack of chips.

Meanwhile, Joan has been divining the blackjack area and finds an empty chair at a table that speaks to her. She pulls her hair into an ancient hairband to keep it from distracting her then promptly loses three hands in a row.

Scooping up her remaining chips she moves on. She sees another open seat at a friendly-looking poker table, they welcome her in assuming the weird-looking oldie is a fish. Right away she draws a pair of kings—a harbinger of good things to come. In the midst of an extended run of great hands, she begrudgingly rises to meet Aaron in the coffee shop as promised, taking her winnings with her.

Designed to resemble a luncheonette where "gents" took their "gals" for an ice cream date, the Parrot is a mob scene, crammed with aging, overweight gamblers looking for a break from the action. Aaron has found a table in the corner and is chatting up one of the waitresses dressed like The Supremes.

"You're late. I ordered us the usual."

Video screens hug the perimeter each airing a different sporting event, silver stools with red-vinyl padding line the wrap-around counter. Besides the fact that it's two in the morning, the place hums like a high school hangout after a winning football game.

Twenty minutes later, with a half-eaten cheeseburger on his plate, Aaron is ready to get back to the tables.

"Do you mind, I'm still digesting," Joan says.

He tosses down some bills and stands to leave.

"We're leaving at nine, right?" she says.

He shrugs.

"Aaron, I told you, we're putting an issue to bed. I've got to get back. I should be there now, the whole team's working on it."

"Excuse me, aren't you the publisher?"

"It's bad enough I've been gone on the film thing. It's not right."

"Okay, okay," he mumbles hurrying off.

Diana Ross begins to clear their table. Her manner speaks volumes: *this guy is such a loser.* "Dessert, hon?" she asks sympathetically.

The naturally-caffeinated Joan uncharacteristically orders an espresso.

"Milk and sugar?"

"Just black, thanks, and the check. Better make it a double."

Joan savors her coffee and thinks back to the years she and Aaron came to Reno all the time.

In those days, back when they had something more going between them and Aaron had a guy he could trust to look after the store, they would spend three-day weekends here. Dining at the best restaurants, taking in a show or two, a splurge at the spa. But now it's just business, there-and-back, not even a room to change clothes. Why incur the expense?

She glances at the screens and is reminded of some iconic Kennedy moments: Jack without a coat on the coldest inauguration day ever, Jackie in her pillbox hat, the children playing in the oval office. Then the image of John-John's goodbye salute appears, that precious little boy, and it washes over her, threatening to take her down in tears.

I will not let them forget. What we lost.

She'll find a way to get that damn manuscript published or she'll make Grace change her mind about running it in the magazine. Or convince Ira to put more of it into his film. She'll find a way to get the story out there, one way or another.

———

Hours later Aaron has put the top down on his car, blasting oldies on the radio—all is right with his world. Joan worries the wind will bring on one of her headaches, she thinks she feels one starting. Or maybe it's the Bee Gees.

"How'd you do?" he shouts over the wind to her.

"You know me. Bet a little, win a little. You?"

"You know me, bet the ranch, trust in the gods."

"So—you scored big, huh?" Joan had guessed as much based on the music.

"Yes, ma'am. You probably saved me some shekels back there, dragging me out when you did."

"We said nine!" she yells, "It was nearly ten!"

"No, no, I'm thanking you! Really!"

They drive for a while until they pass a billboard sign.

"Wanna stop at Denny's, my treat?" he shouts. Joan shakes her head no, but Aaron has his eyes on the road. "Do ya?" he yells even louder.

"Got to get to the office, Aaron, they've probably been there all night," she yells back.

"Okay, okay. Pedal to the metal."

———

Four hundred seventy miles west of the *Atlantis*, Grace and Jeff are in Joan's office reviewing mechanicals, Grace still looking crisp in her weekend outfit, Jeff worse for wear. Other young people move tiredly about, sucking down Red Bulls.

They've all been there all night.

Grace pulls out her "cheat sheet" to check that everything is in proper alignment: *thirty-two column inches for new restaurant openings and food events — check! Thirty-two for upcoming entertainment — films, theatre, dance, festival reviews — two columns devoted to a new downtown civic development, a spread geared for children — check! check! check!*

It's a formula she believes in and revenue improvements seem to confirm. She smiles when she thinks how it makes Joan ballistic.

"Ready for the next one?" Jeff asks her. "Got a couple more. We still planning to wrap this tonight?"

"Yes, the print time is reserved. Why? You have something?"

"Sure do, box seats to the Lakers. Comps!" he toasts with his Red Bull. "So . . .?" he asks again before slinging it over his arm.

"This one's good to go," Grace salutes him.

He's nearly out the door when she adds, "Hey, I want to thank you for all your hard work on this issue, it's not gone unnoticed."

"You're welcome," he says with a smile.

"And a small favor: Can you swing back to the office after the game, just in case there's some last-minute something that I need you to look at?"

"Sure," he says, "no problem."

———————

When Jeff returns near midnight, the office is dark except for a light peeking out from under Joan's door. He finds Grace sitting at Joan's desk, she waves him in.

"It's looking great, maybe our best issue yet!" she smiles broadly at him. "You deserve a lot of the credit." She motions for him to join her in a glass of champagne. "I've been celebrating. To Jeff!" she toasts, finishing off her glass.

He picks up a press proof lying on the table. "Wow—this one came out great. I hope the center spread looks this good—that was tricky."

"I'm so excited about our future together!" Grace refills her glass and puts one into his hand. "Again—to you, your talent, your dedication!"

"To *Relevant*," he smiles warmly and takes a sip of champagne.

"And to late nights, and to blood, sweat, and tears!" she says to no one in particular, or maybe to the rest of the staff in absentia. "I want you to know how I've come to rely on you—you're the backbone of the operation, Jeff!" Grace beams.

He realizes she may be a bit tipsy.

"Thanks, Grace," he says sweetly. "Back at ya. You're taking us into the twenty-first century. Happy to be part." He toasts her and turns to go.

"Yes, I do feel we're in synch on this," she rambles, not wanting him to leave just yet. "Like two peas in a pod," she says, in case he missed her point. "This might sound odd but I dreamt about you the other night," she decides to confess.

Of course, this makes him extremely uncomfortable.

"Nightmares, huh? Ha."

"No. Seriously, sometimes I just can't leave this office behind, try as I might. I spend so much time here, it's always on my mind," she rambles on.

"Yeah, it can be intense," he agrees.

"Intense, yes," she says, picking up the theme. "There's *Relevant*, sure, the pressures of a monthly, but also the board and their investment. They're counting on me. And you know how hard it is to make some of the tough calls, I'm always the 'bad cop' around here, even though I'm only trying to steady the ship, get us out of the hole and to the next level . . ."

Realizing she's likely to go on like this for a while, and with nothing that really needs his attention, Jeff starts inching toward the door.

"But you get that, I know. I count on you to get it. I'm sure you've noticed how I've been relying on you. You've got *it*, that special something, what gets you to the top. I know. I see it. I hope that's something that you want."

Expecting some kind of positive response, Grace repeats, "Getting to the top I mean."

"Oh, I do, yes," Jeff says not knowing what else to say.

"I can help accelerate your career," she says, although now slurring, it comes out sounding like *I can sell your rear*. It takes Jeff a moment to decipher. "It can happen, you've got what it takes," she says again.

"Um, thanks, Grace," realizing she *is* plastered and desperate to get out the door. "Thanks for the kind words. I'll try to live up to it."

"Oh, you're up for it. I can see that," Grace says with a sudden nastiness in her tone she hadn't meant.

"It's really late. I'd better get going." He's got his foot in the corridor now.

"Aren't you even a little curious? I said I'm up for it if you are, Jeff." She's smiling and tilting her head seductively.

"Let's table this for tonight, Grace," he says gently. "Going home for some needed shut-eye, too many all-nighters. I'll see you tomorrow."

And he's gone.

Hey, don't ask, don't get. She shrugs and puts the matter to rest, picking up the next press proof, willing her eyes to focus, and debating whether to pack it in for the evening when Jeff sticks his head back in.

"You okay to drive?"

She doesn't look up as she waves him away.

"Of course," she says dismissively. "I'm fine. And I've still got some work here to do."

CHAPTER EIGHT

Uncle Donny is trying to pay attention. He really is. But having replaced an entire set of dentures with twenty-first-century porcelain, a long and arduous process, he's just not up for a lot of meetings lately. In fact, he had been dozing on the sofa when Joe arrived.

"I bring you the union deal, I fix Orange County and now I'm managing collections, who else you got like me, a go-getter, bringing you all this quality business?" Joe repeats his laundry list of accomplishments.

Don makes a scissors motion.

"I know, I get my cut. But I'm talking about the recognition. The respect. It's time you did what's right by me Uncle Donny. It's past time. This has been going on for too long. And Freddy was two years younger than me when he was made."

Don silently shakes his head and frowns, which translates to *"Age has nothing to do with it and you already know that."*

He takes a cigar out of the humidor, waves one at Joe, who declines, then changes his mind about the cigar and sits back on the sofa. He's starting to really fade.

"Tobeye's all over my ass about it," Joe lets slip the most likely reason they're having this conversation again.

Tobeye is Don's sister's kid. That's how Joe came into the family in the first place, Don doing her a favor. But it was a good move.

There's silence while Don gets up to pour Joe a scotch. And another for himself. "A think," he croaks out, pointing to his head.

A think is family code for *it's possible*—a much better result than Joe got the last time he went down this road.

"Deadbeat?" Don manages to ask.

"Who? Oh, the liquor store guy. Yeah, well he used to play at the *Taj* but Charlie won't seat him there no more, so now he loses at the *Atlantis*. He's still good for a couple g's with us—sports, mainly college, so it keeps him on the radar. We put him on a plan, remember?" Joe winks.

Don smiles and nods. "Ruby?"

"Oh, yeah. The deadbeat's got a friend making a movie 'bout him."

Don smiles again and points to himself.

"Yeah, I remember that story," Joe says, "when you were down in Dallas and met the guy."

Don has a Jack Ruby story that most of the family has heard several times. Whenever the assassination comes up in conversation, which is surprisingly frequent considering how long ago it took place, he tells the same tale about going down to Dallas with Santos Trafficante . . .

"And Ruby was trying to impress us, you know, trying to show us a good time, buttering us up. Had a few shitty night clubs, some coin-ops, and the girls. Wanted to hook us up. You kidding? Wouldn't touch it. Everything about him was third-rate. And on top of that a fagala!"

Don would hold his nose when he said that.

"What's that?" Joe asked the first time he heard it.

"You don't know what's a fagala?" he laughed. "How's this possible? Where'd you grow up? He's a homo, the guy takes it up the ass! This generation, what else don't you know?"

Don's eyes are closing, it's clearly time for Joe to go. He walks him to the door. "Close," Don mumbles putting his two palms together. "Capiche?"

"I gotcha Uncle Donny."

Joe knows exactly what Uncle Donny means. And what to do about it.

CHAPTER NINE

bout one hundred miles west of the *Atlantis*, the Mercedes's oil light goes on. Aaron pulls over to look under the hood but that's mainly for show; he's hopeless with anything mechanical. Nothing seems obviously out of place so he gets back on the highway but now driving slower, deepening Joan's foul mood.

A few miles later they spot a gas station, an old and dusty gas station in the middle of nowhere, a Texaco with the old star logo. And luckily there is someone there who claims to know something about foreign cars.

Anyway, that's what he says.

Gil puts the Mercedes up on a lift and begins tinkering under it. The thing is, at least it seems to Joan, that Gil tinkers really slowly, like this is the only thing he has to do today—or this week—which in fact, may be the case. Sweaty and irritated, she asks Gil if she can use his landline.

"Sure, but it don't work so good neither," he stops tinkering and takes her inside.

"It's me, Joan. Can you hear me? There's no cell service here and this connection is terrible."

Grace is perched sideways on Joan's desk, looking fresh and cool as usual. Through the glass partition, she's been monitoring the staff, watching them run back and forth with materials as the score from *Rent* blasts loudly in the background. Everyone's pumped, focused, happy.

"We're fine, stop worrying, it's a solid issue." Grace puts her hand over the phone to say "no" or "yes" to something. "I had to cut *Coming Attractions* but I'll put it online, it's more appropriate there anyway. It's all under control."

". . . in the bloody desert in the middle of nowhere . . ."

"Oh? Do you need me to do something, send a car?" Grace asks.

Being helpful and magnanimous makes Joan even more anxious.

"No, it's okay, they're fixing it, it's not—"

"Okay then, see you," Grace says, bringing the conversation to a close.

"So aggravated I'm not there. Leave me anything that—"

"What? You're—what?!" Grace ends the call.

Joan walks back into the waiting room. Aaron is sprawled out over an old leather chair with a *Men's Fitness* on his lap, asleep. She plops down across from him in a matching worn-out chair.

"Everything okay?" he asks, coming awake.

"Fine," she says.

"So, okay then," he says.

"Aaron!" She uses the voice he hates, her "teacher" voice, a way of speaking that reminds him of his second wife and not fondly. But she can't help herself. "How is it you don't have Triple-A? What car owner in America does not have Triple-A?" She stares at him through narrowing eyes.

"I had it, but I canceled it. I got tired of paying for nothing,"

"You're missing the point. It's better if you don't need it," her voice rising, "it's insurance, like life insurance. Get it?!"

Aaron's shrug suggests he doesn't carry life insurance either.

"When did you become such an idiot!?!"

Another shrug.

"What's wrong with the car?" she asks a few minutes later, after she's calmed down.

"A hole in the oil pan, easy fix. He's almost done."

Joan points to a beer can near his foot, "Where did you get that?"

"Gil said to help yourself. Want one?"

"No!" now angry again, "I don't want one! We have four more hours to drive—on no sleep—thank you very much."

"I'm not one of your interns," he says. "I'm a fully formed grown-up, I can handle a beer."

Gil enters the office wiping his dirty hands on a dirty rag and leans on the back of Aaron's chair. "Okay, folks, she's good to go."

"Great!" Joan says.

"What do I owe you?" Aaron asks.

"That'll be twenty-five dollars for the patch, plus five for the oil and eleven for the two beers. So forty-one dollars altogether."

Aaron peels off twenties from a large wad. "Here you go, can't thank you enough."

Joan races toward the car while Aaron strolls at a leisurely pace; Gil calls after, "Don't you want your change?"

Aaron waves no and slides into the driver's seat. Joan asks to put up the top—he pushes a button that unfolds it from the trunk, clamps it down, starts the car, and smiles when it purrs.

"Okay. So, tell me, what's new with the Jack Ruby project?" he asks once they're back on the road.

"I never told you the best part, Aaron, I found his sister! She's alive and living in California. I'm going to see her this week. Can you believe it—I found Jack Ruby's sister and she's willing to see me!!!"

———————

Phoebe is in her customary position on the sofa scanning the great room: diagrams fill the blackboard, documents spill over the coffee table, the corkboard is a jumble of visuals—yet there's a holiday feeling in the air.

"So, what'ya think about where we're at?" Ira asks walking in with a large mug of coffee. "Me? This is shaping into a real, complex, bad guy. Someone we haven't seen before."

"Yeah, we're close," she says. "Definitely gaining on three-dimensional. Wonder what's keeping Saint Joan?"

"Oh, she may not come in today, something about car trouble. And then she's going upstate somewhere, remember? Jack Ruby's sister. She probably won't be in much this week."

"Okay!" Phoebe laughs. "A week without crazy. I knew something felt different this morning."

"You know, um, I've started to change my mind about—"

"Oh no you don't! Don't desert me on this. She's toxic. You know it. She slows us down, overcomplicates everything."

"C'mon, she's not that . . . uh, George doesn't like her either."

"Oh really? Really? Brilliant minds think alike. Right, *Ike*?" She'd been saving that for the right moment.

"Look, Pheebes, we just need to finish this up, nail it down. Another two weeks, three at the outset, and then she can go."

"Back to whatever dark and dismal dungeon she crawled out of," Phoebe uses her Halloween voice. "Reminds me, that search. Where were we?"

"The *Chicago Sun-Times*?" Ira suggests but Phoebe's already scrolling.

"Yup, found it."

Joan Ross, investigative reporter for the *Chicago Sun-Times*, was relieved of her White House reporting duties today after the paper disclosed negligent fact-checking in the Iran Contra story and served with a "cease and desist" order from the family of Caspar Weinberger. The *Sun-Times* also cited an earlier transgression where Ross had mistakenly linked ownership of the Dallas Trade Center to the New York World Trade Center owned by a New York City real estate syndicate. After the February 1993 bombing in New York, the paper found no such linkage and was forced to retract its original story.

"Holy shit," Ira says.

"Seems Saint Joan may not be all that *persnickety* herself," Phoebe smirks. "We better make doubly sure about the stuff she's feeding us."

"It's fiction so we don't—"

"Whatever dungeon she came out from, Ira," she repeats, "don't you dare let me down on this!"

She walks over and punches his shoulder. Hard.

———

Joan parks her Hertz-Number-One-Club-Gold car and walks gingerly toward Jack Ruby's sister's house. She can't seem to locate the door, it's hidden by years of neglect and she walks right past it, arriving at the back. She searches for a bell or something to announce herself then hears barking coming from inside.

The place seems so unaccustomed to visitors Joan feels like a trespasser, like she's upsetting its natural balance. Even the weeds seem annoyed by her presence. She prays she hasn't jinxed anything, gotten off to a bad start. She called ahead—what else could she have done?

She peeks in a window and sees a kitchen. She knocks hard, guessing that Eileen, like her now-deceased mother, might be hard-of-hearing. The barking grows louder and Joan pictures a wild animal baring teeth.

"Who is it?"

Eileen opens the door slightly; Joan sees a swinging tail and two worn slippers that belong to Eileen.

"Joan Ross."

She waits for the deadbolt to be released.

Eileen is wearing sweatpants, beads, and bright pink lipstick, which Joan realizes she forgot to apply herself in the rush to get ready this morning. Her small, neat kitchen has orange Formica counters and colorful green appliances, like something out of a time machine. Joan stays hovering near the door—the big dog straining to get her scent.

"Here, sit down. I'll take care of him," Eileen says, leading the dog out of the kitchen and returning quickly. "So how was your trip?"

"Fine. But it was long. Thank goodness for GPS," she adds then wonders if Eileen even knows what she's talking about.

"You got one of them new-fangled cars, huh? Good for you. Saved ya some coffee. Should be hot," Eileen says.

"No, thank you. Do you mind if we just jump in, Eileen? I only have a couple of hours before I need to drive back. I really screwed this up; I thought I could get a hotel last minute but the closest place was over two hours back . . ."

"Yeah, I'm in the boonies," Eileen laughs. "You sure came a long way to talk to an old lady." She motions to the coffee, "Sure? Okay . . . so, let me think. Oh yeah, on the phone I was telling you about my family, my growing up with Jack and the rest of them."

Joan pulls out her pad. "Mind if I take notes? I don't want to forget anything."

Eileen doesn't answer right away.

"Sure, go ahead," she says finally. "Got nothing to hide. Nothing to be scared of. What can they do to me now?"

"What? Did somebody threaten you?"

"Oh, hon, it was years ago, right after Jack went to prison. Three tough guys paid me a visit. Said to keep my trap shut or else!" Eileen chuckles. "Yeah, didn't leave no business card if ya know what I mean. But that was a long, long time ago. They're probably all dead by now."

"So, you're okay with this? We can talk about Jack, pick up our conversation from the other day? My project doesn't include the assassination, Eileen," Joan tries to ward off any lingering concerns. "I'm just here to learn more about Jack's family life, his early days. We won't go anywhere you're not comfortable, I promise."

"Sure, sure," Eileen says, distracted by the scratching coming from the closet. "How about we sit outside since it's so nice and all? I got a table and chairs I hardly use and I can let the dog—"

"Of course, yes, let's!" Joan's allergies had kicked in the minute she entered the kitchen, she's thrilled to get back outside.

Eileen leads them out to the yard, stepping over cracks in the patio. Just as they both get settled, she remembers she forgot the dog.

"Terrible what happens to your memory, right?"

They both laugh as she goes back to retrieve him.

"So, anyways, on the phone, I was telling you about the time my Lenny died," Eileen says as she sits back down. "I think I told you but he wasn't sick or nothing. He's getting ready for work when I hear this loud crash and there he is on the shower floor! We'd only been married a few years, I thought maybe I was gonna end up an old spinster. Then he has that heart attack and dies a couple of days later."

"Tragic," Joan says.

"Here I was, thinking my real life had finally begun, and he up and dies like that." She shakes her head. "Anyways, I'm living down the block from Lenny's family, this is St. Louis, hardly knew a soul. Never worked much, just some waitressing and once in a factory, so when he passes" — she sighs — "Left me some life insurance, sure, got his veteran pay and the house and all. So moneywise it was okay, but I was real lonely. Anyways, a couple of months later I hear from my brother Jack, why don't I come down to Dallas for a visit? Maybe even move there. Check it out, see how I like it."

"That was very considerate, were you two close?"

"Nah, wouldn't call us close. We had a rough time growing up. A lot of kids, never enough money."

"Like a lot of families back then."

"We were eight kids! Jack was what you call the black sheep of the bunch, always in trouble. Hanging out with a rough crowd from the wrong side of the tracks. Not our kind, if you know what I mean."

Joan looks up from her pad. "This would be about the time he worked in the bodega?"

Eileen laughs. "Not sure you'd call it that, he pretty much stole what he could from the back of the store. My folks wrote him off, they had their hands full."

"What about you, how did you get along with your parents?"

"Me? Oh, it was different with me, I was the baby of the family. Papa's little girl. Did what I was told, didn't cause no trouble. Not like Jacob."

"Jacob, that's Jack's real name."

"His given name. Never used it though. Too Jewish."

"Sounds like my folks," Joan says. "Didn't want to be labeled."

"You're Jewish?!" Eileen says peering at her. "Funny, you don't look it."

They both laugh.

"Rosenzweig was my last name originally," Joan explains.

"My, my. Well, those guys at Ellis Island changed a lot of names," Eileen says knowingly.

"Actually, it was my parents who changed it, thought we'd fit in better. They were always kind of"—Joan searches for the right word—"ambivalent. I think my dad thought it would be better for business. Caused a lot of tension in our family."

"Yeah. Well, Jack liked to pretend he was Spanish, could speak it too. Used to speak Spanish around the neighborhood, drove Papa crazy," she laughs.

"Are you saying Jack spoke Spanish?"

"Yeah, pretty good at it too. Had a way with languages," Eileen boasts.

Joan's eyes grow wide, *First I heard of this.*

"Spanish, a little Italian, and Yiddish, of course."

"My grandparents spoke Yiddish."

"That's what we spoke at home," Eileen says. "The only language my mother knew. Kinda put the kibosh on me bringing friends over."

"I can imagine." *Phoebe will be over the moon!*

"Thought knowing Italian would get him in good with the mob."

"Honing his career skills," Joan jokes.

"Yeah, Jacob Rubenstein, very Italian," Eileen laughs. "Also to impress the ladies." She bats her eyes.

"Ah, anyone special you remember?"

"A lot of them back then. Jack liked the lookers, you know, them 'show girls.' Always a blonde on his arm, always showing her a good time, taking her to fancy restaurants, spending money.

That's one thing you can say about Jacob, he took care of his people. Bought me my ticket to Dallas," Eileen says proudly.

Joan smiles. "What about his other friends?"

"Friends—you mean the Italians he was always trying to impress? Dressed like them, tried to be tough like them, but Jack was small and skinny. And they knew he was Jewish. I don't think they took him serious. Nah, I'm not sure you'd call them friends."

"You said he tried to act tough—like how?" Joan asks with Phoebe in mind.

"He walked around like this." Eileen pushes up from her chair and begins to strut, swinging her arms and waving to her "fans." Her dog runs over with an old tennis ball in his mouth, ready for a game of fetch.

They laugh again.

"So tell me about the time you went to Dallas, what was that like? On the phone, you mentioned this was after the July Fourth holiday—so July 1963?"

"Let me think . . . yup, think so. Lennie dies in February and a few months later I go down to Dallas. Yeah, right after the Fourth of July."

"And you stay for how long?"

"About three weeks I guess. Dallas wasn't for me. You know Jack loved it—had this nightclub and all. Everybody knew him there, treated him with respect. I got treated nice too 'cause I was his sister. But Dallas . . ." she shakes her head.

"This was about the time of the Silver Spur, when Jack ran the Silver Spur?" Joan has beaten down her pencil and is searching for another.

"Don't remember the name of the place. Kind of a dump if you ask me. Jack thought it was ritzy, never had no taste," she smiles, enjoying these memories. "And listen, you had a secret? Never tell Jacob. Such a big mouth!" She wiggles her finger and they laugh again.

"So what happens there in Dallas, how come you didn't like it?" Joan prompts.

"Nothing. Just couldn't handle the heat. Dallas." Eileen makes a face. "When Jack got arrested he said not to come back. I wanted to, and . . . well, but I couldn't help him, what could I do? and I didn't need all those questions," she makes the face again. "Those reporters. What a terrible bunch of—oh, present company excluded. You're different from the others, I can see that now." She sends her a big smile.

"Well, thank you, Eileen."

"So anyways, once those reporters figured out I didn't know any more than they did, they stopped pestering me, left me alone."

"Okay. So may I ask you this now?" Joan pauses to collect her thoughts. "Tell me if you'd rather not answer, Eileen, but I have to ask. After all this time, do you still think it was Jack behind the killing?"

"WHAT? Are you blind?! Everybody saw him pull the trigger—it was there on the TV over and over and over—"

"No, of course, I know Jack shot Oswald. What I meant was did he ever tell you *why* he did it?"

Eileen is silent.

"Was it his idea, all on his own?" Joan realizes she's losing Eileen and stops herself. "Let's go inside, you're getting cold."

"Yeah, okay, I'll make us a nice cup of tea. Unless you want something stronger? Let me just deal with the dog. C'mon, Newport, we're going in now."

"Newport? What an unusual name."

"Doc said quit or else. So I gave up smoking and got me Newport. Been a real comfort to me all these years."

"Aah, so if I ever get a dog I'll call him Winston."

They smile at one another, back on solid ground.

"Still miss it, don't ya? My dad lived to ninety and smoked like a chimney."

"My folks never knew I smoked, they would have killed me. Years and years and they never knew," Joan says sadly.

"Hon, bet there was some other things they never knew. Right? Am I right?"

They laugh.

"Everything by the book. No smoking, no drinking," Joan sighs. "My dad died when I was just a teenager, my mom was only in her fifties."

"Oh, that's sad. Red wine okay?"

"Please don't think you need to entertain me."

"It's real nice having company, hon. At my age, I don't get out much and hardly nobody stops by. Nearly nobody left, I'm afraid."

"This must be a hard house to keep up, I mean all by yourself," Joan says, now really looking around.

"Yeah, and it's falling apart. Think maybe it's time for me to go into one of those assisted living places. You know, where they cook and clean for you. Drive you to the docs when you gotta go. Some brochures around here somewhere."

Eileen finds one and passes it to Joan.

"This looks quite nice, *Shady Elms*. Looks very well cared for."

"I thought so too. But been putting it off. They don't take dogs. Been waiting for Newport to . . . well, the beast may outlive me yet."

Joan sips at her wine and tries to get them back on track.

"So, tell me more about your time in Dallas. Were you there when Jack ran the Carousel Club?"

"He had a bunch of clubs," Eileen says refilling her glass. "Buying 'em, selling 'em, mostly they were dumps if you ask me. One time he asked me to come work for him, help him with the books. Ha! His books! Who could make heads or tails out of that nonsense!" Eileen suddenly looks sad. "Look, don't get me wrong, I worshiped the guy. Jacob had a heart of gold, and he was always looking out for me."

"Your big brother," Joan smiles.

"I'm so glad you came, Joan, this is such fun, thinking about the old days. Don't get much company out here."

Joan thinks about how lonely she must be, living so remotely with only a dog for company. She decides to try one more time.

"So, did Jack ever tell you anything about the shooting?"

This time Eileen thinks a while before answering. "No, he never did. I did go to visit him in prison once, but by then he was feeling poorly, really bad." Eileen is suddenly filled with sad memories of Jack.

"Can you tell me about that," Joan asks gently. "He thought he had cancer, right?"

"Well, that's what they told him, but he didn't trust them prison doctors. Who would, would you?"

"Oh no!" Joan says looking at her watch, suddenly startled. "I'm going to have to leave right now if I'm making that last flight out!"

Eileen gets startled too. "Where's my mind? I meant to show you . . . there's this old family album."

She walks into the living room and returns with an album. As she hands it over, a couple of photos fall out from the bottom. Joan rescues them a second before they land in Newport's mouth.

She's immediately drawn to a seven-by-ten photo of a night-club, eight smiling people sitting around a beautifully draped table set with gold-rimmed china and crystal glassware. The women are wearing elaborate cocktail dresses, the men in dark suits and ties. And behind them stands Jack Ruby, arms outstretched, smiling broadly like he's saying, "*See, these are my friends, my crowd, aren't we swell.*"

"His nightclub?" she asks.

"Let me see," Eileen says taking back the photo. "Yeah, that's one of his. See, that's me sitting over there." She shows Joan.

"Look at you! You were gorgeous, so elegant!" Joan says only slightly exaggerating. She strains to see more details in the photo.

"I loved that dress, Jack bought it for me," Eileen says, lost in the past.

"Eileen, do you have a magnifying glass?"

She laughs at the thought. "Why don't you just take this album home with you, go through it with a fine-tooth comb."

"Borrow this, really? Why, thank you, Eileen. I promise I'll take great care." She's amazed at Eileen's generosity.

"I have some equipment back at my office that can help restore old photos, do you want me to try and fix these up?"

"Keep 'em as long as you want," Eileen says, walking her to the door. "And if you can fix 'em up too that'd be great."

"I am so happy we met, thank you for such a wonderful day." Joan goes to take her hand but Eileen gives her a big hug instead.

"Thanks for coming, hon."

"I'll phone you in a day or two if that's okay. I'm sure to have a couple more questions to ask." She knows she's going to worry about Eileen now, now that she sees how she lives, now that she's become fond of the lady.

"Call me anytime. Or listen, you come back if you think it could be helpful. Safe travels, hon."

Joan drops the Hertz off and sprints to the terminal. She makes it just as they are closing the doors. And while she's anxious to look through the photo album she resists, not wanting to risk peering eyes from nearby seats. Instead, she reviews her notes, what Eileen told her about Jack, about Eileen herself, alone in that house in the woods. What would a move to Shady Elms entail? Maybe she can help her get ready for that. She should make that happen soon, before . . . well, Joan would rather not think about that.

———

Up in McCloud, Eileen's finished dinner and is watching tv in bed, Newport at her feet. She too is reviewing the day, a busy one, with that lovely lady's visit and the trip down memory lane. She suddenly remembers there was something else she wanted to show Joan—not just the photo album. What was it? She thinks and thinks and finally gives up, ready to call it a night. She shuts off her light and pulls up the covers and then—she remembers! The box. Yes, the box Jack gave her for safekeeping. Now, where oh where did she put it?

———

Joan's home phone has a message light blinking; Aaron wants to know if she's available for a game Thursday night. She calls him back to confirm.

"An amazing woman and so generous! I learned so much I didn't know. Not only did Jack Ruby speak Spanish, the guy spoke Yiddish! Can you imagine, Yiddish? And she gave me an old photo album, there are a couple of shots that could be important. I'm going to try and restore them when—"

"Joan, listen," he interrupts. "You're not gonna believe this. I just found out that a friend of mine, Joe, don't think you know him—anyway Joe knows someone who knew Jack Ruby!"

"What! Oh my god! How?"

"Joe says that his Uncle used to be in the Mob. He's retired now, an old dude, but he was a big deal back in the day. Anyway, he says that his Uncle Donny went to Dallas at some point and met Jack Ruby there."

"Uncle Donny . . . Donato Escarolla?!? Oh my god, Aaron, if this is Escarolla!? He was the top man—you got to get me in to see him. I'm serious. I'll never ask you for another thing in my entire life."

"Okay," he says.

"I swear, he's the real deal! I'll go anywhere, anytime!"

"Hey, relax!" Aaron snaps. "I'll ask him, okay? I don't know where this guy lives anyway."

"It doesn't matter where he lives. Call Joe now then call me back."

"CALM DOWN, will you? I don't have his number, it's in the store. I'll call him tomorrow."

"Please. Please, Aaron. Swear you won't forget!"

"I promise. Jeez, I'll call him tomorrow."

"Call me the minute after you speak to him."

Grace hasn't missed Joan one bit. The magazine is running smoothly, their latest issue looks great, and best of all, Jeff has had a change of heart.

Grace isn't sure what brought that on but she's trying not to analyze it too closely—she's just enjoying it for what it is.

Sometimes there's a muffin waiting in the morning, once flowers were delivered to her (Joan's) office, and just today, Jeff texted an evite to dinner when he found out his roommate would be away.

Luckily, Grace had dressed in something chic this morning. Something youthful. Something he's sure to like if things progress as planned. Her plans.

Jeff looked a bit flustered all day, a bit red in the face, so when he says he has to leave early, Grace says, "Sure, happy weekend" as if she won't see him again until Monday.

His cottage in Santa Monica is disappointing, more run-down than imagined, although she really has no idea of what's possible on a creative director's salary.

It's clean at least.

She brings along a bottle of her favorite rosé, which Jeff accepts graciously but without true appreciation. He is standing in his kitchen finishing up a roast. It smells delicious, Jeff often boasts about his cooking.

I should have brought a red, she thinks. *Or two*, she smiles to herself.

He hands her a glass of champagne he has waiting, remembering the champagne she offered him that night in the office.

"*Salud*," they toast.

"Smells really yummy in here," she says.

She's already decided to let him be the aggressor, she's going to be playing it cool. But the warmth and aroma emanating from the kitchen, and with a handsome young man being so gracious—well, she's already pretty excited.

She walks around his living room, sipping champagne and admiring the art on the walls.

"Love this," she says about the lighthouse and he agrees, it's one of his favorites. Glenn, his roommate, is a fine artist who sometimes freelances for the magazine and it's his work that lines the walls. She completes the tour while Jeff plates the roast with small potatoes, carrots, and another vegetable that she can't put her finger on.

The table has been set with a giant tossed salad, warm bread, and Jeff brings the remaining champagne along with two new glasses for the rosé.

They never make it past the salad.

He rises to put some on her plate and ends up kissing her neck. He's not sure how that happened but he is sure she's okay with it. Before they know it, they are backing into his bedroom.

Grace's surprise is a silky thong she ordered from Victoria's Secret for the occasion, it requires no other *accouterment* and seems to be very appropriately selected. Later, they'll return to the table to enjoy the rest of their dinner.

Jeff's roast is delicious. Everything about this evening is delicious.

CHAPTER TEN

Joe enters Aaron's liquor store carrying two Dunkin' coffees and a thick brown envelope tucked under his arm. He places the envelope next to the cash register and slides a coffee down the counter to where Aaron is standing.

"Deposit this when the bank opens tomorrow. Then wait twenty-four hours and do a wire transfer into this account for the same amount." Joe points to a number scribbled on the top of the envelope.

"You read my mind," Aaron says sipping the steaming brew.

"Yeah, yeah, you're welcome."

"This is kosher, Joe. I can pull this off?"

"Piece a cake, Aaron. Got my man Phil on the inside. Hey, I brought you a picture of me on the swim team," he puts down his coffee and pulls a photo from his jacket. "See, that's me!"

Aaron sees a group of handsome and fit young men standing in front of an Olympic-sized pool, each wearing a UCLA swim cap. "You the mascot?" he says, eager to assess Joe's mood.

"Har. Har. Very funny."

"What's with the caps?"

"You never been to a swim meet? That's what you wear, shmuck."

"And what, you shave your legs too?"

"God, I was buff then," Joe says grabbing back the photo.

"By the way, I just spoke with my friend, Joan. You know, the one who's making the movie about Jack Ruby . . ."

"Sure, of course. Uncle Donny knew Ruby."

"Yeah, so you said. Well, turns out, my friend would love to meet your uncle."

"Who?"

"Uncle Donny."

"Oh no, he's not my uncle, Aaron. That's his name."

"Huh?"

"Uncle, Donny. It's like . . . like . . . President Bush."

"President Bush? Bush isn't president."

"But that's what you say when you see him on the street, right? 'Look, there's President Bush!'"

Oh okay. "So if she wants to meet um—*him*—you can make that happen, right?"

"Just where is she with her little fairytale anyway?"

"Well, she met Ruby's sister, learned some cool stuff about his family life, him growing up and all."

"Wow!" Joe says. "Gonna make a call, be right back."

He steps outside and Aaron decides to peek inside the envelope. It's just what he thought: wads of high-denomination bills tied up in rubber bands. Aaron's not sure what a million dollars looks like but . . .

"Uncle Donny says set it up, he'll meet your friend," Joe's back in a flash.

Aaron suddenly feels queasy about this development. He busies himself opening a delivery crate, trying to think it through.

"The guy loves talking about the good old days, makes him feel young," Joe says, sensing the change in mood.

"Is this something I shouldn't be doing?" Aaron asks finally, "I mean I don't want to get Joan into anything."

"What ya talking about? These are bedtime stories, Aaron. Fairy tales. Uncle Donny's an old guy, we're just keeping him happy is all,"

"So . . ." he takes a deep breath. "Anything in it for me?"

"Hmmm," Joe takes a second look at Aaron. "Lemme run it up the flag pole," he says as he's leaving.

"Yeah, you do that," Aaron says.

"And put that envelope somewhere for safe keeping. You don't want it laying around. Just in case you get a customer in here someday."

CHAPTER ELEVEN

ra and Phoebe are working late so when the doorbell rings, Ira answers expecting Chinese food.

"I couldn't wait," Joan says.

Over dumplings, kung pao chicken, and house fried rice, she takes them through her meeting with Eileen.

Phoebe has positioned herself across from Ira so she can look at him when Joan speaks, the tuna pita experience still very top of mind. This leaves Ira sitting across from Joan, but since she's quite inept with chopsticks, it's much less of an open-mouth chewing issue.

"And another thing," Joan says stabbing at a dumpling. "His mother had emotional problems and that was hard on the family. In and out of hospitals, even a nervous breakdown once. Some of the kids went into foster care but Jack was left to fend for himself."

"Yikes," Phoebe says. "How old was he then?"

"Eileen said twelve, maybe thirteen?"

"That can't be good," Ira says.

"She called him the black sheep of the family," Joan carries on, searching for a fork or spoon but finding neither on the table. "His

78

folks wrote him off, couldn't cope with all his issues—they had all these other kids to worry about."

"So, let's just think about this for a minute," Phoebe says, pushing back from the table. "Here's a boy, left on his own, on the street. Folks have nothing to do with him. He's not even a real teenager yet, it must have felt like desertion."

"And he's short and skinny and you know how little guys can get complexes, they act tough but it's an act," Ira says.

"So, he tries to fit in somewhere. No wonder the Mafia looks good to him, it's like family," Phoebe says. "Joan! This is key to his whole motivation—a small, lonely kid, trying to find a place to belong."

"You hit the jackpot," Ira says, "there's a lot more here to work with."

"So, tell us about the sister," Phoebe asks.

"Spry, funny, old but you'd never know it. And generous! She gave me all these photos, who knows what we can learn from them."

"Incredible," Phoebe says, stifling a yawn. "Guys, I'm beat, let's call it a night."

"You hardly ate anything," Ira says to Joan as he packs up the leftovers, "take this home with you."

———————

Something about tonight's dinner makes Ira nostalgic, he keeps thinking back to his family growing up—*the Chinese food,* he figures.

His folks were Hollywood royalty back in the day. Mom was a singer in an opening act for some of the biggest bands on the road. She toured the country extensively with her two sisters, Aunt Phyllis and Aunt Rose, until Rose contracted measles and lost her voice.

His dad had dreams of becoming a professional baseball player—a catcher—but flamed out in the minors; instead, he had a long career as a well-regarded sports reporter.

Ira and his brother George were both athletes growing up. George was a natural at tennis and Ira flourished in basketball. But when some of his teammates caught up to him in height, Ira started spending more time on the bench; later he switched to golf. But that didn't work out either—golf was just too slow. Neither brother ended up with sports as a career, although George still kills on the tennis court, they leaned into entertainment like their mother's side of the family.

George's first acting job out of college was on a TV soap, the show ran for years and was an even bigger hit overseas. TV led to small parts on low-budget films, then bigger films, then credits above the title. He began directing and producing and remains an international favorite today, respected for his philanthropy as much as his artistic talent. The trajectory of George's life has been a steady rise and he's been smart and careful with his money.

Ira is smart too. But less careful.

His writing skills led to some decent early jobs, but he decided to forgo salary to work on a spec film that never got released. After that, he spent a year as a speechwriter for a California guber-natorial candidate (his guy lost in the primaries), then flailed around for a while until George sent a screenwriting job his way.

That was his lucky break.

The film was a hit, won a couple of awards, and Ira spent a decade writing sitcoms and romcoms that scored at the box office. But he never developed the necessary toughness for the business, and after *Bridges Down* and the divorce, he fell apart.

He still has trouble sleeping, drinks more than he should, and vacillates between that easy-going guy with legions of friends to a cranky introvert apt to fly off the handle at the smallest provocation.

The pressure on him now is crushing. *Long Road to Havana* has got to be more than good—it's got to be great. He's keeping an eye on that prize and there's no way Joan Ross—or anyone—can get in the way.

———

Phoebe's driving home when she sees Tom entering the estate from the other direction. She waves but he doesn't see her, he's half-turned to someone sitting in the back.

Escorting another princess to the palace, she thinks.

George is waiting for them by the fountain, he's brought along two champagne flutes, his charming smile and sparkling eyes. The Escalade pulls up and he tilts his head inside to welcome his guest.

"Laine, so wonderful to see you again."

———

So, George prefers the company of men. At first, it was an occasional thing, a sometimes thing he'd take advantage of when traveling—away from LA. But as he grew older, the company of men became the companionship he most desired.

And so what? This had long stopped being an issue in Hollywood, no longer making news. But his business manager, the one who made George a millionaire by the time he was thirty, the one responsible for him earning more money in residuals than he can spend in a lifetime, the one who allowed him to build this estate, buy the loft in Tribeca, the apartment overlooking Lac Leman in Geneva, anything—*everything*—his heart desires . . . for some reason that guy insists George keep his sexual preferences under wraps.

That it could significantly damage his career.

So he does, he keeps it secret. Not even Ira is aware. Only Tom.

CHAPTER TWELVE

Joan has started phoning Eileen every night before bed, she knows she'll be awake. Eileen sleeps only a couple of hours each night, Joan herself doesn't sleep much either. Sometimes their calls go on and on, talking about all sorts of things—the way friends do late at night.

Lately they've been discussing the various adult living homes Eileen's visited, *Shady Oaks* still the favorite.

Eileen likes to hear about Joan's workday, loves hearing about the young people, loves all the crazy things they do.

"So we took a poll and everyone voted to bring their dogs into the office," Joan tells her.

"What! Who ever heard of such a thing?" Eileen can't believe she's not joking.

"Luckily, Grace nixed the idea. So now everyone's angry with her, they call her the pet nazi!"

They laugh.

Eileen tells Joan about the time she brought home a stray, mangy dog from the neighborhood. Her mother wouldn't let it inside the house, she screamed she had barely enough food to feed the family.

"That must have hurt," Joan says.

"I brought it back to where I found it. I was so afraid it would be mad at me, but the mutt just took off. Ha. Stuff we did as kids."

"Did I ever tell you about the time I became very religious?" Joan asks. "It was a phase—probably just to piss off my mother—I might have been eleven or twelve. Started saying prayers over dinner, going to synagogue, keeping the Sabbath. They thought I'd lost my mind. But then the Bay of Pigs happened and then the assassination and . . . well anyway, all those empty rituals in the face of everything that was going on."

"I would have loved to have known you then," Eileen says. "We weren't very religious, but Jacob!—he wouldn't wear a yarmulke, not even at a funeral!"

"Well I grew up hearing that Jews were the most persecuted people in the world, so when I learned that Jack Ruby was a Jew, I couldn't believe it—a Jew capable of cold-blooded murder!"

"I know. I couldn't believe it either. Even after I saw it with my own eyes!"

"It kind of tripped me up, made me question everything I thought I knew, everything my parents had told me. I got moody and withdrawn. And later, when I was old enough to date, I went for the 'bad' guys, you know, the ones I knew they'd hate."

"Don't know much about kids, Joan, but that sounds pretty normal to me."

"Yeah, maybe . . . Well, here's some news, something on a happier note. I may have a chance to meet someone who knew Jack!"

"Really?"

"Yes. It's a friend of a friend of a friend. Claims he was in the 'mob' back in the day and says he knew your brother."

"Well, Jacob certainly had contacts there," Eileen says.

"So I wanted to know if there's anything you'd like me to find out for you, anything you'd like me to ask this guy. If I get the chance to meet him and all."

Eileen's quiet for a moment. "Thanks, hon, but I think I know as much about that as I need to."

"Oh, sure, I totally understand. And he's got to be ancient, right? Probably won't remember anything anyway."

"Like me," Eileen says.

"Are you kidding—you still got it, my dear, you're as sharp as a tack. I only hope I can keep it together when I'm your age."

"Well, thank you. Sometimes it's a struggle."

"Yes, I was thinking about that, about how hard life must have been for you after Dallas, that must have been dreadful, seeing him go to jail and all. Cops, reporters, everyone throwing questions at you. After all you'd been through with Lenny."

"Yeah," Eileen sighs. "But you get through it, right? You had it tough too, losing your parents at such a young age."

"Well with my dad, it was one thing. We pulled together after that," Joan says, "but then when my mom died—geez. We were on the outs, barely speaking. One time, I told her I hated her. It started over something silly, but then I called her a two-faced liar. Swore I'd never be like her. God, the look on her face."

"That's old history now," Eileen says.

"That look! I'll never forget it. I never apologized, I didn't realize I'd never get the chance . . . oh . . ."

"That's life. Trust me, she knew. Deep down in her heart, she knew. Lenny wasn't much for words neither, but I knew how he felt."

"I never told anyone that story before."

"You can tell me anything, hon. Nothing surprises me. At my age, I think I've seen it all."

"So, that reminds me. I've been going through some of my old files . . . did Jack ever mention Dorothy Kilgallen to you?"

"No, that doesn't ring a bell. Oh wait, isn't she the *What's My Line* lady?"

"Yes. And you and I are about the last remaining folks on earth who remember that show. I was watching some old film of the shooting. You can find a lot of this on the internet now. There's a piece of live footage where a reporter gets a policeman to move— leave his post!—so he can get a better shot of Oswald sprawled on the pavement. The cop does it too, he accommodates him, it's like bloody theatre, the whole thing looks staged!"

"Jack never told me anything. Really. I never understood why he shot Oswald. I know you have your theory about him getting in good with the mob, and sure, he always wanted that but . . . I just can't see him shooting anyone. Just like that—in front of people! In front of the whole damn country!"

"I hear you. Maybe one day we'll know."

"Nah, I doubt it. We would have heard already, someone would have said something."

Joan hears Newport bark.

"I'm gonna take the dog out and say goodnight for now, hon. You get some rest, you hear."

"'Night, my friend, talk to you tomorrow."

CHAPTER THIRTEEN

Aaron is at the register, ringing up a sale, when Joe walks in. He pretends interest in an expensive Merlot, stalling until the customer leaves.

"Wasn't you supposed to call me? What, you lose my number?"

"I was just about to," Aaron says, "but you know why? 'Cause when I did the bank run this morning guess what—Phil was MIA!"

"What?! What'ya mean?"

"Phil, your bank guy, missing in action, nowhere to be found!"

Joe's eyes grow wide.

"Nobody seemed to know anything. What's up with that?"

Joe gets quiet, thinking about what could have gone wrong, whether this is something he needs to worry about or if it's just Aaron being a fuckup as usual.

"You went to the right branch?"

"Yeah, Joe, it's not my first rodeo. What do I do with your *deposit*?" Aaron asks testily.

Joe's still thinking, weighing his options. "Don't do anything until I figure it out," he says finally. Then he remembers why he came in the first place. "What about the girlfriend, Aaron? Does she want to meet Uncle Donny or not?"

"You bet she does, she doesn't stop hocking me about it."

"So then call her now, let's get this going," Joe says. "Uncle D's having a little dental work, but he'll be available next week. Let's make a plan."

"How about next Tuesday?"

"What's wrong with Monday?"

"She might be just getting back to town. She's thinking about going away for the weekend."

"Oh yeah, where she going?"

Aaron turns back toward the register like there's something there that needs attending.

"She's got a friend in Northern California she goes up to visit sometimes."

"Yeah, Jack Ruby's sister. You told me about her already. I still can't believe that old dame is alive."

Aaron decides to take the plunge.

"You said this connection might be helpful to me, Joe. Personally." He looks him in the eyes. "Help me clear up some of what I owe. So what about it?"

"Ya gotta give me something to work with, Aaron, like, what's she doing up in Northern California for example?"

"Well, like I said, that's the sister, an old lady, you know—she goes to help her out, give her a hand."

"I mean something important." Joe gives him a steely stare.

"Um, well, she found a photo," he says finally.

"Oh yeah, what kind of photo?"

Joe's expression is making him nervous.

"I don't know. She said it was very faded, like you can't see who's in it . . . maybe from a nightclub, hard to tell . . ."

"So why don't you give me the photo and I'll show it to Uncle Donny, and maybe he'll recognize somebody," Joe says still staring at him.

"Oh, I don't have it." Aaron walks around the counter hoping to end this conversation.

"Hey, I just got in some outstanding Nebbiolos. Very rare. From Cape Town . . . South Africa," he says after a beat.

"Yeah, I know where Cape Town is Aaron."

"Why don't you bring Uncle Donny a bottle, it'll put you in his good graces."

"What the fuck! Don't change the subject!"

Aaron puts the bottle back down.

"Would it help if I found out some more stuff about the old lady," he finally asks, "or the photo?"

"Uh-huh," Joe says. "That would be helpful. And why don't you call your friend now while I wait? You can see if she's free for Tuesday," Joe asks. But it doesn't sound like a question.

"Okay," he says.

"And I'll take one of those Nebs."

CHAPTER FOURTEEN

Joan is standing at Uncle Donny's door when she gets a serious case of nerves. She thinks she might throw up, she can't remember the last time she felt like this.

The day that Grace arrived at *Relevant*?

The time the bank threatened to shut them down?

When she got fired from the *Sun-Times*?

Oh, the printing fiasco.

I'm like, what, thirty years old???

She's standing on the hard concrete of a factory that stinks of oil, leaning over an ancient linotype printer.

"Hey kid, don't get so close, you'll fall in."

The owner is a big fat guy who smells of cigars and thought a tie would cover his protruding stomach. And he's not pretending that he's not aggravated to be dealing with someone who knows nothing about anything, especially printing.

He keeps asking when Berta will arrive.

She already told him Berta's not coming.

The printer is groaning, the pages fly by, making it hard to distinguish one from the next when young Joan spots something amiss, something out of register. The color cyan is bleeding off the page. She tells him to stop and check.

"WHAT!" he yells over the clanging machinery, "STOP THE PRESS? Are you crazy? Do you even know what you're ASKING?!?"

She watches the speeding pages a bit longer to make sure.

She's sure. She yells over again to stop the press.

While it's clearly a big deal, he can't talk her out of it. She is the client after all. He finally signals the press operator and the machine grinds to a halt.

He pulls a sheet and they stare at it intensely.

It's perfect.

Joan feels the butterflies and then her face turns hot and she runs looking for a bathroom finding only a men's room that's luckily vacant.

And throws up in a urinal.

Aunt Berta laughs so hard when she tells her the story that it makes the whole terrible nightmare worthwhile, just to hear her laugh like that.

That was more than two decades ago.

Joan takes a deep breath before ringing the doorbell. Berta reappears. "What's with the nerves? Baby, you got this."

Classic Berta.

She wonders how old Escarolla really is. "Old" is what Aaron said. He may have been a big deal once upon a time, but now he's just an old man wanting to reminisce about old times. That's what he said.

Joan knows she's good with old people, they get her right away. Sense she's trustworthy and dependable and she's a very good listener, a skill she picked up as a reporter. Younger people like her too, at least some of them, the ones that aren't turned off by her intensity. *Although some don't,* she chuckles, thinking about Grace. She takes another calming breath and reaches out just as the door swings open, and there is Uncle Donny. For a split second, she fears that he's seen her standing there the whole time.

"Come in," he says through a mouth of very white teeth. "Happy you could make it."

She stifles a nervous laugh.

Uncle Donny is wearing some kind of expensive tracksuit with an emblem she doesn't recognize and exotic sneakers, a little sparkly. It makes him look friendly and a bit odd. Joan is glad she took the time to look professional. And remembered the lipstick.

"You must be the gal making the movie," he says smiling and nodding.

"I am." She holds out her hand, "Joan Ross."

"Pleased to meet you. Carmen Donato Escarolla. Call me Don."

It takes some convincing, but Don finally stops trying to ply Joan with a sherry, a drink he's convinced is appropriate for *a beautiful woman like Joan from Hollywood.* Joan has never, ever, been called beautiful, and even though she knows it's a lie, and even though Don is *only ninety-three and in excellent health—prime of his life, never better!* she takes an immediate liking to the man.

"So who's financing the film?" he gets right to the point.

She explains about the studio and George which leads to a discussion about Ira and Phoebe; Don asks about mezzanine debt and alternative funding, they have a surprisingly sophisticated exchange that ends up lamenting the digital world and how everything has changed and not much for the better.

By now, Don has convinced *Joan from Hollywood* to have a glass of wine, "an excellent Meursault, a gift from your friend with the liquor store." As he pours, he tells her a story about his dear friend Arnholt Smith, a finance mogul with a serious wine cellar. Arnie owned a huge and successful bank back in the day.

"US National, remember that one?"

"No, Don, can't say I do."

"Maybe before your time," he smiles.

US National was one of America's largest independent banks before it imploded in the '70s, taking Arnie down in a myriad of lawsuits. The IRS, the SEC, Fannie Mae, the FDIC, everyone wanted a piece of Arnie. Ultimately, he was convicted of embezzlement, fined $80 million, and sent to jail.

"Eighty million dollars!" He shakes his head sadly, "that was a lot of money back then. And then he dies behind bars. Poor guy."

They compare and contrast that to Bernie Madoff and Joan learns that Don avoided investing with that *gonif* by the skin of his teeth.

"He wouldn't take my account," Don laughs, "thank the stars above."

Then it's back to more US National stories.

"Arnie loaned me money when I was first getting the business going, when nobody else would. And he made sure to teach me the basics of finance, a crash course in what not to do, that's always served me well."

"Maybe he should have taken his own advice," Joan says.

"You're right!" he winks at her. "After I was making a little money, he let me join his Wall Street Club. Just a couple of guys. We met once a month in the conference room at the bank. Arnie brought up a couple of excellent wines from his cellar and had a chef prepare us dinner. Always delicious, authentic, from the old country, you know? Not this Italian-American thing—'veal parmesan.' Over my dead body."

She laughs, hoping to encourage him further.

"And boy, he could spot a winner, Arnie. Had a nose for investing in quality companies. I was lucky he let me into the club. We made a lot of dough—oh, except for that one time, yeah, when he made a bad call. Okay, sure, that was a pretty terrible outcome now that I think about it. Regardless, it was a privilege to be included in his tight little group."

And this is also how Don reconnects with Jack Ruby because he too did his banking with US National.

"And that's why you've come, right?"

Don first met Ruby years earlier when Santos Trafficante was showing him around Dallas, Santos being another of Don's 'dearest friends' from back in the day.

"All the Chicago guys were trying to carve up Dallas for themselves. Vending machines, strip joints, laundries—you name it. Ruby had the 'in' with local authorities and it was all up for grabs."

"Did you get involved with any Texas business?" she asks.

"Nah, Santos did, but I like to stay local. More than enough business for me right here in LA. Oh, that reminds—" Don stops abruptly as a young man appears, walks past Joan, and whispers something in Don's ear; he shakes his head and frowns.

"Oh, excuse me, Joan, something's come up, something unexpected. I am sorry but we need to cut this short today, I am obliged to deal with this other matter."

Joan feels the rug being pulled out from under her.

"We'll reschedule quickly. I'll have Joe speak to your friend and arrange it. I'm so sorry. At least allow me to show you out."

Back in her car just minutes after she left it, Joan replays the meeting in her head—what did she learn? *Not much*, she concludes *but* she did make a good impression and he *did* offer to invite her back. So there's that.

She drives home planning for a swift return. She pours herself a scotch and starts a bath, hoping it will relax her enough to prepare for sleep later on; then she remembers she left her tape recorder in the car and runs out to retrieve it. She doesn't notice there's been a tiny tracking device placed on her left fender—an exact match to the bracket surrounding her license plate. A very skillful job.

Two nights later, she and Aaron are driving to a poker game when she asks if he's heard from Joe.

"I'm anxious to get back there."

"Oh yeah. Joe stopped by, said how's next week? Don's getting some more dental work done but should be okay by Tuesday."

"Definitely!"

"Okay, I'll tell him."

"Anytime Aaron. I'll rearrange my day if I have to. It's very important."

"I know, I know."

"Day or night, I'll make it happen."

"Okay already."

"So where's the game?" she asks.

"The glove compartment."

Joan rifles through a mountain of papers until she finds a half-torn napkin.

"Tarzana? Again? What a schlep!"

"Last time it was Encino and what do you care—I'm driving."

"So, um, thinking about this, Tuesday morning would be better than Tuesday afternoon. He's an old guy, just had some dental work, he's likely to fade during the day. Probably wakes up at like five or so, that's what happens to old people. They don't sleep, Eileen only gets a couple of—"

"Are you on something?"

"WHAT?!"

"You're babbling like you've taken something. Some kind of— oh no, don't tell me you're drinking coffee again, please not that!"

"I'm not on anything, Aaron. I'm just really excited to get back with this guy."

"Well, sit back and relax, will you? You're making me nervous."

"Relax? Not a chance. Too much is happening. Besides Escarolla I uncovered something about Jack Ruby that I don't think anybody knows!!!"

"See, that's one of the reasons I love poker, it's so distracting."

"I think Ruby went to Cuba two or maybe three times, not just once like everyone thinks."

"Like everyone thinks? You mean everyone who's as obsessive-compulsive as you are and still living in the '60s? And still thinking about the Kennedys?"

He's only half-joking.

"The next exit, stay to the right. So, I was speaking with Jack Ruby's sister yesterday—"

"Hey, save this for the ride home. I need to get in the zone, I'm looking to make some money tonight."

———————

At one a.m. Joan is driving while Aaron's reliving a successful night and replaying some of his better hands.

"I knew he had nothing, he's such a shitty bluffer."

"I never have the stomach to go all-in," she says.

"When it's just him and me, you think he realizes I always win those pots?"

"I think he's stupid, Aaron, probably too stupid to be playing with us, someone should tell him."

"Let his wallet tell him. Let's hope not too soon. You notice the tell?"

"No."

"C'mon." Aaron makes a sound like a sniffle. "Like when you got to blow your nose but you don't got a kleenex." Aaron tries again—louder. "It means he's got bupkas, maybe a low pair. Does it every time. A money-maker." Aaron takes a deep, satisfying breath. "So, what did you want to tell me about your pal Jack Ruby?"

"That he made a few trips down to Cuba, not just one."

"Yeah, so what?"

"Well, if it's true and if I can prove it, it's a very big deal. I mean *very* big. Ties a lot of loose strings together," she says keeping her eyes on the road.

"Yeah, well I still don't see the big deal here."

"A lot of families back then, mob families, ran casino operations in Cuba. But when Castro takes over, he throws those guys out, he's pledged to clean up the island. So, they need to get rid of him, get rid of Castro to hold onto their action. So they come together to hatch a plan. They recruit a couple of guys from each family, including Ruby, form a coalition, and go down there to take out Fidel. But he's crafty and he's onto them, he's onto the CIA too.

No one can get near him. But these guys keep trying, that's why Ruby keeps going back."

"Wait—you're telling me they put *Ruby* on Castro's assassination team? This guy's an amateur, you told me that a million times, they have him collecting on numbers or something, he's no hit man."

"I know. It doesn't make sense. Maybe because he's expendable? Anyway, here's where the story starts getting really interesting. The attorney general's office, which is run by Bobby Kennedy now, starts going after organized crime; they're bringing in the bad guys one by one, putting them in front of the justice department. Remember that Jimmy Hoffa trial?"

Aaron laughs. "Yeah, a classic!"

"It makes Hoover and the FBI look really bad—that's what they were supposed to be doing. But it's only part of the problem, the other part is the mob itself, they're not about to sit around letting a Kennedy put an end to all their fun. They were running the show down there in Cuba, that's millions of dollars out of their pocket, they plan to get that back. But they can't with Bobby all over them. And if that's not bad enough, he starts leaning on their remaining business—it's unacceptable!"

"Kennedy was supposed to look the other way, be more accommodating, I mean, since they helped Jack win the election and all. I remember something about his father rigging the voting booths in Chicago."

"Everything's possible in Chicago." She motions to a cup holder and Aaron passes her the water bottle.

"So, anyway, the mob's keyed up to get Bobby off their backs, get rid of him once and for all. They start planning a hit. But then they decide to go after JFK instead. Because, if they kill Bobby, they'll still have Jack to deal with and he's the president, but if they 'cut off the head of the snake, the whole snake dies.' Right? So, that's the plan. And they'll use the same team they assembled for the Castro hit—they each know one another, know how they work, who does what. With their pals high up in Intelligence, it won't be hard to create an opportunity to get it done."

"The visit to Dallas?"

"Yup. They set Oswald up as the shooter, let him take the blame. Ruby's their insurance policy to make sure Oswald doesn't squawk—you know, if the secret service or cops don't get to him first."

"Who was that guy anyway?" Aaron asks.

"Oswald? I'm not sure. Ex-military—maybe a bit unbalanced. It's a weird story. You know he gives up his American citizenship to move to Moscow, marries a Russian lady, has a kid. And then he decides nah, he wants to move back to the good ol' USA. So the Feds say, 'sure, okay, come on back'—they give him back his passport, his citizenship and help him get resettled. HUH? What's that all about? Regardless, on paper, Oswald is the perfect candidate for this job, right out of central casting."

"I sorta remember some of this."

"So, Oswald shoots Kennedy as planned and John Connally— that was probably a mistake. Or maybe he thought he was Bobby? Wow. I never thought about that before."

"Huh?"

"Well, at one time Bobby was supposed to go on this trip because Jackie and Jack were having problems, probably due to his philandering, but then she changed her mind and decided to go at the last minute. It happened fast, maybe the 'team' didn't know about the switch? Anyway, Oswald shoots them both, Jack Kennedy dies, John Connally recovers, and Bobby, at home in Virginia, is very much alive. And he's attorney general so he's going to get to the bottom of it."

"*And* he's got a ton of resources."

"Right. So regardless of anybody else's so-called investigation, particularly the FBI, he's rolling up his sleeves. This is his brother we're talking about and everything about this smells. And don't forget, Bobby is an expert on the mafia."

"Right, right."

"So the mob needs to get rid of Oswald before Bobby can get to him, and interrogate him. Here's where Ruby comes in. He's friendly with the cops there, waltzes right into the Dallas police station—"

"Shoots Oswald, shuts him up, problem solved," Aaron says.

"Right. So now Ruby's a hero, he finally makes it into the big time. Of course, later on, they'll get rid of him too, before he can make trouble. Get rid of all the evidence, tie up all the loose ends. That's how they like it."

"But wait a minute, Ruby's in jail."

"Yeah so he's a sitting duck, they can get to him whenever they want. Dorothy Kilgallen interviewed him in prison and he told her the guards were poisoning him, making him swallow pills every day."

"Who?!"

"Dorothy Kilgallen—you know, the *Hollywood Reporter*."

"Never heard of her."

"*What's My Line*?" she asks hopefully.

"Nope."

"The point is, a reporter gets an exclusive interview with Ruby in jail and he tells her that the guards are giving him pills, and the pills are making him sick."

"And you believe all this?" he asks.

"Well, he does die in prison shortly after. Cancer."

"So?"

"He's only fifty-six," she says.

"Okay, that happens."

"But then Kilgallen commits suicide right after she interviews him!"

"Really?"

"Yes. Except there's no suicide note. So she works all day, taping her TV show, attends this big black-tie event that night, and then goes home to kill herself in a spare bedroom she's never stepped foot in. She's fifty-two."

Aaron's quiet. She signals to exit.

"Jeez," he says finally.

"Exactly. No loose ends, Aaron. That's how they like it."

"And you got all this from piecing together a couple of trips to Cuba? This is some incredible story you're on to."

"Some of it I knew already, it's in my manuscript, remember? The one you told me you read. The one no one will publish."

"Um, I started it—"

"How is it that no one seems to care about this crime? The crime of all crimes!!! It's fifty years, I mean it's *over* fifty fucking years . . ."

"You okay?"

"And now here I find new evidence, important links. Enough to force me to rewrite the thing! But why should I when no one gives a damn!"

"And you know you're on solid ground here?"

She finds a spot, parks, and turns to look at him. "Meaning what?"

"You know, you're not sticking your neck out?"

"What do you mean sticking my neck out?!?"

"You know," he says sheepishly, "The *Sun-Times*?"

"GOD Aaron, what has that got to do with this!"

"Sticking your neck out—stirring up trouble."

"Oh please, if I didn't stand on principals who would I be, not Joan Ross!!! I would have never gotten into this line of work if I couldn't tell it like it is."

"Excuse me, I forgot who I was talking to. So what kind of evidence you got?"

"I *got* a photograph with Jack Ruby, Santos Trafficante, and Lee Harvey Oswald all sitting *together* in a nightclub in Dallas! And that's just the start. For Christ's sake, Aaron, I'm gonna blow the *roof* off this story!"

"Okay, can you lower your voice please, this is a residential neighborhood. So, this is the movie you're making with those Hollywood people?" he asks, trying for a friendlier tone.

"No. That story ends when Ruby goes to Cuba."

"Why? The rest of it is what's so interesting, I mean the whole assassination thing."

"Of course it is! But it's these producers—they're scared to death of going anywhere near the assassination, I don't know what their problem is. Maybe they're afraid to be compared to Oliver Stone."

"Well, what about the writers, can't they help?"

"They're just kids, Aaron, writing a screenplay. Another screenplay in a long list of screenplays, most of which never see the light of day. After this, they just move on to the next one."

"So, convince them, turn on that Joan Ross charm," he smiles, turning on the Aaron Spencer charm.

"Save it for strangers," she says.

He laughs. Then she laughs.

"Look, in some ways, I'm thinking this may be a good thing, a blessing in disguise. I get to tell the story the way I want to tell it."

"The magazine? I thought Grace shot you down."

"I'll take another run at the book. Add the new stuff and find a publisher with the guts to get it out there. That's why I need Uncle Donny. I think he knows more of this story. A lot more. And he's probably ready to unburden himself, that's what happened with Eileen," she opens her car door. "And time is not on our side."

Aaron slides into the driver's seat. "You know you gotta be careful Joan, you could be playing with fire. Who knows what goes on with those people?"

"Thanks," she smiles and closes the car door softly. "Don't forget about Tuesday, Aaron. Anytime. I can't wait to get back there."

CHAPTER FIFTEEN

Jeff finds many reasons to check in with Grace at the office every day.

He thinks *Relevant* needs a new photo enlarger.

She agrees.

He wonders if they can afford a new wireless system, there's a special offer but they'll need to switch providers.

That's okay.

He's found a deal on paper stock if they commit for a year . . . a top editor suddenly becomes available . . . a start-up wants to sublease their unused space . . . and on and on.

Grace is having more fun at work than she ever thought possible. Instead of losing patience with all these interruptions, the questions and decisions that stop, start, and waylay her concentration, she likes being annoyed by Jeff—she finds him simply endearing.

Can't seem to get her fill.

Sometimes, when they're alone, he's able to slip his hand down her dress.

One time he was able to slip his hand up her dress. But mostly there are other people around, so he can do nothing but look at her.

And that can be enough.

Jeff has been to Grace's home *for dinner* a dozen times, so she's surprised when he invites her back to his cottage that night. She prefers her well-appointed condo and assumed he did too, but agrees to go remembering the time he cooked that fabulous dinner for her.

"Is there a roast in my future?" she asks coyly.

"I think you'll like this dish very much," he says.

She brings two bottles of red and doesn't bother to ring his bell. So she's surprised to find him in the kitchen, stirring something on the stove with nothing on but an apron. He turns to kiss her and she can't help but notice his erection.

"Happy to see me?" she kids. Then Glenn walks into the kitchen, nude as well, and she realizes they started the evening without her.

As it turns out, she spends most of the night in bed with two young men. Occasionally they are one on one, sometimes all together in creative configurations. She is new at this but they are not. It is an evening she will never forget, a dinner even more memorable than the roast.

She's a bit shaky on her drive home and looking forward to a long, luxurious soak in her tub. She fills it to the top and slides down into sudsy water, reliving the night. She can't believe what she's done, that it wasn't all a dream.

At the office the next day, she's amazed at how well rested she feels on so little sleep. She tries jumping into some paperwork but has difficulty concentrating because she's keeping an eye out for Jeff.

Finally, she sees him rush by. He waves hello and motions that he can't stop now, he'll come later. She comes right then, in Joan's chair.

CHAPTER SIXTEEN

"Had a nice time? Bet you were the big winner!"

Even at one a.m., Eileen is extra chipper to hear from Joan.

"Did okay," Joan says modestly. "Aaron was the big winner. But I took an expensive steak dinner off him on a side bet."

"Steak? Can't remember the last time I had one. Now that you mention it, I'd love a steak, I'm so sick of chicken."

"Okay. So next time I visit we're going out for a big, juicy T-bone."

"You're on!" Eileen says. "With baked potatoes and creamed spinach."

"Of course, all the trimmings. Aaron's taking me to Musso and Frank's, ever hear of it? It's this fabulous steak restaurant, very popular, in the same location since before you were born."

"Not possible," Eileen kids.

"And very big with the movie folks."

"So when you see Robert Redford, give him a big kiss for me. What a dreamboat," Eileen says dreamily.

"And I've got news. I have a meeting coming up with the man I was telling you about, the one who knew Jack. You know, the guy who used to be in the Mafia." She is testing to make sure Eileen really doesn't want anything to do with this.

"Do I need to tell you to be careful with these characters, hon?"

"You're sweet to worry but you know I can take care of myself," she says.

"Yes, you certainly can."

"So, I just wanted to make sure there's nothing you'd like me to ask him. You know, since he knew Jack and all."

Eileen's quiet for a moment.

"No," she says finally. "But that reminds me, I keep forgetting to tell you this . . . Jack gave me a box for safe keeping which I totally forgot about until, well, until recently. I remember thinking that I needed to put it in a special place, and I did, but that was so long ago and now I can't remember where it is. Isn't that something? I think you should come up and help me look for it, it could be important."

Joan considers that this "lost box" may be, in fact, just a ruse. Eileen's been lobbying for a return visit.

Eileen swears the box is "here somewhere"—she just needs Joan's help to find it. *Before* she puts the house on the market.

Joan opens her calendar to find a couple of good dates. "And this reminds me, I've been meaning to ask, I want to make sure I have it right. Are you sure you were in Dallas on July sixth and *not* May sixth?"

"Ha, you asked me this already."

"I know, it's important. Was it July?"

"Lemme think—Yep, July."

"You're one hundred percent sure?"

"One hundred percent." Eileen laughs again. "You know how hot Dallas gets in July? Holy moly, you never forget that!"

Now Joan laughs too. "Okay. So I'll see you in two weeks. Meanwhile here's a homework assignment: find us the best darn steak house less than an hour's drive from your place."

"I'll ask Buddy tomorrow," Eileen promises.

"My treat!"

———

Eileen's neighbor Buddy, who lives in the house closest to her, still a half-mile away, is her resource for what's happening around town. She's known him since he was a baby, he'd call her "Nana," as his real grandmother lived far away. When "Nana" came down with the flu a couple of years ago, Buddy was there every day to make her tea and take Newport out for a walk. He hooked up her cable and tried again and again to convince her she needs a cell phone, to no avail.

Joan's tried to talk her into it too, for security.

"Maybe Joan will take me to the phone store when she comes up," she says to Newport. "I'll ask Buddy where that is. Oh, and a steak restaurant," she says patting her dog, "just wait 'til you get those leftovers."

———————

The next morning Joan arrives at Ira's cottage early, he's still in pajamas.

"C'mon, it's not even 7:30!"

"Just ignore me," she says and heads for the blackboard. *"Havana, casinos, families"* —she's trying to block out the espresso aroma wafting from the kitchen—*"1958 Castro in"* —she hears the microwave beeping—*"trip three, July 1963, if Eileen's correct—"*

"You heard from Eileen?" Ira asks blowing on his steamy mug.

"We speak every night," Joan turns to face him. "The thing is, the wife of one of Ruby's compadres said her husband traveled to Cuba with Ruby in December. She's positive because her anniversary is in December and the guy wasn't there to celebrate. Eileen swears Ruby was there in July. He couldn't have stayed all that time, he was making several trips down there! None of the research ever turned that up."

"Yeah, okay," Ira says between sips of his coffee.

"Don't you see, he's making all these trips to Cuba, I've tracked three at least. None of the researchers know this."

"Okay." Ira raises an eyebrow, "So this is why you need to get here . . . ?"

"You know the theory that J. Edgar Hoover manipulated the mob into taking out Castro in exchange for dropping some racketeering charges? Hoover was crazy paranoid that Castro was poisoning the US with communism. You got to remember what the FBI was back then, a lot different from now, Hoover did whatever he wanted, left the mob families alone for the most part. *Let them kill each other off.* That was his motto. So he lays off the mob if the boys will take care of Castro. And Ruby's on the team because he *habla español*! That's why he's there, that's his main asset. And that's never come up before—historians know nothing about that. Plus he's got no police record to speak of, he's a nobody, so—totally expendable. So he and the other guys go down to scope out Castro, get the lay of the land and they return again to do the deed—but they can't get it done, they can't execute the plan! So then Ruby returns *again* that July, to give it one more try. That's why there are all these trips to Cuba—oh my god!" Joan has little spittle foaming on her lips.

"You should take up tennis or yoga, it'll be good for you."

"Feels like Chicago," she is muttering to herself but Ira hears.

"Chicago?"

"I had this big story, before I came to LA, before *Relevant*."

"Yeah I saw something about that when I researched you," he says.

"You researched me? Really! On your internet? Well, don't believe everything you read there."

"So, okay, what happened in Chicago?"

"I cracked this story about a big food scandal; one of the major food companies in town was importing fish from Asia but claiming it was 'All-American'—I spent two years of my life on this story. Following trucks around in the middle of the night, reviewing manifests. And I was just a kid, Ira, just a cub reporter, I cracked the story—me! The day after it ran, my editor called me in. Said she had gotten some complaints and didn't trust my sources, which was crazy. I would never play games with my sources. The real problem was that the fish company was spending big bucks advertising in the paper every week, so she took it to my gutless publisher and I was history."

"I bet that crap goes down a lot," he says sympathetically.

"Look, I exposed a fraud, laid it out on the table like good reporters are supposed to—and they shot me down."

"I must tell you that's not what I read on the internet."

"Oh?"

"Something about a mistake on the Iran Contra thing."

"WHAT? It fries my butt to know that people can make stuff up out of thin air then it follows you all your life. The internet!"

"Maybe I got it wrong, I wasn't paying that much attent—"

"God damn it!!! And did you read about me having a nervous breakdown and them carrying me out on a stretcher because that was on the internet too? All over the internet." Tears start running down Joan's face.

"Don't get so upset, this is decades ago and probably all made up—"

"Hi, kids," Phoebe says as she enters the kitchen, closing a dripping umbrella. "Ira, where should I put—something the matter?"

"No, nothing's the matter," Joan says between heaves, "we're just talking about how I had a nervous breakdown in Chicago as reported by the World Wide Web."

"I'm sorry to hear that," Phoebe says not knowing what else to say.

Ira insists they sit down at the breakfast table. He brings Phoebe a coke, refills his mug, and pours Joan a big glass of water even though she says she doesn't want one. They sit quietly for a while.

"It wasn't a nervous breakdown. Not really," Joan says eventually. "It was later on, after the fish story, I took a job at the Sun-Times and was working on an important piece—got blind-sided by someone with 'inside information' that turned out to be very flimsy. Unreliable. Not wrong necessarily, just . . . I made a mistake, I should have . . . anyway, years of building my reputation and then one bad data point. The paper threw me to the wolves."

"People don't always want to hear the truth," Phoebe says.

"You're right," Joan nods. "We battle for it, at least I do at *Relevant*, but it's not always worth the fight."

"So how did you come to work at the magazine?" Ira asks.

"You didn't read that on the internet?" Joan asks snidely, more like her normal self. "It was a lucky break really. Just as everything was crashing down on me, Berta, my father's cousin, she owned a magazine back when it was a really big deal for a woman to own anything. Like Katherine Graham and the Washington Post. Anyway, she offered me a job writing features and I grabbed it. One thing led to another, next thing you know I was editor in chief. Berta got sick about ten years into it and left me the business when she died. It had already started to slide. She had a lot of good years before, well, before the media landscape changed, and I've been fighting to keep it afloat ever since."

"So many magazines are gone now," Phoebe says. "How I miss my *Metropolitan Home*."

"How about *Gourmet* and *McCall's*?" Joan says, "never thought we'd lose those!"

"And *Jane* and *Teen* and *Young Miss* and *Mademoiselle*!" Phoebe rattles them off. "I wrote for all those books."

"I didn't know you wrote for pubs."

"Oh yeah, the first ten years of my career, in New York. I loved it. *Sassy*! Now that was the best. It's just that film and TV paid so much better," Phoebe sighs.

"Yes, so may we please get back to earning our keep," Ira says.

"There was this editor at *Sassy*, he took a chance on me, I was right out of college," Phoebe smiles, "I'll always be indebted to him."

"We all need someone like that in our life, don't we?" Joan agrees in a rare, reflective moment.

"Ladies!" Ira tries again.

"Okay," they say in unison. Then laugh.

––––––––––

The liquor store hasn't seen a customer all day. Aaron has restocked shelves, straightened the back room, put an order in with his favorite importer, and run out of things to do. He's seriously weighing closing early when Joe walks in, dripping wet.

"Climate change," Joe says mockingly, shaking his head.

"What's with the bank, Joe?" Aaron says, annoyed to be stuck at the store now.

"Cool your heels, I'm all over it," Joe says, taken aback by Aaron's tone.

"You know I'm sitting here on all your *merchandise*."

"I said I'm on it, didn't I? Your job is to keep it safe 'til I tell you what to do next." He's cruising the aisles, leaving wet shoe marks all over the floor. "And lose the attitude pal." He eyes a bottle of 1985 Pomerol half-hidden on a low shelf. "You saving this for me?"

Aaron's day goes from bad to worse.

"You was supposed to call me about your girlfriend, Aaron, the one *dying* to get back with Uncle Donny." He pulls out his cell. "You lose my number or what?"

"Um," Aaron says slowly, "I've been thinking about that. Having some second thoughts. Let's just forget about it for now, okay?"

The rain starts coming down hard, growing loud, bouncing off Aaron's roof.

"Okay? I said let's forget about it," he repeats.

"No, I heard you." Joe bangs the wine on the counter, "I just don't—forget about it? I got the guy teed up for this, he's up my ass, so we just FORGET ABOUT IT?!"

"Well, can't you tell him she changed her mind?"

"NO! I can't! I'm already on thin ice with the man, I told you!" He takes a deep breath. "You're missing the point here, Aaron. It's not up to her and it's not up to you. Uncle Donny wants a meet, there's gonna be a meet. Your job is to deliver this broad, you don't want to see him lose patience."

"I don't want any trouble," Aaron mumbles.

"It's about a movie, right, what's the big deal? They have a little talk, she asks him questions and he answers, that's what happens." He waves his finger, "I got no room for more fuckups," and stomps back up the burgundy aisle.

Aaron is not quite sure what to do. He'd like to leverage this, get some relief from these guys, but not by throwing Joan under a bus.

Joe suddenly reverses course and stomps back to the counter.

"Now give me a case of red and a case of white. Nah, make that two cases red. You can mix 'em up but none of the crap like the last time. Screw caps? You wanna see screwed? I'll show you screwed!"

"That's a lot of wine," Aaron complains but it's just posturing.

"Yeah, we're having a party this weekend, a birthday celebration. Uncle D put me in charge of refreshments."

"Okay, well then maybe you'd—"

Aaron's screen door swings open and an umbrella appears.

Oh shit! "Can I help you?" he asks.

"Yes, Aaron, you can help me. Today is Tuesday. Remember?"

Aaron reaches behind him for a bottle of Absolut.

"Yeah, we can talk about that later. Okay?" he says carefully.

"Do I have a choice? Should I bring something tonight—salad, dessert?"

"No, I've got it under control, just come by around six and—"

"Hey, are you Joan?" Joe interrupts, "the writer friend, the one making a movie?"

"Yes, I am," she says.

"OMG, I heard a lot about you."

"You have? All good no doubt," she smiles her charming smile.

"About the '60s, right? I love the '60s, those cars, them go-go girls." Joe pantomimes and they all laugh. "I told Aaron here that we need to get you back with Uncle Donny quick, he feels so bad he had to cut that meeting short. He's really looking—"

"You're Joe!"

"That would be me," he bows ceremoniously.

Aaron's never seen this side of Joe before.

"I can't wait to get back to see your uncle. Aaron was supposed to—"

"It's not his uncle, that's his name, Uncle Donny," Aaron offers.

"What?!" Joan looks at Aaron like he has two heads.

"It's like President Bush . . . never mind." He retreats behind the counter to put her vodka in a bag.

"There's so much I want to ask him," Joan turns back to Joe.

"I bet. I hear you're working day and night, uncovering a lot of new information. That's pretty exciting," Joe says with a wink.

"This story means a lot to me, it's years in the making."

"Oh yeah?" Joe says just to keep the conversation going.

"Not just the film, I'm also writing a book, a tell-all about the '60s. What *really* happened back then. I want to be to the Kennedy years what Woodward was to Watergate!"

"Nice. Well, Uncle Donny sure knew a lot of important people back then, a lot of the players. I bet he can help."

"I'm counting on it. Listen, why don't we go right now?" Joan pivots toward the door.

"Ah, you know, he's not always up for visitors. But don't worry, I'll work this out with Aaron and you'll get back there very soon."

"Okay. The sooner the better."

She takes her package and heads for the door. Then remembering her manners she turns back. "A pleasure meeting you Joe."

"The pleasure's all mine," he smiles back.

Joe takes a long slow look at Aaron and chuckles. "So that's your lady friend."

"Not like you're thinking."

"A bit on the intense side." Joe's still smiling and nodding. "Looks like she got you wrapped around her little finger."

"Whatever."

"Tomorrow soon enough?" Joe asks, checking his phone, "Because we can't keep her waiting, her 'journalistic integrity' is at stake! A film! A book! Bob Woodward! Pretty intense, Aaron, you better watch your step. You don't want her kicking your ass— that's my job."

"Okay, okay already."

Joe continues to rib him while Aaron loads up his car with the wine. Three trips in the rain. On the last pass, Joe takes a call.

"The Feds? No way! Holy shit! A nightmare, okay *my* nightmare, I'm on it. Listen, tomorrow okay for a meet-up with Brenda Starr?"

"We're good," he says to Aaron.

"Huh?" Aaron asks wiping raindrops off his face with his sleeve.

"The meet. Four p.m. tomorrow. She comes alone." Joe gets into his car. "No more fuckups, Aaron, I got no room for fuckups. Capiche?"

CHAPTER SEVENTEEN

At four p.m. on Wednesday afternoon, Joan is met at the door by Uncle Donny, she follows him into his beautiful den.

"Sorry for the last time. Today, I promise, I'm yours, all yours." He gives her a big smile, a mouthful of teeth. "What can I get you? You prefer red wine if I recall."

This guy flirting with me? Even though he's ancient, Joan feels a thump in her chest.

A young man appears out of nowhere to pour the wine.

"*Salud!*" Don says.

"Thank you, this is very nice," she says.

"I always have a little something this time of day, it is my ritual. When you get to be my age, and in such good shape—I may have mentioned that I'm in terrific shape—you don't change your rituals. Why tempt the gods?"

They both chuckle.

The assistant disappears as silently as he had come.

"So how can I help you, what would you like to know? Let me make up for the last time."

Joan would love to ask him just to tell her everything he knows about Dallas and the assassination of JFK: did he know any of the participants; did he know who gave the orders; who ran the cover-up; what happened to Ruby in jail?

That's what she wants to ask. But she won't, she'll just let him talk for a while, see where it goes.

She also left her recorder and notebook in the car, he might not be as open or free-spirited if he thought he was 'on record'—she picked that up on her first visit.

"Why not just tell me what you remember about Jack Ruby? You were telling me how you met him, you and your friend down in Dallas that time. Why don't we pick it up from there?" she prompts.

"Aah yes," Don smiles as he sips his wine. "Santos Trafficante. Now there was a true gentleman. And very popular with the ladies," he tips his glass toward her. "Looked like Dean Martin—handsome, smooth. Everyone wanted to be his friend. Just like Arnie, I mentioned him to you, the bank owner, Arnholt Smith. They had a way about them. Between them a million friends. Difference was Arnie treated everyone nice, all his customers like family. Santos was very selective if you know what I mean. I think I have a picture of him around here somewhere."

Don starts to rise when the assistant reappears to look for the photo.

"Anyway, that's how I got reunited with Ruby. Arnie threw a party at the Adolphus hotel and Santos and I flew down to Dallas."

Don explains that at the party, which had hundreds of people, Arnie personally walked them around, introducing them to everybody.

"That was his way. So some of these guys I knew from before. Santos knew a lot of them too, but that didn't mean he liked them; the man slept with one eye open, if you know what I mean."

Don grows quiet. She can feel his mind working. Deciding whether to tell more.

"Sounds like Santos was a smart man and a good friend," she says to encourage him.

"Yes, that he was. On both counts. How I miss him," Don says smiling sadly. "And boy did he hate Ruby! Ha—the more that guy tried to cozy up, the more Santos tried to get away. He basically followed us around the whole night. Did you find the photo?"

His assistant shakes his head no.

"Then never mind."

He leaves quietly.

"Ruby." Don's face changes, like something went wrong with the wine.

"Always trying so hard. Threw off some bad energy. Of course, Arnie was nice to him." Another sad smile.

"Sounds like quite a party," she says wanting to keep him focused, sensing him drifting away.

"Yes, yes! Hundreds of people, did I mention that? Some heat there too. That often happened back then. But they kept to themselves for the most part. Looked a little out of place, you know, with their Robert Hall suits and wingtip shoes."

"My dad shopped at Robert Hall," she smiles.

"It was a challenging time for a lot of guys," Don says graciously.

"A couple of them looked familiar, but . . . lemme think, that's not what I wanted to . . . oh yeah. There was a bunch of local guys, Texas ranchers or maybe they were oilmen, you know, with cowboy hats—and one of them was bragging how he owned most of downtown. Worth millions, he said. Including the School Book Depository. Remember? From the JFK thing?"

At the mention of the School Book Depository Joan inadvertently sucks in her breath. She feels the room pulling away and fights to stay in the moment. Don doesn't notice or pretends not to. He keeps talking.

"There was this guy there who owned a security company, Ace Security I think, something like this, he's one of Arnie's clients. I forget his name or maybe I never knew it. Anyway, he's there talking with Ruby all night. All night! Everyone else is trying to avoid it. Seemed like a nice guy though, maybe a little rough around the edges. Anyway, a couple of years later, I learn it was *his* company in charge of protecting Robert Kennedy at the Ambassador that night—the night he gets it! Remind me not to hire that company!"

Joan works her face to stay neutral.

"Turns out the guy supposed to be watching out for Bobby had a rap sheet a mile long, that wouldn't have been good if that had come out at the trial, right? Luckily one of Arnie's bank partners made it disappear, this was Carlos Marcello's skinny cousin Milo. Arnie and Milo had a lot of gambling interests together, like in raceways and some hotels when there was gambling in them which was mainly run by his good pal Mickey Cohen out of New York . . ."

Joan is working to get her breathing back to normal. Don is spewing names and stories that she's trying to mentally file away so once she's back in her car she can write it all down.

The wine isn't helping.

"Another big-time pal of Arnie's was Nixon—you know, the president. They knew each other from back when Dick ran for governor and Arnie put a lot of money into his campaigns, a lot! Starting with local ones and ending up . . . well, you know how it ends up. But still, a good investment for Arnie when you do the math."

It suddenly occurs to Joan that Don could be playing her, having fun at her expense, you know, the big-time *Hollywood movie lady*. But she rejects the thought, he seems like he's on the level, just emptying out old stories in whatever way they occur to him. Not censoring himself, not trying to help her make sense of it either. Just dumping it out, dumping it all over her.

Santa Anita keeps coming up.

Joan dislikes horse racing but when Don mentions Sirhan Sirhan in passing, because he trained to be a jockey there, she changes her mind. This is definitely something she needs to know more about. She's going with Aaron the next time he asks.

"Probably where he met the guys," Don says and she tries to ask "what guys?" but he keeps rambling on.

The assistant reappears, holding a tray of canapes. Don explains they're 'gougères'—cheese puffs—flown in frozen from France.

"Heat up like a dream. Try one, you must."

It melts in her mouth. This may be the best thing *Joan from Hollywood* has ever eaten in her life! And she's not just being polite. She instantly feels elated, what a fabulous blend of cheese and . . .

"What else is in here?" she asks.

"Air," he says with a smile.

"But isn't there some kind of herb? Cumin?"

"Caraway," he says, "like in rye bread."

She laughs and tells him how her mother would toast rye bread, smear it with Velveeta, and then cut it into small squares for guests.

"The height of sophisticated entertaining," she jokes. They being a Chicago family with an umbilical cord into Kraft.

"Hey, that reminds me of Jimmy, he was from Chicago. What a character!" Don switches effortlessly to Chicago Jimmy stories.

Jimmy did this, Jimmy knew that, Jimmy paid this guy, that guy, to show up, to go away.

She tries to imagine who he's talking about while Don seems to take for granted that she does. And at the same time, she's just amazed she's getting all this information from him. She thinks back to Eileen and decides it must be a similar phenomenon, growing old with no one to share your memories with. She pictures Uncle Donny trying to talk to Joe, the kid with ants in his pants. She makes a mental note to stay calm, positive, and keep smiling.

Jimmy did this, Jimmy planned that, Jimmy Jimmy Jimmy.

A light goes on in her brain—could this be Jimmy Hoffa?

She tries to rewind what she's just heard putting Hoffa into the story but more stories are still coming, it's a hopeless cause. She'll try to recollect all of it later. It's the best she can hope for.

That, and another tray of gougéres.

In his same matter-of-fact tone and same relentless cadence, Don now explains how, in '62, Jimmy made plans to assassinate Bobby Kennedy, who was then the attorney general because he was trying to throw all his friends in jail.

"As if that was possible," he chuckles.

But still, Bobby was making their lives very difficult and finally, they had had enough. Enough was enough.

So Jimmy put a team together but he didn't know that Marcello also had a plan, and his plan wasn't targeting RFK but JFK. And so Santos has to convince Jimmy to let him take the lead on this, take out the big cheese. So it wasn't until '68 that they could get to Bobby, get the little bastard.

She is remembering to stay calm but it feels like a tidal wave is rushing over her, overwhelming her. She may drown at any moment. Did she just hear that Donato Escarolla was involved in the assassination of Bobby Kennedy?

Was that what HE JUST SAID?

Finally, finally, he stops speaking for a minute and there's an opening to ask him a question. She blurts out the first non-threatening thing she can think of: "So how did you manage all of this, Don, keeping so many balls in the air?"

He very much likes this question, it shows she's been paying attention and he's flattered. He smiles broadly as he lights a cigar.

"Yes, those were the days. And the nights weren't bad either," he winks lecherously, she laughs on cue.

"No, seriously. You are right, there was a lot going on. Well, lemme think. Yeah, the thing was, we had a lot of good people around back then. Inside guys and outside guys, guys you could trust. I had a lot of resources. Like I had Arnie when I needed capital. I got it. And the families were all organized nice so you weren't always looking over your shoulder, but if you needed muscle, it was there. And we had Eddie giving us air cover, you know, keeping the suits off our backs."

They move on to Eddie stories.

Now it's *Eddie this, Eddie that, Eddie Eddie Eddie.* Don is reliving the Eddie days and Joan is again scrambling to figure out who he is talking about. It's not until he says *"fagala"* that she realizes she might have it.

"I didn't trust the fagala even though he saved my ass more than once."

Joan knows Hoover was gay.

Don stands, this time as his assistant appears, explaining he needs to get ready for dinner. "Another of my rituals, Joan, dinner at six-thirty sharp."

Two-and-a-half hours have flown by. She never asked the questions she prepared but then Don has been telling her things she'd never have had the nerve to ask. Just emptying out memories without reservation, like a kindly old uncle that maybe, she thinks, he's actually become.

He walks her to the door and asks her opinion on electric cars. "There's a beautiful model coming out of China, pricey, but I'm told a good investment. Runs on solar, how about that? I'm thinking about investing in a dealership." He wants her opinion since you *Hollywood people* are early adopters.

"Can't wait forever to see a return. Don't even buy green bananas anymore," he jokes.

She motions to her station wagon. "I really don't know much about cars Don, as you can see."

"An oldie but a goodie," he says graciously but with an eyebrow raised.

The attendant arrives holding a small, gold drawstring bag with three frozen gougéres carefully wrapped inside.

"A bit of a swag 'cause you *Hollywood folks* expect that kind of treatment," another joke from Don. "Am I right?"

They hug. Don says he had a great time talking about the old days and Joan should come back again real soon.

On the road, she spots a Taco Bell and drives to the back where no other cars are parked, pulls a pad from her backpack, and clicks open a pen. She can't wait to write everything down, two-and-a-half hours of pure, unadulterated Carmen Donato Escarolla. Amazing stuff, all of it, absolutely astonishing.

"Thank you, Uncle Donny!" she says aloud.

She would have preferred to process it first, organize it in a logical way, but she doesn't want to risk forgetting anything so she just starts scribbling away.

She'll get most of it, she prides herself on being a keen observer with a first-class memory. She quickly fills up two pads as darkness begins to fall.

What this keen observer hasn't noticed is the guy who arrived right after she did with a plate of nachos, sitting down at a nearby table and picking at them slowly. Nor did she notice when he walked by her car on his way to the trash to check if the tracking device was still attached to her left rear fender.

The following day, Joan packs up a wheelie with sweatpants and tees and leaves to spend a few days with Eileen. She remembers they have a reservation at a steak restaurant, which is sure to be dreadful, but requires something beyond sweats; she reopens her case and lays an old silk shirt and a pair of slacks on top.

On the drive up, she calls her bookkeeper. Since the magazine is nearly out of the hole, at least for now, she'll ask to be put back on full salary—she needs to pay down some debt before it becomes a serious problem.

"My goodness, child, it's so nice to hear from you. And your books are in such good shape—that new gal must be a wizard!"

When Joan gets to Eileen's they go straight to work looking for Jack's box. They start in the basement, plowing through years of accumulated junk. While not a big house, Eileen has kept everything.

Even when an item is unsalvageable there's often a tense negotiation before it can get tossed.

"You never know when you'll need it," Eileen cries when Joan demands something be placed on the throwaway pile.

"You don't need it if it doesn't work!"

Joan also insists on boxing up many items for charity, everything Eileen won't be taking with her when she moves. It ends up taking the whole day but at least the basement's done.

The next morning they tackle the two hall closets and the living room built-ins where Eileen keeps books and mementos and where she found the photo album from Joan's previous trip. The day ends with nine cartons packed to the gills, one sore knee—Eileen's—but no box.

Then it's on to the master bedroom with its walk-in closet and small adjoining bath that is falling apart. Joan wonders how Eileen manages with the temperamental toilet, the leaking showerhead, the chipped sink.

"Oh you get used to it," Eileen pooh-poohs.

It takes the good part of the afternoon to sort through her wardrobe. Some of her ancient clothing is threadbare, other pieces look like they've hardly been worn—one has a price tag dangling from a sleeve.

"Twenty-four dollars for this dress, that's a pretty good deal," Eileen boasts.

"Not if you never wore it," Joan kids.

Several outfits result in a spiel of laughter. "Can you believe I ever wore this thing?" Eileen says more than a few times.

"I got a couple of those goodies in my closet too!"

Over their fancy steak dinner, they plan out the next two days and then collapse together on the living room sofa back home. Joan can't get over how Eileen keeps up with her, she marvels at her stamina, a woman more than thirty years her senior.

"I'm used to doing everything around here," she explains.

Joan tells her she has no intention of driving that long boring trip back to LA without finding Jack's box. "I promise," she says hand to heart, "no matter how long it takes."

The next morning they tackle the guest bedroom where Joan is staying, a small room with a twin-size bed and a three-drawer dresser. The room is simple, practical, with a lovely view of the garden. Joan's already mentioned how cozy it is and how comfortable the mattress is, she even turned it upside down to see the manufacturer.

"You're my first overnight guest in all these years!" Eileen tells her.

It doesn't take long but across the hall, the guest bathroom and linen closet are another story. Eileen has kept dozens of items she no longer uses but is reluctant to throw away: half-empty bottles of shampoo, mini tubes of lotions, empty prescription bottles, etc., etc.

The linen closet holds not just sheets and towels, but rolls and rolls of toilet paper along with paper towels, blankets, and pillows, an ironing board that's rusted shut, and a matching rusted iron. There's a box labeled "Newport" that sparks Joan's imagination but turns out to be just a collection of beaten-up doggy toys, teething bones, and god knows what else—she resists putting her hand farther down in it.

"Don't be a weenie," Eileen says as she digs into the box. "Nah, just some biscuits Newport decided he was too good for."

"God, Eileen," Joan yells down to her the next morning when she finally goes up to the attic. "There's a ton of winter gear up here—hats, sweaters, coats." She's surprised by how it's all just tossed about.

"Oh, Lenny's things. I forgot. Didn't know what to do with them."

Joan debates whether to drag everything down to box up or just leave the mess for the next homeowner to deal with. Her allergies decide for her, she can't take a minute more in the dusty space.

"No box here!" she yells as she descends the ladder, eyes watering.

Eileen has offered to make some tea and by the time Joan is settled back in the kitchen, she sees all the cupboards have been torn apart.

"I thought maybe in the cupboard with the tea bags . . ." Eileen puts her head in her hands, more embarrassed than upset.

"Let's have that tea," Joan says calmly. "It's here somewhere, it didn't just evaporate, we'll find it." She smiles, "This happens to me too."

Eileen puts the kettle on, collects the tea bags, sugar, milk, cups, saucers, and spoons, and takes a large canister down from a cupboard.

"These should still be fresh, just bought 'em," she says, laying out bakery pastries on a plate. They wait for the kettle to whistle.

Buddy, Eileen's neighbor, has been driving her to the big Albertson's in Chico to shop. Buddy just received his learner's permit and is required to have an adult sitting next to him while he practices, his parents are thrilled not to be the ones for yet another practice drive. The ten dollars Eileen tips him each week is icing on his cake, he'd gladly drive her anywhere for free.

Dipping biscuits into their tea, they discuss what needs to be done to get the house ready to sell. When Joan suggests Eileen may want to update some of her appliances to appeal to today's buyer, Eileen rises wordlessly and goes to the freezer.

Inside is the box.

"I did put it in the cupboard because I'm in the kitchen all day and could keep an eye on it, but then Newport grew so big, and I worried that maybe, somehow, he could get at it, so I moved it to the freezer."

The box is very cold. They wrap it in dish towels and wait patiently for it to come to room temperature.

———

At *Relevant*, Grace sits in Joan's chair, chatting with her sister on the phone.

"But not that smart, and the sex, well, it's become a bit *routine*—besides, the magazine is the only thing we have in common. All the man talks about is sports—this team, that game, who cares? How about taking me to the ballet or the theatre, wouldn't that be a nice, grown-up thing to do? Some adult conversation for a change? I'd settle for a restaurant with a tablecloth."

Grace has been trying to distance herself from Jeff for the past several weeks, trying to avoid him when she can. She's ready with a reason not to accept one of his many invitations—to get together after work, take in a Lakers game, grab a drink at a bar they won't be seen at.

Either she's tired after a long day or she's promised a girlfriend to go to a movie. Or she needs to stop at the mall for a gift, or . . .

Always a ready and rotating excuse at hand.

But Jeff's been getting more and more insistent.

She remembers when she found him irresistible, anxious to get something going between them, even letting him know that time they were putting an issue to bed. He's so less attractive now that he's clamoring for her attention.

"I'm going to have to end it soon," she says.

Last Friday, when he suggested a special dinner *including* Glenn, she thought, *That could be amusing,* and agreed to go. But then when she really thought about it she regretted saying yes, had to come down with a sudden case of 'food poisoning' and leave the office early.

How does he not know it's over?

Jeff's young with youthful enthusiasm and she's an accomplished woman of the world. They're on different planets; she's going to have to end it soon.

It won't be the first time she has to tell a man they're destined to be just friends, never a pleasant conversation but one she can handle nevertheless.

This might be a bit more awkward since they'll continue to see each other as coworkers at the magazine—well actually, not coworkers, he works *for* her, she's the boss. Fortunately, no one (besides Glenn, an occasional freelancer) knows anything about them. So everyone can keep face and go about his or her business.

She thinks about how best to stage it, where she might tell him, when it would be best. He might get upset. He wears his emotions on his sleeve, she's seen that more than once. Tears up at movies and when the Lakers blew the finals he cried. Aloud! So no one can be around just in case, she'll have to make sure. Probably best done in a public place. Maybe she'll even write out her speech, she's done that before, memorize it so it sounds sincere.

That's just what she decides to do tonight after work.

But in walks Jeff, carrying photos for her review and plops down in the guest chair across from her. He's got that look, the one that says he's not taking "no" for an answer. So it will happen now, he'll force her hand by demanding they get together tonight.

And so he does.

And so she says, "We should talk," and walks over to close the door.

"Uh oh," Jeff kids. "Did I screw something up, am I in trouble, teach?"

Grace smiles.

"No, nothing like that. It's about us, Jeff," she tells him, deciding to wing it. "I think you know how fond I am of you, how much I enjoy your company, but I've been thinking we should table our affair for now. You're a young guy, a good-looking guy and you should be hooking up with a young, fabulous lady, someone your own age."

She thinks "hooking up" was a good choice of words, that's what his generation says.

Jeff gets very red and closes his eyes tightly.

Grace hopes that it goes quietly so no one can hear. But when he opens his eyes, there are no tears. What she reads in his face is fury.

"*My own age,*" he says mockingly. "What makes you think I don't have women my own age when I'm not with you."

Grace is not sure what to say or where this is going so she doesn't say anything, she knows this is a tactic for diffusing difficult situations.

Jeff gets up and walks very close to her. "Haven't I been making you happy? I've tried, Grace, I've tried. Here at work. In the bedroom?" He leers at her, "I thought this was working out for both of us. Isn't this relationship just what you had in mind?"

Grace is extremely uncomfortable. She should have made time to prepare, she should have known better.

"Look, Jeff, you're a great creative talent. You know, working under me you've had a lot more responsibility, taken on a bigger role here, I'm not going to change that, I'm—"

"Under you, yes. I thought that's how you wanted it," he snorts.

Grace wills herself to ignore his comments, to stay focused, to finish this up, and get rid of him. Now that she started it. "I'm not talking about changing anything here at work, just about putting a pause on our personal relat—"

"Oh, Grace, let's find a way to keep this going. For both our sakes." He puts his hand on her shoulder. That's often the way it begins, before he slides it down, down, down.

She's chilled to the bone. "It'll be okay, Jeff. Really, it will," she looks up at him, looking him straight in the eyes, looking earnest. "I just want you to be okay, to know you're still the leader of the team, the—"

"You're so good at this, I'd hate to see it come crashing down on you. I mean, once Joan hears about what we've been doing. She might not like it. Our meetings after work and here in her office." He starts walking around, gesturing. "On her couch," he sneers. "On her desk. Her chair! No, I don't think she'd like it one bit."

She sees that he's enjoying this.

"On so many levels I don't think she'd approve," he grins, but maybe also tearing up. "I can see her disapproving face right now," he says, finally, stopping to stare at her.

"I know you're upset," Grace says trying for a sympathetic tone, "and maybe a little hurt too, but I promise you—"

Jeff makes the face he would use to appease a child.

"You don't seem to appreciate the situation. You're not thinking it through. You don't *get it*! I go to Joan and tell her you propositioned me, told me you held my career in your hands if I didn't—"

"I DID NOT," she yells back. "What are you talking about?"

Jeff has his hand on the door, ready to leave. He's about to say something else, thinks better of it, and stomps out slamming the door behind him. He's read the same book about diffusing difficult situations that she has.

Grace is shaking visibly as the last pane of glass topples to the floor. She rushes to the bathroom to collect herself. For some reason, all she can think about is how she'll explain the broken glass to Joan.

———

Jack's box is nearing room temperature, at least warm enough to handle; Eileen opens the lid and peeks inside.

A ticket stub. Some roulette chips. A bunch of old coins. A pair of tarnished cuff links, a couple of collar stays, a matchbook, a blue silk pocket square.

"Rick's Starlight Lounge," Joan squints at a faded coaster. "Hey, this might be Cuban money . . ."

"A perfectly good train ticket from Dallas to Chicago, so wasteful," Eileen tsks-tsks.

"These look like regular keys," Joan says as she picks up a set of keys linked together on a chain. "But what's this?" She separates out a small key with a strange shape.

Eileen has no idea. "Bunch of junk," she complains.

"Something's written on it, I can't make it out. I should have brought my magnifying glass," Joan says squinting at it.

Eileen laughs. "Look at you, Miss Marple. Just take the box back home with you, you can go through it with a fine-tooth comb."

"Really, you'd let me take this home?"

"Nothing but junk. I can't believe I was so worried about finding it."

"I'll let you know if anything ends up being valuable," Joan says thinking about the old coins.

"Hon, I got no use for a train ticket to Chicago."

"Jack gave you this box to take care of, Eileen, there's probably something of value in here, or at least something he thought was valuable. Regardless, I will take it with me, thank you very much, and I will go through every single item very carefully."

"One less thing to worry about."

That reminds Joan of something she's been meaning to say. She takes a deep breath.

"And, Eileen, this has been on my mind for a while. When you decide to move to Shady Elms or one of those other places, I would like to take Newport. I know we've just become friends and all, and maybe you'd want someone else to have him, maybe your neighbor's kid, but I love dogs and I'll take very good care of him." Joan never had a dog before and is terrified by most of them, but she's taken a real liking to Newport. "He's so easy and friendly and I could use the company," she adds. "I'll take him whenever you're ready and bring him with me when I come for a visit."

Eileen is thrilled to hear this, she gives Joan a big hug. "What a load off my mind! I thought maybe Buddy, but he's off to college soon and . . . oh Joan, this is just the perfect solution. And to think, he'll be going to a nice Jewish home."

Joan bursts out laughing—they both laugh so hard they cry.

A bit later, Eileen adds, "I feel like I've made a best friend in my old age."

"Me too, and so has Newport," she pats the dog's head.

They're thinking aloud about dinner when Joan's cell phone rings.

"Will you be coming into the office at all today?" Grace asks in a low voice.

"I'm out of town, Grace. Why? What's up?"

"Tomorrow then?" Grace asks, sounding like someone else entirely.

"Well, I can," Joan says. "But you'd better tell me what's happening, what's wrong? Is something going on at the magazine?"

"Um, it's a personal problem."

"Oh?" Joan says repeating, "you have a personal problem you need to discuss with me." *With me???* "Why not tell me now?"

"No, uh—it's a personnel problem," Grace says and Joan's internal alarm bells go off.

"Okay, I can be there tomorrow afternoon, can it wait until then?"

"I guess it will have to," Grace says as she hangs up.

———

Joan spends a sleepless night worrying about the magazine.

The later the hour, the crazier her fears—someone died in a car accident—someone has an incurable disease—there was a fight, a fire—what?

She slips out of bed at 5 a.m., packs up her wheelie, and carries Jack's box to the door on tiptoe. Not even the dog stirs.

She stops in Solvang for breakfast and orders a double espresso with her scrambled eggs. "To hell with it," she says; there are still three hours left to drive.

Joan charges into the office expecting to see Grace, but she's not there and the office seems weirdly quiet. She's about to lose her mind when she sees Grace coming out of the ladies' room, nose red and her normal composure gone. They lock eyes and walk into Joan's office in silence, Grace shuts the door and sits down heavily in the visitor's chair.

"There's a small problem," she says finally, trying to smile.

Joan steels herself for the bad news. "I'm listening."

Grace starts—then stops. She hems and haws. Joan is getting ready to jump over the desk and strangle her when Grace finally says, "I made a mistake. I was seeing someone from the office. It was stupid, it breaks all the rules and I knew I shouldn't have but, well, I stopped."

"So that's it? You were dating someone who works at *Relevant* but now you're not. That's it?" Joan is skeptical since Grace's demeanor is telegraphing there's more to the story.

"Well, yes, that's it. It's over. It's just . . . he seems to see this differently."

"Okay, Grace, let's start from the beginning and lay it all out on the table, let's stop playing games here."

Grace explains how she's been having an affair with Jeff. Joan stifles a laugh at the thought of Jeff and Grace together.

"And when I realized I needed to end it, that we shouldn't have started it to begin with, well, he became belligerent."

"Belligerent? How?"

"He said I had started it! That I propositioned him. He said that I said if we had sex it would be good for his job, that getting involved with me would be good for his career."

Grace's face is bright red and she pulls a tissue from her pocket.

"Why would he think that?" Joan asks. "What did you say to him?" She's already guessing the answer.

"I never said *that*. I mean, I don't know why he thinks that." Grace whimpers, "I mean, I did tell him I thought he had talent and that he was important to the business. And I let him know I found him, um, attractive . . . and he knew I was available, I mean, that's common knowledge, but I never said having sex with me would . . ."

"Where's Jeff now?" Joan asks over the alarm bells going off in her brain.

" . . . Or maybe it was because I told him that he was special and because he saw how successful I am and—"

"Where is he NOW?!!"

Grace begins sobbing. "He threatened me! He's threatening to sue me, to take it to the board, to court . . ."

Joan's head begins throbbing. Her stomach is doing somersaults. The last thing they need now is a lawsuit, not now! Now that they've finally pulled themselves out of a hole. Still, she keeps her face neutral.

"Okay, Grace, here's what we need to do. You go home. Leave the office and don't come back until you hear from me. I'm going to get some counsel on this, some advice, this is a serious issue and I want to handle it properly."

Grace is staring at Joan, mouth agape and tears streaming.

"He started it. *He* did, not me. *He* asked me to dinner, I said okay just—"

"*Go*. Now."

"But . . . but . . ."

Joan stands. She's trying not to jump to conclusions, trying not to take sides, but she knows Grace and she knows Jeff. She can imagine the truth. She's about to scream "GODDAMN YOU, GRACE" when Grace spins on her heels and leaves.

CHAPTER EIGHTEEN

Phoebe is cruising the kitchen, thinking about lunch, when she runs into Ira on the phone with George.

"Attached. Wow! Okay, wink wink. Absolutely!"

He shoots her a big grin.

"Plus one? I'm good. Cool. Yes, yes!"

"What's that all about?" Phoebe asks as she slides a potpie into the microwave.

He's about to tell her when Joan comes running in.

"Kids! A long trip to McCloud but was it ever worth it!" She dangles a bunch of keys on a chain. "Look what I found!"

"Keys?" Ira asks.

"These are Jack. Ruby's. KEYS!!! Can you believe it?! I don't know what they are for, Eileen doesn't either, but it just so happens I know the best locksmith in the Valley and if anyone can figure it out it'll be Brad!"

"Nice," Phoebe says gesturing to Ira about the potpie—he motions back he'll pass—so they all walk into the great room together.

"Well, I have some great news too," he says just as the microwave beeps.

"Wait, wait, wait," Phoebe says.

She returns with lunch and they settle into their normal places—Phoebe and Ira on the sofa and Joan sitting across from them in a straight-back chair.

"So, George's representative at the studio was contacted by an agent of an up-and-coming actress who is thinking of attaching herself to *Long Road* if we can accommodate a few of their requests," Ira smiles. "This would be quite the coup and the timing is perfect, it would get us over the finish line."

"What kind of requests?" Phoebe asks, spearing a fork into her potpie.

"George says it's nothing much. Very reasonable. Fifteen lines. George suggests we write her in as one of Ruby's girlfriends, maybe his main squeeze."

"Who is it, would I know her?" Joan asks.

"George told me but I forgot the name. I never heard of her—but George says she's well thought of, very dependable. Very attractive."

"Well, he would know." Phoebe smiles. "What else?"

"What else what?" Ira asks.

"What else is on her list of requests," Phoebe says knowingly.

"Oh yeah. She also wants a certain amount of screen time and some visual stuff, but George says that'll be up to the director, we don't need to worry about it. But he did suggest not being stingy with dialogue so we can get her tweeting and making the rounds, you know, PR and such."

"Shouldn't be too hard since George *suggests*." Phoebe smiles.

"Great! Oh, and one more thing. You're both invited to his gala. March 15. He's being honored for his philanthropic work, actually, it's GoodWorks getting a humanitarian award. Anyway, George suggests we put it in our calendars now so we don't forget and we can confirm later as the date approaches."

Phoebe looks at Joan. "*Suggest* is George-speak for 'do it or else!'"

"And it's plus one, so you can bring that Aaron guy if you want," Ira says.

"Oh no, plus one, ugh," Phoebe snarls.

"Thought we could go together—you can wear your purple thingy."

Phoebe laughs, "I just had it cleaned!"

"Aaron'll be delighted to come and the magazine can cover it too," Joan offers.

"George'd love that!"

"So this is big-time formal?" Joan suddenly looks worried.

"Hey, you can wear whatever you want," Ira says.

"Yes it is," Phoebe says. "I'll lend you something if you like, you'll just need to hem it. Unless you're okay wearing six-inch heels."

"And losing fifteen pounds? No, no thank you. I've been looking for an excuse to beef up my wardrobe, this is it."

"Happy to go with if you need another pair of eyes," Phoebe says.

"Really? Seriously? How about Wednesday after work then? I think Macy's is open late."

"Wednesday is good but Macy's is not. Nordstrom's is having a sale, that's where we should go."

"You're on!" Joan says as her cell phone rings. It's her lawyer so she steps outside to take the call.

Ralph gets right to the point.

"Dodged a bullet here Joan. I was concerned the magazine might be liable but I double-checked with my colleagues who handle these cases and they confirmed that since it's her company, the investment firm, who are the actual owners of *Relevant*, they're the responsible party. I'm right about this, Grace is not a *Relevant* employee correct, the investment firm pays her salary?"

"They do," Joan says.

"Good. So it's their problem, you're off the hook."

"Oh, thank you, thank you! The last thing we needed now was to be dragged into some awful sexual harassment suit. This woman has been a thorn in my side from day one, I can't thank you enough, oh my god, thank you!"

"You're welcome. Here's what you need to do. One: call your contact over at the investment firm, don't assume Grace has told anyone there anything about this. Let them know they need to get their own attorneys engaged *now* before this thing spirals further out of control. If they don't have the right lawyer for this, have them call me. As I said, we have a robust sexual harassment practice here."

A whole practice?!

"Two: phone Grace now and tell her she is no longer welcome at the office. If she has left any personal items you will ship them to her, she is not permitted back on the premises. Understood?"

"Okay."

"I mean *now*. If she puts up a fuss, gives you any problems at all, you just hang up and call me right back and I'll get a restraining order."

"Okay. Anything else?"

"Three: if anyone at the office asks about Grace, where she is, or what happened, you just say she had a 'Personal Problem To Attend To.' Give no details. The less said the better on this. Okay? It's clear?"

"Yes."

"That's it for now. As I said, you're one lucky ducky, this could have been the *Titanic*," Ralph says, signing off.

Joan walks back inside grinning broadly.

"Your locksmith?" Phoebe asks.

"No, but this is just as good."

She fills them in on what's been happening at the magazine.

"With everything you've told us about this Grace person and how she behaves at the office, with you, with your staff, I'm not surprised. She's despicable!" Phoebe says.

Joan nods in agreement.

"I've been in those situations myself, all it takes is one rotten apple—talk about toxic," Phoebe says.

"And now you're rid of her forever," Ira says.

"I am," Joan grins broadly.

"Poof, Grace be gone," Phoebe laughs.

"You're on a roll!" Ira laughs too, handing her back the key chain.

"So?" Joan asks, fondling the keys.

"Sorry, they just look like keys to me," Ira shrugs.

"Okay, so this one might be for a door and then this one for a deadbolt, right? Typical. And this one," Joan says, referring to the third, "might be for a car because that's what car keys used to look like. But what about this little guy? I don't know but it's sure not a house key. You?"

She passes it to Phoebe. Phoebe shakes her head. "Dunno."

They discuss possibilities for a key this size: Gym locker . . . jewelry box . . . an old skate key . . .

"Safe deposit box, that's what I'm hoping for," Joan says.

Ira returns with a sandwich as Phoebe is still turning the key over in her hand.

"Just spoke to George again," Ira says. "He's going to call your lawyer now, what's his name again?"

"Ralph. Why?" Joan asks.

"He wants to explore buying *Relevant*. He said he would take that private equity firm out, replace their capital with his," Ira smiles at her. "He thinks now might be an optimal time to negotiate with these people."

"I bet it would," Joan smiles back.

"What's his motivation?" Phoebe asks.

"Not one hundred percent sure but, you know, George has had some serious problems with some of the news outlets in the past, the tabloids, Fox. The lies they report about him. And they follow him everywhere, make every day a battle. He respects your magazine and probably doesn't want to lose another credible vehicle like *Relevant*," Ira says.

"Wow!" Joan says as she texts him Ralph's contact info.

"What a guy," Phoebe says.

"Yeah. You want half a sandwich?" Ira asks Joan.

"No thanks, Ira, I already ate lunch, like two hours ago."

They laugh.

"So, you two come up with anything?" Ira asks, referring to the key.

"A safe deposit box?" Phoebe passes it to Ira.

"Interesting," he says.

"Wouldn't it be amazing if this little key breaks the whole story wide open," Joan says.

"What do you mean, we got the story, it's done. We're just tweaking, doing some fine-tuning," Ira says as Phoebe nods in agreement.

"I know. Not *that* story," Joan says. "*My* story, the rest of it. What really happened in Dallas, who really killed Kennedy, who covered it up? The part you guys didn't want to touch. I've started to revise my manuscript."

"And so you should," Phoebe says.

"Yeah. Who knows where this will take you?" Ira says, still holding on to the key. "Maybe to other stories from back then, maybe to a pot of gold."

"Why don't you serialize the book and put it in the magazine now that Grace is no longer an impediment?" Phoebe asks thoughtfully.

"I'm sure you can work out the rights with George, especially if he ends up owning *Relevant*," Ira says.

"It's a possibility. But I've got some new leads I need to follow, get to the bottom of. This key, for example, I'm hoping it won't lead to a dead end."

"C'mon, it probably opens up some smelly old gym locker. You've got tons of material to work with—all that new stuff from Eileen—the photos. And that old Mafioso guy you're gonna meet, right? He may give you something. Don't kill yourself over this one little thing," Ira tosses the key back to her.

Joan never mentioned she's already met Uncle Donny, she never filled them in on those meetings. And she's not even sure why not—they're certainly not going to muscle in, they have no interest in this whatsoever. She's just been following an instinct.

Her phone rings again, this time it is Brad.

"No, earlier than that," she says. "Maybe the '60s? It's hard to see, wait a sec," she picks up Phoebe's reading glasses and walks to the window for more light. "Okay, it's 54824—no, that's a seven—54827," she says squinting. "Brass, four prongs, about an inch long. I'll email you a photo when we hang up. Really? Wow. Gosh, imagine that! Hey, I might know someone in DC who could maybe trace the bank. Let me do a little research, give me a couple of days."

She returns Phoebe's glasses and picks up her backpack.

"Going to do some digging in my Rolodex. I'll be at the magazine if you need me. Do either of you happen to know anyone at the Treasury Department?"

"Treasury?"

"Rolodex?"

Ira and Phoebe laugh.

"Are you back tomorrow?" Phoebe asks, realizing she's growing quite fond of Joan.

"Not if you don't need me. If this is a safe deposit key, and Brad thinks it might be, I'll be digging into that." She swings on her backpack.

"Well, if anyone can figure it out, it'll be you, the pit bull," Ira jokes.

"Joan, I've been meaning to ask, do you ever hire freelancers? Now that we're wrapping up here, I'd love to get back to some magazine writing," Phoebe says.

"Sure, we're always looking for talented writers. But we pay by the word so it's not very lucrative, Phoebe."

"I know, I remember. Luckily, I'm in better shape these days. Let me pull together some samples for you to look at, I'll bring them Wednesday," she calls as Joan heads out the door.

"Good luck with the key," Ira yells.

"If it's the last thing I do!" she yells back.

———

Joan is flipping through her Rolodex, looking for the lady she met years ago who worked at Treasury—she can picture her face but can't recall the name—when Jeff sticks his head in and asks if she'll have a beer with him after hours.

"It is after hours," Joan says. "What time you have in mind?"

"No time like the present," he says, and they walk over to Bernie's, the watering hole around the corner.

"So, I guess Grace is gone for good?" he says jumping right in.

"I wanted to speak to you about that," Joan riffs, "but I didn't want to make it awkward or . . ."

"That's okay, I know the legal eagles probably said to say nothing to nobody."

"Actually that's exactly what they said but without the double negative," she kids him.

"That's not what I want to talk to you about. What I need to tell you, and this is kinda hard for me . . ."

Uh oh, Joan thinks.

"I'm leaving. Glenn and I—we want to start over. Someplace new. Get out of LA. We're thinking San Diego maybe."

Joan takes a sip of her beer. While she's relieved that this is not more about Grace, this is terrible news. Jeff is her best guy, a true talent. Before Grace compromised their relationship, Jeff was her right hand, her go-to. He gets *Relevant,* her *Relevant.* She had hoped they could get back to that.

"Bummer," is all she manages to say.

"I know. I'll miss working here. Twelve years! Gonna miss the work and my peeps, the craziness. And you, you know how much I loved working with you. I won't leave you in the lurch tho', Joan. Promise. I already have feelers out for my replacement. It won't be hard."

She raises an eyebrow to disagree, but for some reason, no words are coming out of her mouth.

"This has been an incredible experience in more ways than one," he continues. "I learned so much. I really must thank you for that. I feel like I can go on to a lot of places—not a competitor, not another magazine, don't worry, there aren't any of those around anyway . . ."

She chuckles.

"But maybe an ad agency, there are a couple good ones down south, maybe a studio. That's what Glenn's looking into. Anyway, I wanted you to know about this once we made up our minds. Glenn and I are going to try and make something out of our . . . well, I know you wish the best for me."

"I do," she manages to say. "You know I do. It's just . . ."

"Bummer," Jeff smiles. "Yeah, I know."

"Can I try and talk you out of it? Now that Grace is gone, now that we can get back to putting out the magazine the way we used to . . ." she's trying not to sound desperate.

"It's really not about that. Her, I mean, that was the catalyst, sure, but I've been thinking about this for a while. It's mainly about . . . life." He stands and starts to put some bills on the table. "I'll be in first thing Monday, we can talk more if you want."

She shoos away his money. "Okay. Have a nice weekend, send my best to Glenn."

"Will do. Oh. And don't bother to thank me for getting rid of Grace, by the way. That was all my pleasure." He winks, smiles, and leaves.

She's stunned. There are many possible meanings to Jeff's parting comment—some innocent, some not—she starts running through the options but decides she really doesn't care what was implied, she's just thrilled to have Grace gone.

And devastated about him.

She thinks about their early days, when he was a young art director and she was an editor. Berta became ill and asked Joan to step in, she had no choice, she was forced into taking the reins. Trying to figure out the business side of the magazine while still writing, editing, and then Berta died and . . .

God, that was chaos. He never complained about the mess I was making, the crazy hours. I'm sure he realized I didn't know what I was doing. Never called me on it, just the opposite, hung in there with me through it all.

And she remembers sitting here with Jeff, in this very booth, when Grace joined the operation.

"So how about I tinker under her BMW?" he teased. "I know enough about cars to be dangerous."

They laughed. But there were days she thought about taking him up on it.

He found another way.

———

Joan walks back to her office, back to her Rolodex, still thinking about the past. She pries a pillow from her couch, places it on her chair behind her back, and gets ready for a long night.

She shakes loose the three by five cards from an ancient metal wheel and covers the table with hundreds of Rolodex contacts; she starts going through them, one by one. The person she's looking for is in here somewhere.

The cards have yellowed with age, some written in pencil have nearly faded away. But after midnight she finds the one she's been looking for:

**Margot Harris, Program Analyst,
US Department of the Treasury.**

Margot's face appears in her mind, a young woman with a serious nature and an impish grin, a face from a thousand years ago.

She remembers how they met.

JFK had once issued an executive order creating a new currency backed by silver. He was planning to move the money supply back to the Treasury Department and rein in the power of the Federal Reserve.

And then he was shot.

That's why Margot had come looking for her. She knew Joan was researching a book and thought she should look into this executive order, thought it could be the motive for the assassination.

"Kennedy never trusted the Feds. He thought those guys were thieves in three-piece suits," Margot had said.

Joan worried it might be just another fringe theory floating around then, most with little substantiation or consequence. After wasting many hours looking into it, her instincts were right: a dead end.

She wonders if Margot could still be working at Treasury, she really needs someone to help Brad locate the bank. She scoots over to her computer and scrolls around, landing on LinkedIn. There are twenty-seven financial professionals listed with the name Margot Harris, she decides to tackle this in the morning.

Across town, Phoebe is also digging through her past. Sitting crossed legged on the floor of her closet, she searches her portfolio for magazine articles written years before.

She can't find her *Sassy* articles. She sets her weight against the metal drawer of the file cabinet and tugs it open. A *Sassy* folder sits right on top and inside are dozens of issues! There are bound to be a couple of good articles here she can add to her collection for Joan.

She remembers the editor that championed her work, a meeting where he debated with his editorial team whether to run one of her articles or someone else's. How he had fought for her! And how thrilled she was to see it in print. How proud.

She even called her mother to tell her about it.

Was that the last time we spoke?

She recalls her mother being pleased, giving her a few "go get 'ems" and then switching the subject to Phoebe's love life.

"So who's the lucky fella got you running all over town?"

Her mother seemed to confuse her with Carrie Bradshaw—a swinging city gal whose only worry was what to wear out to dinner that night. This was all happening while Phoebe survived on ramen noodles in a tiny apartment with a roommate she couldn't stand.

Worse, her mom seemed jealous of her life in the "big city" — it had been her own dream growing up.

Just one of the many things that plagued their relationship.

Phoebe would like to find one more article to add to the pile. She pulls out another folder from the file and is shocked to see a bottle of red wine sitting underneath.

She had totally forgotten about it.

There are some plastic cups and a metal corkscrew buried nearby, the cork slides out in one clean motion. She pours herself some wine after using her T-shirt to wipe the dust off a cup.

"To old times," she toasts aloud. "Hmmm, delish."

She gets up to go to the kitchen for something to eat, she's not used to having wine on an empty stomach. Or even a full one.

She passes through her living room, remembering the day her treasured furniture arrived: the walnut coffee table, the sectional sofa and two semi-matching chairs she seldom uses. How she had splurged! This was back when she and Ira were writing hit comedies, one hit after another.

We should have tried harder to make it work. I know I'm no Miss Utah but . . . never mind. He's your friend, your best friend, let's face it. But where the fuck is love?

She finds a ham-and-cheese sandwich that looks edible and takes it back to the living room, refills her cup, and plops down into one of the chairs she never sits in.

It's the last thing she remembers.

CHAPTER NINETEEN

"Is she on to something or what, Aaron?"

Joe is cruising the aisles, picking up a couple of fancy reds.

"Your girlfriend drives all the way to McCloud just to keep some old bag company? Doesn't compute, you better not be holding out on me."

"I told you, she's an old lady she needs help. Take her to the doctor, help her around the house, things like that. No big deal. Hey, any news about Phil?" Aaron asks, mainly to change the subject.

"Oh yeah, that's a sad story, I forgot to . . ." Joe takes a step back to look at him solemnly. "Phil had a heart attack, yeah — in his cell, a couple of days after they brought him in. Imagine that? He never did take good care of himself. Fat as a pig, right? You saw him. Maybe the stress of getting locked up. Anyway, we had a small service yesterday, guess I forgot to invite you."

"He's dead?" Aaron gasps. He flashes that Phil's demise is tied to Joe's occupation and his own situation — but he can't allow himself to go down there. "What about the deposit?" he says instead. "I'm sitting on a lot of cash."

"Cool your jets. Your job is keeping it safe. You fuck with that, you don't wanna know what happens."

Joe starts perusing the bourbons. "So, what's up with the girl-friend, give me something I can take back to Uncle Donny."

"Like I said, nothing, there's nothing to say."

"You sure?" Joe asks, moving in close.

Phil's face appears.

"Well, let me think," Aaron says. "Okay. She told me that they sometimes reminisce, you know, look through old photo albums, talk about the old days. There, would Uncle Donny like that?"

"Keep thinking," Joe says, still not smiling.

"Okay, um, once in a while she'll hear something interesting about Ruby's childhood. Once she found something, like, you know, some memorabilia that was from Ruby."

"What kind of memorabilia?" Joe spits out the word.

"Well, um, one time she found a coaster from his nightclub."

"Oh yeah?"

"Another time they found a key, uh, keepsake, I mean." Aaron realizes this entire line of conversation has been a bad idea.

"Keepsake? What the fuck does that mean?"

"I don't know," now desperate to backtrack, "like a . . ."

"Like a corsage from his first prom?"

"Something from his family maybe?"

"You slay me, Aaron. Keepsake. A real comedian." Joe puts an expensive single-malt scotch on the counter. "You're a Real. Funny. Guy."

———

Later, when Aaron replays this unfortunate conversation in his mind, he'll remember Joe mentioning *McCloud*. He doesn't recall ever hearing that name before, Joan never told him exactly where 'up north' this woman lived. *Right?*

———

"This is important, Joe. You say the broad found a key?" Uncle Donny asks, pouring him a scotch.

"Yeah, that's straight from the deadbeat's lips. Well actually he said 'keepsake' but that's him blowing smoke, he knows he shouldn'ta told me nothing. Hearing the news about Phil loosened his tongue," Joe laughs. "Just like you said."

"Hmm," Uncle Donny says.

"Why, what's the big deal?"

"Ruby kept a safe deposit box, he was always bragging about his money, about all the dough he was socking away, how he was getting ready for retirement. It's possible this key goes to that box."

"So? I still don't get the problem."

"It's not the cash. He kept some of our papers in there too."

"Oh, you want me to go get them?"

"Shit."

"I can go get."

"If somebody smart finds those papers, they might connect some dots, dots that connect to me. To us. And that broad's smart."

"So what'ya want me to do, Uncle Donny, go take the key away from her?"

"The tail still on?"

"Oh yeah. We know where she goes, who she sees, and what she ate for breakfast. We got her good," Joe says.

Uncle Donny goes over to his humidor, takes out a cigar. Tamps it, lights it, and puffs on it for a few minutes, thinking. Thinking.

"Time to stop the train, Joe. This thing is getting out of control. That broad needs to stop butting into our business! Let's just take care of it now."

"You mean take her out?" Joe asks. He never had to do that before.

"The lot of them. Both broads and the deadbeat. They have out-lived their usefulness."

"But that guy still owes us big time."

"I know, but we need him gone. No loose ends. Trust me on this. We'll take his inventory, that'll make up for some of it."

"So how about I stage a robbery at his store that goes bad?"

"Better if you get them all around the same time. That way no one's talking to the authorities about the other guy. Look, the old lady is a cakewalk, it's the dynamic duo that'll take a bit of planning."

"Maybe a car accident with the two of them?"

"Sure, but it's not as easy as it sounds. You keep an ear open for when they'll be together, you know, driving down some dark quiet road at night. Maybe he'll give you a heads-up, you're friends with—"

"I wouldn't exactly say friends."

"You know what I mean. Find out when they'll be together, it doesn't really matter where. Just get it done. And soon."

"So you—you want me to handle it?" Joe asks again.

"If you're not up for it, I'll get someone else . . ."

"No, no, I can do it."

"I got guys who do this all the time, Joe, don't—"

"I said I'll do it!"

"Okay, okay. You want to be made, right? Here you go, on a silver platter. Take Tommy if you need to. But I don't want to hear another word about it, I'm leaving it to you to handle," Don looks at him intently. "And you're sure?"

"Consider it done," Joe says. "And thank you for trusting me with this, you won't be disappointed."

"No, I won't, Joe, because you won't let me down."

CHAPTER TWENTY

Eileen is looking for the paperback she just put down one minute ago when Newport starts barking loudly.

"Okay, okay." She pats his head and speaks in a calming voice, the one she uses when creatures at night set him off, driving her batty with incessant barking.

She peers out the window but sees only darkness.

"It's nothing."

She walks into the kitchen to look through the window over the door, hoping to see a coyote or bobcat she can frighten off.

Nothing.

She debates putting him down in the basement (*driving me crazy!*) when she thinks maybe she does hear something, like the wind cracking through the trees or tires coughing up pebbles on her driveway. She returns to the kitchen window and sees the outline of a large moving object, a dark-colored van trying to execute a three-point turn in a narrow spot by the garage.

A lost driver!

So easy to get lost out here, in the boonies. It even happened to her once, trying to find one of the retirement homes she was checking out. The Uber driver got them totally twisted around, heading in the wrong direction. She was an hour late for her appointment.

"Hush, Newport."

That was her first time in an Uber, last summer. Or was it two summers ago? Buddy insisted she try it instead of that old rickety taxi with the nearly bald tires she would call before he got his permit.

What kind of name is that, Uber—Arab?

Newport's barking brings her back to the window.

Guess I'll set him straight.

"Quiet! I'll be right back."

She pulls a jacket over her bathrobe and goes out to help this lost soul get back to civilization.

———

Joan can't wait for a long soak in her tub to shake off the day. She makes a beeline for the bathroom, speed-dialing her phone on the way.

C'mon, Eileen.

The water reluctantly sputters out from the faucet. Lately, it's been taking forever to fill.

This is almost as bad as Eileen's.

She walks back to the kitchen to fix herself a vodka.

Maybe time to look for another apartment, something from this century.

She plucks Ruby's keys from her backpack and walks back to check the water. She carefully lays the keys in front of a photo taped to a tile on the wall. The lab guys did an amazing job of restoration, both Ruby and Oswald are as clear as day. She'd like to find out who the others are, the patrons sitting around the circular table, she's not ready to release them back to obscurity.

She sheds her work clothes and slides into the tub, half-full. Cold tile momentarily shocks her system until she's down into the warm bubbles.

Aaah.

With time to think, Joan can finally review all she has going. She laments being so tired, really drained. Days at the office never used to exhaust her like this. She decides it's the price she's paying for being gone so much, for having to reassert herself with staff, renew relationships.

And wasting time searching for Margot Harris.

Of course, she couldn't still be at Treasury, she's probably retired by now.

She thinks about George acquiring the magazine; Ralph said he made a very generous offer and the PE firm was probably going to take it.

"Too good to pass up."

She'll be happy to have a new investor, one that doesn't come with a Grace breathing down her neck. She only knows George from what Ira and Phoebe say about him, but it's all good.

She could never retire.

Now all she needs to do is find a new creative director.

Jeff said there were some promising candidates, but that's Jeff being Jeff, always optimistic. Joan knows he'll be difficult to replace.

She separates the small key from the others.

Safe deposit box?

So far this has been a disappointment. She's not sure that Brad is up to the task. Who else does she know?

She realizes she's nodding off.

C'mon you lazy bum, you need to eat something first!

She leans forward to fetch the keys, careful not to get them wet. She hits the redial button on her phone, again there's no answer.

"What the heck, Eileen?" she says aloud. "How long does it take to walk a dog at night?"

———

"Yes, sir, I'll tell her," Ira says. "She should be here any minute. Is this the best number to reach you on?"

Joan comes into the kitchen carrying a large envelope of retouched photos. "Look at what I brought—hey, something wrong?"

"We've got a problem," Ira says quietly, calmly, taking a deep breath. "I just took a call from the Redding Police. Something happened at Eileen's and they've taken her to the hospital."

"Oh no! What happened, what's wrong?" Joan drops the envelope and rushes over to where Ira is standing.

"A neighbor boy came over this morning, supposed to take her someplace, to the um, market? But she wasn't . . . he found her on the floor—unconscious. It's not good." *Where the fuck is Phoebe?*

"Oh my god, she's got no one up there, Ira. Oh my god, that's why she didn't answer the phone, I tried calling her last night, I should have known. Oh my god, do you know where they are taking her, which hospital?"

"Gosh, I forgot to ask. Let's just take a breath here."

"They said *unconscious*? That's what they said?" Joan asks, just as Phoebe enters.

"Who's unconscious?" Phoebe looks first at Joan then Ira. "George?!!"

"It's Eileen," Ira says.

Joan is pacing frantically around the cottage, picking things up and putting them down, looking for her backpack, finding it, then looking in it for something, putting it down.

"I'm going up there," she says finally.

"Let's just call them back," Ira says. "I have the number, this way you can get more—"

"But she's all alone!" Joan cries.

"Just wait, we'll get more information, you're too upset."

Joan won't hear of it.

"I thought she was walking the dog. Her phone just rang and rang," she turns to Phoebe, who is desperately searching for something hopeful to say.

"A neighbor boy found her on the floor," Ira repeats. He looks at Joan again and says more forcibly, "Please calm down. She could be fine. You should just wait to—"

"WAIT!!? I'm not waiting!" Joan explodes in tears. "If I drive straight through I can be there by . . . oh my god, Eileen."

"I'll go with you, I'll help drive," Ira says but she is already out the door.

Phoebe is still trying to catch up to the scene, asking a barrage of questions Ira doesn't have answers to: "Was she ill? Does she live alone? How old is she? Didn't Joan say something about a nursing home?" He goes into the kitchen for another coffee with Phoebe at his heels.

"You know, you don't look so good yourself. You okay?"

Phoebe wasn't planning on telling him—telling anyone—about last night. But he knows her too well.

"Well, don't beat yourself up," he says once she's confessed. "Everyone falls off the wagon once in a while. Just get back to those meetings, they really seem to help. Don't you have a sponsor you can call?"

"I already did. But I'm so mad at myself Ira, I don't even know why I did it. I am feeling good about things, really, it was just—I don't know—spur of the moment!"

"Okay, so that's all it is, you get a pass. I give you a pass. Just promise you'll go to a meeting and talk to people who are knowledgeable."

Phoebe walks over and kisses him on his forehead. She grabs a Coke from the refrigerator.

"I'm worried about what's going on," he says taking his espresso back to the great room.

"Well, let's just finish up those revisions," she says. "Joan promised to call us once she knows something, it'll take our minds off waiting."

"You don't think stirring up the Ruby story has anything to do with this, with Eileen?" he asks.

It catches Phoebe by surprise.

"I—uh—I don't know. I mean, how would it? It's not in our script and, even if it's in Joan's manuscript, well, that's still in a drawer. I mean, how would anyone even know about the sister?"

"Right. You're right. Who knows about Jack Ruby's sister? Nobody. Besides us I mean," he says.

"Unless she told some friend. Maybe that guy, what's his name?"

"Aaron with the liquor store? Does she have any other friends, she never mentions them."

"No girlfriends," Phoebe says. "That's what she told me the night we went shopping. She said she wished she did."

"Plus, let's face it, this sister has to be very old. Like ancient," he says.

"Right, very old."

"Shit like this happens to old people," he says.

"I don't think I can face these revisions right now," Phoebe says.

So they sit and wait to hear from Joan.

———

One week later, Joan is making another trip up to McCloud, this time it's to finalize funeral arrangements. She also needs to start disposing of Eileen's estate.

There's no one else to do it.

The trip before was a mad rush that resulted in her arriving too late to say goodbye to her dear friend. Now she's driving much slower, not anxious to get to where she's going.

Eileen had once mentioned she'd like to be cremated. So Joan located a funeral parlor and is meeting with a rabbi in Chico to organize a simple service.

She'll also meet up with a real estate broker, finish packing the house and donate what she can to the Salvation Army. Since Buddy is heading off to college, he asked for some of Eileen's kitchen items: her microwave, toaster, and a few pots and pans. Joan will keep the photo albums and other mementos for herself, along with the cardigan sweater Eileen wore the first time they met.

She'll also spend hours trying to locate Newport.

She had planned to bring the dog back with her the last time, but despite searching everywhere and putting up posters, she couldn't find him. This time she'll broaden her search and add a reward. She's debating whether to make it $300 or $400 when Buddy calls, he's learned that Newport is dead.

"Left to die on the side of the road. A neighbor thought this was the dog she saw animal rescue pick up the day Nana went into the hospital," he gulps.

"Are you sure it's Newport?"

"She said she thought it was Eileen's dog."

"And she's sure he was dead, Buddy?"

"That's what she said. She said they picked up the roadkill!" he sobs, "that's what she said to me. Roadkill!"

Buddy loved Newport almost as much as Eileen.

Joan makes a mental note to stop at the police station anyway, just to double check.

"The door was ajar, the dog wandered out, that road is pitch black, we see it all the time," the cop tells her.

"But Eileen would never leave her door open," Joan argues.

"Lady was getting on in years," the cop says. "It happens."

———

She drives back to LA in a fog, stopping at a diner, but when seated she just stares at the menu. Once she gets home it all comes crashing down on her. She can't sleep, can't concentrate on anything. A few days pass and she worries that she'll never snap out of it.

But when she awakens this morning she feels a little better, her head is clearer and she's got an appetite. She decides to run some errands and then spend a few hours catching up at the magazine. Maybe even stop at the cottage if she has any energy left.

"What a surprise, great to see you!" Ira says when she walks in.

"You holding up okay?" Phoebe asks. "We want to tell you again how sorry we are about Eileen, it's just devastating. We're here to . . . well, if you need us to do anything just . . ."

Joan drops her backpack and turns to face them on the couch.

"I think I got a problem guys," she says.

"What's wrong?" Ira and Phoebe ask at the same time, although Ira has actually said "What's wrong *now?*"

"I think I'm being followed," she says.

"You sure?" Ira asks, trying to keep doubt out of his voice.

Phoebe knows what he's thinking: Joan's been a nut from day one and this business with Eileen couldn't have helped much.

"Well, I think so. No—I know so. I'm being followed. I was followed here."

"What do you mean by followed?" Phoebe asks.

"There's been a blue Taurus in my rearview mirror all day. I thought maybe it was gone for a while but then it came back."

"Well Taurus's are pretty common," Phoebe says trying to cheer her up, "Maybe it's just one of those crazy coincidences."

Joan shakes her head. "That's what I thought. I was driving around, doing errands, I went to the office but I kept seeing it. I dismissed it, you know, Taurus. But later when I left the magazine to come here I thought maybe I saw it again, the same car! So I drove way out of my way, past your exit and doubled back. It was gone but then, don't you know, it showed up again, right near the turnoff for your road!"

"You sure?" Ira asks again, unable to help himself. "Taurus is like the most popular car in the country. And blue—"

"Camry is the most popular car, Ira! And I'm not delusional. Somebody is tailing me. They tailed me here!"

"You need to realize you've been under tremendous pressure lately—"

"I'm NOT CRAZY, someone's following me!"

He reminds her about the time she thought her phone was tapped.

"Yeah, well, it is and the more I think about it, I think I've had this car thing since Eileen's. I mean I've been so upset, I haven't been paying attention but when I think back . . ." she is pacing in circles around the great room, "you don't think this has anything to do with that—with Eileen do you?" Joan asks with a sudden tremble in her voice, "Oh my god, do you . . . ?"

The room goes quiet.

"Eileen was an old woman," Phoebe says sympathetically. "Close to ninety, isn't that so," she adds.

Joan continues pacing.

"Did you ever mention to anyone that you met Jack Ruby's sister, became friendly with her?" Ira asks.

Joan stops to think. "No, just you guys. And Aaron. But he doesn't care much about that stuff, about my work I mean. Why do you ask, do you . . . ?"

"Nothing, no reason. Never mind," he says.

"It's probably just a coincidence, Joan, this happening so soon after Eileen, but regardless, I think we should take it seriously. Don't you, Ira?" Phoebe says.

It gets quiet again.

"Why don't we switch cars for a few days, see if that doesn't solve it?" Ira says finally.

Joan turns to him and brightens. "That's a good idea, Ira. An excellent idea."

They discuss the logistics of a swap.

"You know I'm not suggesting the Lamborghini," he says.

It breaks the mood. They laugh.

Phoebe ventures to ask how Joan likes having Eileen's dog at her place.

"I don't have him, I couldn't find him. They told me he got run over!" Joan says, plunging back to remorse.

"Oh no," Phoebe says, looking at Ira for help.

"The cops weren't positive but they found a dog that fit his description near—look, it probably was hers," Joan sighs. "They said she left her door open, that's so not Eileen."

"She shouldn't have been living alone at that age," Phoebe says.

"If she had moved into Shady Elms, this never would have happened!" Joan says.

"You're still coming to the gala Sunday, right?" Ira asks.

Phoebe stares at him. "Maybe she's not feeling up to a party, Ira."

"Oh no, I'll be there, of course I'll be there. Listen, life goes on," Joan sighs again.

"You're sure, you don't need—" Ira says.

"No, this is important to you. I wouldn't miss it for the world."

"Super, so we'll all be there together," Phoebe smiles.

"And we finally get to meet the mystery man," Ira winks. "Okay, you know how to drive a Prius? Ever drive one?"

"There's a first time for everything," Joan says, motioning him to toss over the keys.

"Hmm," Ira says, "I'll come with you, show you how it works."

"Don't be silly, Ira, a car is a car."

"This one's a little different," he says as he escorts her out.

———

"You don't think this business of being followed is somehow related to Eileen?" Phoebe asks Ira a bit later.

"To her mental state? Wouldn't surprise me. And not just that— how about that business with Grace? She's been through a lot lately."

"You're right. I wonder if she shouldn't see someone."

"Maybe you can find a way to suggest it?"

"She doesn't seem to be, you know, overly self-reflective. But I'll look for an opening."

"Wait a minute. Were you referring to her poking around the Jack Ruby story?" Ira asks a moment later.

"It's crossed my mind. But I'm just being paranoid, probably caught it from her. It's definitely contagious."

"Please never bring that up, we can't be adding a whiff of guilt into that crazy cocktail," he says. "'Specially now, when she's got my car."

"George's car, you mean," Phoebe smiles.

———

Joan drives to Aaron's liquor store straight from the cottage, checking frequently in her rear-view mirror. Thankfully no one's been tailing her and Aaron hasn't closed up for the evening yet.

"You must be hitting the bottle pretty hard," he says. "Not that I'm *not* happy to see you."

"It's been a trying couple of days."

He takes Joan's hand. "You have to remember she lived a long, full life."

"I know. I know."

"What was she, like in her nineties? That's a nice run, I'll never make it to that," he says with a smile.

"No, you probably won't. Me neither. Not sure I'd want to anyway," she says with a heavy heart.

"Cheer up. Let me introduce you to Mr. Tito, a much better choice in vodkas." Aaron takes a bottle from the shelf but Joan argues that she can't taste the difference. He slips it into a bag anyway and then refuses to take her credit card.

"Listen, I need to give you a heads-up about Sunday. There's a chance I won't make it," she says a bit more chipper. "I may have to fly out of town."

"Wow! You found it?"

"Well, my guy's getting close. We got a lead on a bank in Texas that changed hands a couple of times, I'm hoping it was the old US National, that would be very promising. Brad isn't sure. But if it is, then I want to be with him first thing, the minute it opens on Monday. If not, it's back to our original plan, Aaron, I meet you at five p.m. in front of the VIP tent. And don't forget, it's formal."

"Black tie, red Converse, got it."

"And wear socks this time. I still remember that press dinner where I spent the whole night staring at your ankles."

They're quietly looking at one another.

"Come here," he says and hugs her.

Joan begins to cry. She croaks out "Newport" but he knows that's just a ruse. Joan is missing her friend and feeling awful about it, maybe even blaming herself somehow.

"Everything you've told me about her, everything you did, you gave her life at the end of her life! You made her your friend, you made her laugh. Look, it was a positive send-off. Please stop feeling so bad. She was an old, old person and old people die."

"Thanks, you are a good friend." She heads for the door. "Hope you don't mind me saying I hope *not* to see you on Sunday."

"Fine. Just take it easy with Mr. Tito," he calls out as the screen door slams.

Aaron starts shutting off some lights, preparing to close—when the door swings back open.

"Wait!" Joe yells.

"Ugh," he says under his breath.

"Here." Joe thrusts a large padded envelope into Aaron's arms.

"Why are you bringing me more—"

"Hold your horses. We got you a new Phil," he says. "The other side," he adds when Aaron looks confused.

"Roger Rodriguez," Aaron reads on the envelope flap. "What—Century City? That's like hours from here!"

"Yeah, so? Roger's branch manager. He knows all about you. You think you can find Century City?"

"I'd better leave now," Aaron says sarcastically.

"What else is new? How's your girlfriend? She back up north again?"

"Her friend passed away, she's pretty broken up about it."

"Wow! Ruby's sister kicked the bucket? No shit. But yeah, I guess. Must have been pretty old, right?"

"Yes, she was. Joan says she feels lost without her."

"Ah, that's so sad. So why don't you take her out for a nice date, wouldn't that cheer her up? Or make it worse?"

"Har har. Actually, we're going to a big Hollywood shindig on Sunday. A tribute to George Baxter—her film friends invited us."

"Oh, excuuuuuse me," Joe says extending his pinkie finger.

Aaron grunts, "And that's the worst Steve Martin impression ever."

"You got something nice to wear friend. Just saying, cause this"—Joe gestures to Aaron's chino's—"won't do."

"Yeah, a monkey suit. I hate these things but . . ."

"You're a good sport. Cheering up your friend. So make sure you put that someplace safe over the weekend, maybe take it home with you?" Joe says, gesturing to the envelope.

"No, no, I'll put it with the other one in the safe. In the office."

"You got a safe! I didn't know. You never mentioned you got a safe. I need the combination."

SHIT.

Aaron rips a piece off the envelope flap and writes the numbers down.

"Here. Don't lose it."

"Oh, I won't," he smirks. "And you don't forget the bank first thing Monday. Roger's expecting you."

"Maybe the traffic won't be bad real early."

"No, it will," Joe smiles. "Have fun at the ball and say hi to Cinderella for me. Tell her Uncle Donny was saying how his door is always open, love to see her again, talking about the old times, blah blah blah."

"Yeah, okay, I'll tell her."

CHAPTER TWENTY-ONE

ra, looking debonair in a black tuxedo and blow-dried hair, is working the room, stopping at every table to make small talk, inquiring after new projects, new houses, new babies. George invited an A-list of industry folks and most of them have come, drinking wine, toying with salads, and feeling ever-so-smug about their involvement with GoodWorks, one of California's most prestigious charities.

Technically each guest is a volunteer, doing his or her part to improve the planet, a markedly different activity from their regular dog-eat-dog world.

Actually, most have written checks rather than donned overalls to 'pitch in' . . . sometimes even fulfilling an unspoken obligation. Mister Hollywood and all.

George is in the green room prepping for his speech. If he can get through his notes one more time, he'll speak without any prompts at all.

The emcee has been trying to command attention but guests are flitting from table to table, the place is a buzz. Finally it quiets as he begins speaking about 'the man of the hour.'

"So after realizing that George isn't the one-dimensional *bleep-bleep* he pretends to be, some of you started digging into your pocket and kicking in some serious dough," the crowd chuckles predictably at *bleep-bleep*. "And George was able to expand into Chad and Nigeria. Wait until you see the difference you have made in the lives of the children of N'Djamena, you will be so proud to be part of this effort. We're about to roll a short film that will transport you to that school as well as lay out plans for GoodWorks's next chapter, our expansion into Mali. Watch the film, enjoy your dinner, and I'll be back to bring up tonight's man of honor, George Baxter."

The house lights begin to dim slowly.

Phoebe is nursing a Coke Zero, stewing over how Ira is always left out of the GoodWorks's accolades. After all, he does much of the work. She knows this first-hand: him running off to solve a passport problem for one of the volunteers; setting up the conference logistics with educators in Africa; postponing a weekend away to solve a bureaucratic snag.

Just last week he even pulled her into it, subbing for him at a preproduction meeting so he could fly off somewhere to pitch-hit for George.

She had been quite busy at the time, but how could she say no to Ira?

Phoebe has been working full-time with Joan at *Relevant*. Writing and editing and trying to erase Grace's fingerprints from the operation. Often that means modeling good office behavior — Grace managed through fear and intimidation — so Phoebe smiles a lot, keeps her door open, and tries to bring comradery back into the place.

Incredibly, she often finds herself acting as Joan's right hand, making some of the many daily decisions about the business. She likes it, it makes her feel validated and grounded and maybe is helping to put the drinking genie back in its bottle for good.

She laughs watching Joan and Aaron at the party, trying every exotic drink the bartender has suggested. She watches them pretend not to stare at the rich and famous, pretend not to ogle at the 'beautiful people' including the young actress with a role in *Long Road to Havana*.

As the lights dim, they join her back at the table.

"So this is what Hollywood is all about," Aaron says. "Big stars, big drinks, big boobs, I'm loving it." He turns to Joan. "You look very nice by the way, you should wear your hair like this more often."

"That's her doing," Joan points to Phoebe. "Her stylist touched up my color. But these things are driving me crazy," she says tugging on fake eyelashes, "how does anyone—Hey, a text from Brad!"

"What kind of phone is that?" Aaron asks.

"Android," she says as she reads the text.

"New?"

"Yes, my whole life's on it. Oh shit. It's probably not the bank. Shit, shit, shit."

"Just a small setback," Aaron says. "Not the end of the world. You'll keep at it."

"I know—but I was hoping. Oh well. Live to fight another day." Joan is still texting when Ira finally makes his way back to their table.

Phoebe has gone to the ladies' room so Joan looks up to introduce the two men.

"Heard a lot about you," Ira says, shaking Aaron's hand. "Glad to see you're real."

They laugh, acknowledging a shared Joan moment.

"GoodWorks is amazing, you and George should be very proud. All that great work you do, I didn't realize!" Joan manages to sincerely deliver this compliment while still texting.

"You know," Aaron says conspiratorially to his new friend, "I could easily get used to this, beats peddling booze any day."

"It's not all cake and champagne," Ira says as Phoebe reappears. "Phoebe will back me up on that."

"I'm off champagne but no cake? I'm outta here!"

Joan puts her phone down to raise her glass. "This calls for a toast: to Ira and George and your wonderful foundation."

They clink glasses.

"And to *Long Road to Havana,*" Phoebe adds.

They clink again.

"George loves it by the way," Ira tells Joan. "He's trying to fast-track it through the studio."

"That's great," she says as they hear the first music cue intended to bring Ira back to the dais. He decides to ignore it and make a stab at dinner.

But more toasts are to come.

"And here's to your excellent magazine." Phoebe toasts Joan. "I'm even more impressed with *Relevant* now that I've come to know it better."

They clink again.

The second music cue sounds just as someone's phone rings, they look to Joan but this time it's Aaron's. He walks toward a window to get out of the action.

"We couldn't have done *Havana* without you, Joan," Ira says between bites, "I hope you know that."

"Happy to contribute, but guys, that baby belongs to you."

"Got a lot riding on it," he says as he reluctantly puts down his fork to head to the podium.

Joan turns to Phoebe. "I'm so glad to hear you're enjoying working at the magazine. It's so nice having you there, you bring a fresh point of view. And I like your persistence in going after a story. It reminds me of me."

"It's been great fun, Joan. I'm loving it," Phoebe says. "I mean, I know we clunked heads a couple of times on the film, but I can't tell you how different working with you is now . . . you've got a great mind, you're a good listener and I'm just learning a ton! I really do hope there's more I can contribute."

They clink again.

Aaron returns and Joan sees something's wrong.

"That was my security company. Some guys broke into the store, trashed the place, god knows what they took. I gotta get back there," he gathers up his things and slugs down the rest of his drink. Phoebe and Joan mutter condolences.

The emcee picks up the mic and begins a long and flattering George Baxter introduction.

"You know what I miss about *Havana*?" Phoebe whispers to Joan. "Those early mornings when you got to the cottage before—"

"WHAT THE—" Aaron passes a security cop that looks oddly familiar. He turns to look at him again. "FUCK!"

Joe fires his silenced gun straight into Aaron's chest. He falls twisting backward, slipping downward, and is dead before he hits the ground.

Joan sees him fall and jumps up.

"Aaron?!"

Joe's second shot turns Joan 180 degrees and with a questioning expression, she starts to fall. Phoebe catches her midway and they slide to the ground together, Joan's blood pooling over them.

Everyone now realizes there's an active shooter in the room and the place explodes. Guests scream, they dive under tables, there are calls for police, for ambulances, for someone, anyone to *HELP, HELP, HELP!!!*

It's pure pandemonium.

Tom shoves George and Ira out a side door. They rush past two genuine security guards who are running from their sideline stations into the ballroom, trying to catch up with the gunman.

Phoebe has Joan cradled with her shawl over her wound. "You're all right," she whispers. "You'll be fine."

The shawl is quickly turning red.

"Joan, please, hang on."

A guest with medical training rushes over to Aaron to try and resuscitate him. Someone kneels by Phoebe's side, feeling for Joan's pulse. Ira fights his way back to their table, threading through the chaos.

"The ambulance is on its way, they're almost here," he tells her.

He puts an arm around Phoebe and they both cradle Joan's head. She's moaning but thankfully breathing as the EMT arrives.

CHAPTER TWENTY-TWO

Brad lied to Joan. The bank he found in Ft. Worth could very well be "the" one. He'll know as soon as it opens for business.

He lied to stop her from flying out to join him, he knows from experience what a pain she can be—difficult even in good times. So he set her expectations low and if it turns out that this is the right bank, she'll be over the moon!

First thing Monday morning, he's at the bank and quickly finds the branch manager; she takes his authorization documents and then disappears to check if the box is one of theirs.

She returns with a smile and escorts him down two escalators through a dingy hallway to an old vault; they enter the safe deposit room.

She inserts her master key, then Brad's key, and turns the lock.

It opens!

Brad realizes he's been holding his breath the whole time.

He thanks her, carries the box carefully into a private cubicle, and closes the door.

The box is large and heavy and crammed to the top. Without looking, he shovels everything into a reusable Walmart bag he brought with him and quickly summons the branch manager to escort them back out.

Once inside his car, Brad can't resist putting his hand inside the bag. He fishes around and runs over a large padded envelope that feels like it has bills inside. He pokes around again to see what else seems interesting. He feels other padded envelopes along with a mountain of loose papers down near the bottom, some with the raised engraving of old stock certificates. He decides to leave everything undisturbed for the moment, not wanting to risk a closer look.

He heads back to the motel where he can dump it out on his bed.

He spots a local drive-thru and orders a double cheeseburger to take back with him, wondering if he shouldn't treat himself to a nicer meal to celebrate. Instead, he adds fries and a chocolate shake. He and Joan can really party back in LA.

Brad counts and recounts Ruby's fortune several times, he can't believe how much money was in the safe deposit box. He briefly worries he is now tainted by some dastardly business, how else could Jack Ruby accumulate so much cash? But he puts it out of his mind, focusing instead on how happy Joan will be once she learns of his success.

After finishing up his burger, Brad scrolls to find an earlier flight and sees a breaking news bulletin. There's a clip of a shooting in California, a few seconds of a shaky home video from a terrified partygoer at a fundraising event.

Joan's last text had been from a fundraiser.

No names are released but Brad gets an awful, sinking feeling.

It's not like her not to have called today.

He turns on the tv and sees a video of a security guard, his cap casts a deep shadow over his face making him hard to recognize. There's a crawl asking for tips leading to his arrest. Brad scribbles the toll-free number on the pad by his bed. He has no idea as to the identity of the guard, but he is very worried. He can imagine how Joan might be a target. He can think of a motive. His eyes travel over to the Walmart bag.

All night, Brad debates whether to call the tip line but what could he tell them?

He's hundreds of miles away from everything he knows with a bag full of cash and only an inkling of the story. Brad's just a simple locksmith with a small shop in the Valley, Joan roped him into helping her, an old friend, and he couldn't say no.

Now he's completely at sea.

The next morning, he tries phoning her again, and this time—thank god!—she answers.

But it's not Joan.

"Intensive care," Phoebe tells him in a voice that's been crying. "It's bad. They're not sure she's going to make it." He hears muffled sobs. "Aaron didn't."

Brad has heard about Phoebe from Joan, and has even met Aaron a couple of times in the past, he didn't know that they were back together, and now he's dead, and Joan . . .

Man, oh man.

Phoebe tells him she knows he's been trying to find the safe deposit box.

He decides to stick to the story he told Joan earlier.

"Dead end," he says. "Should I keep trying? That's what Joan texted me last night."

"She has great faith in you," Phoebe says between tears. She gives him the room number and tells him to ask for her when he gets to the hospital. And to bring a photo ID, the place is loaded with cops and he won't get in without it.

But Brad doesn't go to the hospital from the airport, he has a change of heart on the plane. He decides to stash the bag somewhere safe before rushing over to see Joan.

Then, once he's back home, he changes his mind again.

Not sure she's going to make it. Isn't that what Phoebe said?

So he'll wait a day or two to see if Joan survives her injuries. He figures that if she doesn't . . . and that's not what he's hoping for, not at all, not by any stretch of the imagination! . . . but with Aaron gone, he being the closest thing Joan has to family, then he will keep the money.

Why hand it over to the government? That's definitely not what Joan would have him do.

She would have split it with me. I did all the leg work, she'd never have found it if it wasn't for me. Plus all my expenses—this trip. Plus possession is nine-tenths of the law and . . .

Of course, if she does survive, and is compos mentis, because it's possible she could survive but not remember or think clearly, then Brad will bring her the Walmart bag and they can celebrate a fantastic success together!!!

He pictures that happy scene in Joan's hospital room, a fairy tale scene with balloons and confetti and him smuggling in a bottle of champagne, tossing $100 bills all over her as she laughs and laughs.

PART TWO

CHAPTER TWENTY-THREE

Phoebe is already having a bad day when she notices Ralph in the lobby.

She was late getting to the office and missed out on a parking spot. Then she found only dregs in the coffee pot and still doesn't know how to work the damn thing. Plus all the papers screaming *"read me"* that actually need her attention and . . .

"May I?" Ralph asks at her door.

Not this.

"Last night, in her sleep. At least she went peacefully."

Phoebe has tried to prepare for this day, praying it would never come. For weeks it seemed like Joan might be improving, but then . . .

She looks at Ralph looking back at her.

She wants to tell him how heartbroken she is, how utterly, hopelessly destroyed, how she just wants to lie down right here on the rug and cry and scream and—

But she can't, she's supposed to be in charge.

Ralph pretends interest in the magazine covers on the wall. It makes her even sadder to think how much of Joan's life was tied up in this place.

She tries to speak but stops herself, afraid she will sob.

Two young women carrying mechanicals appear at her door.

"We need a decision," one says.

"Critical," says the other.

Phoebe motions them to wait.

She's lucky to have staff like this, they really care about the magazine. And are willing to stick with her through all of this. They even managed to turn out a pretty good issue this month. A very solid issue. Joan would be happy.

"I need to be going," Ralph says softly.

So, no, Joan's not returning. Not that she can't keep this going. She can. She proved that already didn't she? With this issue. But . . .

"Phoebe?" Ralph says.

We'll dedicate the next issue to her, swap out that feature on driverless cars that she was so bullish about, that's not coming together anyway. I'll ask . . .

"Phoebe," Ralph says a little less quietly.

Get a hold of yourself.

"Here, this is for you."

She knows what's inside. The keys to the kingdom.

———————

Joan summoned Phoebe from the hospital a few days after the shooting.

"The kids know what to do," she had said. "They just need to see an adult in the room. Just while I'm recuperating, couple of weeks. Can you do that for me?"

Later, after some setbacks, they had another talk. This time, Ralph was present. Joan wanted him there in case the worst should happen.

———————

"The magazine's in good shape," Ralph says as he rises to go. "That's not always been the case. Regardless, you've no personal liability for debt if that should change."

"Thanks, Ralph," she says sadly. "I'll try to keep us afloat."

He leaves her with documents and papers to sign so she walks them over to a notary they use. On the way she thinks about this seminal moment and the circuitous path she took to get here. How she got her start in magazines—then a lucky break into television—a move to California and her partnership with Ira on films.

And now here she is, back at magazines.

Her magazine!

Incredible.

Ira has been her rock these past months. He calls every day, today she needs him more than ever. They commiserate, share favorite Joan stories, funny moments, laughing, crying, and comforting one another.

"You know how exhausting each day is, I'm hanging on for dear life. Well, how was it she kept up this crazy pace for all those years?"

"You should have seen her at the Landmark Committee hearings, the pit bull!" he laughs.

"I used to think she was like my mother, self-absorbed and manipulative. But she wasn't like that at all, not really, not when you got to know her. She was really interested in her people. Boy, I'm going to miss that."

"Yeah, me too," he says.

"I'm not sure how to break the news."

She looks over to Joan's boxes that are filling up her office. Some are from the film project, she'd been meaning to store those. But there's really no place to put anything.

"And that's not including all her new material, the stuff that still needs to be transcribed and fact-checked," she says to Ira. "Talk about a resource suck. And, oh, by the way, her handwriting is atrocious."

Was atrocious.

Oh boy.

"Hey, do you have another minute, want to run something past you, something for the magazine. We've been working on a series about electric cars that's not really coming together, I'm thinking to replace it with something else."

"Yeah, so?"

"Well, I'm conflicted because Joan asked me to do that, you know, the electric car piece, she was going to make it into a big multi-issue thing about conservation, saving the planet."

"Well what would you replace it with?" he asks sensibly.

"About the changes LA has gone through over the past decades. How it's changed. A kind of retrospective. We'd start in the '60s with Vietnam, then the assassinations, you know—what Joan collected, and then move on to some of the other big events and social movements—gangs, drugs, Watts—then AIDS, 9/11, racial equality, #MeToo. Where it's taken us, how we got here. How each impacted LA kind of retrospective."

"So, maybe you end up at electric cars, looking forward."

"You're a genius, Ira. That's perfect!"

Phoebe's new cub reporter starts soon. Young, bursting with energy and crazy smart, Louie's the only young writer she's been able to attract—today's media majors are interested in everything but print; she hopes he'll stick around.

"So, here's your first job—everything Joan. Organize her stuff, her writings, her research, her notes. It's a big job, you think you can handle it?"

Louie nods and goes off into the abyss.

Phoebe is still trying to get to the bottom of Joan and Aaron's murders. She can't believe how little cooperation she's getting from the LAPD, they broke speed records to 'solve' the case and close the books. She has decided to commit some of her own *Relevant* resources to continue looking into it.

When Joan was in the hospital, she was visited and interviewed by an LAPD detective on two separate occasions; unfortunately, she was of little help to him. She never saw the shooter, she had been looking at the speaker on the dais at the time and only caught a glimpse of Aaron falling *after* he was shot.

She also told him that she was sure Aaron had not been in debt to the mob. Yes, he played poker occasionally, went to a casino a couple of times a year—so did she! But Aaron never complained to her about money, or being in debt, or anything like that. She was his best friend and would have known if he was having money problems or in trouble with the mob or any of it—she told the detective he was barking up the wrong tree.

That was the sum of her contribution.

This same detective had interviewed dozens of gala guests and got similar, unhelpful testimony—they hadn't noticed anything amiss until after "some man fell down." Once shots rang out, they were too busy scrambling for safety to see anything or anyone. Unfortunately, that was basically Phoebe's and Ira's testimony as well.

There had been some video footage—a security camera in the parking lot picked up someone running away from the arena—his back to the camera—and a mobile phone caught the shooter running through the ballroom. But a baseball cap left his face in deep shadows—ultimately neither visual rendered him identifiable.

And worst of all, no bullet fragments or expended shell casings led the police anywhere. There were no identifying marks on the ammunition and no weapon was ever found, a true "tell" of organized crime.

But the cops had the motive: Aaron was a committed gambler, he owed the mob a fortune and he wasn't paying them back.

His bank records confirmed a sad financial state: his house carried two mortgages, his business had maxed out its credit line, there was no insurance, no savings, and $450 in a checking account.

That his liquor store was also rampaged, his shelves ripped clean, lent additional support to their theory.

Payback time. Textbook.

When it came to Joan, the police decided she was just collateral damage, someone in the wrong place at the wrong time. Perhaps the shooter thought she might be able to identify him. She and Aaron spent a lot of time together, maybe she could have picked him out of a lineup.

Either way—plenty of bullets in a revolver.

Open and shut.

Phoebe tried to convince them that Joan could have been the intended victim, not Aaron.

"Look, she had evidence that was extremely damaging to the Escarolla family and was writing a book about it. So, let's say the Escarollas got wind of that, that she was writing a tell-all, including their role in several high-profile murders. Well, they couldn't let that happen, could they?" she pleaded. "So maybe they decided to go after her and maybe Aaron got in the way?!"

She told them about Jack Ruby's sister, how Joan had befriended her, and received more incriminating evidence which, on top of the sister dying suddenly, had gone missing.

Talk about motive.

The detective was polite, listened carefully, and thanked Phoebe for stopping by. And that was that. No minds had been changed.

Phoebe would like to find Brad who disappeared around the same time as the shooting. He's listed on Joan's phone as "Encino Locksmith" but that phone number is no longer in service. Phoebe wonders if he's purposely keeping off her radar. Maybe he knows about the Escarollas and got spooked by what happened to Joan and Aaron.

Maybe he's planning a different future for himself, one where he survives.

She sent Louie to Encino to see if he could find anything about the shop or Brad or his whereabouts. So far it's been nothing but dead ends.

She's promised herself she won't give up. Maybe once Louie's finished with Joan's files and the transcripts she'll ask him to do a few more reconnaissance missions. If he hasn't quit by then.

CHAPTER TWENTY-FOUR

ONE YEAR LATER

Relevant needs to move. Phoebe can't cram another desk into another inch. And they can finally afford it, the magazine just had its best financial outcome in years.

But can she cut the umbilical cord?

Joan's favorite magazine covers still hang on the walls, Phoebe has kept her old couch, her taped-up, scruffy leather chair, and the office door still has no glass.

Yeah, it's time.

"Hey, Louie," Phoebe buzzes the intercom before remembering he won't be there, he's picking up a Vespa before coming into work today. A gift to himself, a reward for an upcoming promotion. She asked him to wait on it, let her officially make a big deal over him at the party on Friday; instead, a moped in the parking lot will alert the staff he's moving up in the world.

Either way, he's earned it. Their ground-breaking expose, "Who Killed The '60s," *Relevant*'s most successful series ever, was only possible because of him. Scouring Joan's files, pulling the information together, fact-checking everything; then checking it again. An enormous achievement for a young reporter.

Phoebe admits that she favors Louie, he's become her right hand. She finds herself thinking of him first whenever an interesting or challenging new project crosses her desk.

She also finally feels like she's hit her stride as managing editor—no longer a stand-in—meeting the high standards that Joan and her predecessor, Berta, set for the magazine. And she's even taken on more of the business side of the business too; George's hands-off approach taken to an extreme.

Two nights ago, after a hectic day followed by a long dinner with a media mogul exploring a podcast platform for *Relevant*, just as she was ready to pass out from exhaustion, Joan's face appeared in the mirror, laughing, telling her she was a wimp. A lightweight. To step it up and stop whining about it.

"God, I miss you," she says to the mirror. "And can you send me more Louies."

Phoebe's not invincible to stress. She's had problems in the past with exhaustion and substance abuse so she's making time for yoga and AA meetings to keep her on track. She knows she should do more, but some nights she can barely make it to bed.

Louie offers to take her for a spin on his bike, but Phoebe begs off, there's a trainer waiting for her at the gym. But that's not where she'll go after work. She'll meet Grace Yuen, an ex-employee who has been demanding an audience for weeks. Phoebe suggested they meet after hours, out of the office.

The woman was toxic, her staff would freak out if they saw her.

"Sorry to hear about Joan's passing," Grace says sipping at her Chardonnay. "I mean, dying like that! Terrible. I read the eulogy you wrote, it was very nice, very complimentary. I actually don't remember Joan like that, but I get that you're supposed to speak well of the dead."

What a sweetheart, Phoebe thinks.

"You know we never got along. Joan couldn't take advice from anyone, didn't listen to anyone, impossible to manage. But still," Grace takes another sip. "To die like that." She puts on a sad face.

"What is it that you want to talk to me about, I've got lots to do tonight," Phoebe asks. But Grace isn't quite through with her own testimonial.

"She never appreciated that I saved that magazine. She had been running it into the ground and the investors—"

"Enough. She wasn't perfect, okay, who is? That doesn't let you off the hook. I know all about you and your . . ." she searches for the word, "carryings-on."

"Oh, please, that's all hearsay from Joan, don't you believe it," she says. "There's a lot more to the story. From my side, I mean. But that's not why I wanted to meet. I've got something I think you'll be interested in."

"I'm listening."

"Do we need to sign an NDA on this? Or can I have your word that you won't reveal where you heard it?"

"If you want an NDA I'll sign one. But why don't you tell me a little bit more about it because we might not need one, I might not be interested."

"Oh, you'll be interested all right," she says.

Phoebe points to her watch.

"You know that issue on California charities that we were working on, the one that never ran—it was around the same time as when, well everything—"

"No, I don't know what you're talking about. What about it?"

But as soon as Phoebe says this she does remember something about charities, something about George asking Joan to feature his non-profit on the cover—something like this.

"Well, one of the not-for-profits we were looking into, GoodWorks, you know—your screenwriting friend has something to do with that, maybe he's on the board there I don't know. Anyway, I heard that it's a sham. They never give the money away—it's just a front for illegal activity. We didn't get far enough along investigating but you should look into that, there's something not right—"

Phoebe rises. "See, we don't need an NDA after all. Baseless, damaging innuendo is not what *Relevant's* about. You should remember that at least."

"Hear me out. This person says they're still at it, laundering money, that's what they've been doing with their donations, they're crooks—"

But Phoebe is already gone.

Serves me right for lying to Louie. She heads for the gym after all.

CHAPTER TWENTY-FIVE

rad has returned to his chaise lounge without the newspaper that sent him into the house in the first place; he spins to retrieve it. The fact that his house is a far distance from the pool is the only mistake the builder made with the place, the only thing he would change if he could. It's a long trek in the hot sun.

"Can't remember shit these days," he says, shaking his head.

Tonya calls out for an iced tea. "*Per ferver,*" she yells in her version of Spanish.

Brad finds his paper and pours her tea. The icy glass is refreshingly cold against his sunburnt chest; he cradles it carefully so as not to drip on his link to civilization.

Then he remembers he forgot to apply lotion this morning, the one for fair-haired folks who burn easily.

"Man, oh man, where's my mind?"

"Here, let me," Tonya says, as she starts greasing him up.

Brad lives in a beautiful home just a short hop from the best beach in Nicaragua. But Brad doesn't like sand so he rarely ventures beyond this incredible backyard.

And why should he—the place has everything a single guy could ask for: a master suite the size of his old apartment, a home theatre, a pool, a matching cabana. Even a small putting green. All nestled in a ritzy neighborhood of expats, some American, all with serious money.

That's who Tonya thinks Brad is—a *gringo rico.*

He's happy to play along. He probably is *rico* anyway, at least by Nicaraguan standards.

"Sveetie, you do my back?" Tonya bats her eyes seductively.

Brad finds the lotion she prefers, the expensive, imported stuff, and massages it slowly into her warm back. Its heady aroma hits him hard, it smells delicious, enticing. It awakens his desire.

She feels it too—Tonya's like that—and leads him to the "hoochi cabana" near the pool, built for this very purpose.

"You write down passwords," she says once they're finished. "Since you so forgetful. And make copy for me, I keep safe where I keep mine."

Brad nods and smiles.

Yeah right, like I'm gonna do that.

———

Being a locksmith by trade, Brad has installed a special combination lock on his bedroom closet, that's where he keeps the cash. Every Monday he pulls out a few bills—not a lot—just enough to get him through the week. He's not much of a spender except when Tonya's around—when she insists he take her shopping or for a big night out. Then he pulls a couple extra and chooses the venue carefully—a different beach town, a different restaurant, mixing it up, just in case.

At first, he would count the cash after each withdrawal but now he doesn't bother. His memory may be spotty in some areas but Brad knows to the penny how much money is left in the closet.

Nor does he bother with the papers stuffed at the bottom, attendance records from a club and stock certificates from a company called Ace Security. He was excited to find these at first, but when he googled around, he saw it had been out-of-business for decades.

He was about to throw the whole mess away when he noted some interesting names on the club roster: Escarolla, Marcello, Trafficante—old Mafia family names he recognized. And another: Jacob Rubenstein—he knows that's Jack Ruby's real name since it was Ruby's safe deposit box he found up in Texas.

He decided to keep all the papers stuffed in the bottom of the bag. He doesn't want to jinx anything.

―――――――

Brad opens his paper to the sports section and inhales the photos, scores, and stats. It's what he misses most about his old life, his teams.

Tonya asks for the style section even though he knows she'll mock it.

"You call this style? This like school girl," she says, ripping out something she'll search for online.

Brad starts on the crossword as the sun begins to go down; Tonya rises to replace their ice teas with gin and tonics.

"Maybe I should go back to work," he says, having made few inroads with the puzzle.

She makes a face. "What for, you got plenty of money."

"To keep me sharp, you know. And make weekends feel more special. Instead of spending every day in paradise," he says, spreading his arms open wide.

"Oh, you kid," she says.

But no, Brad's been thinking about this for a while. He thinks it may be this very lack of structure, this lack of routine, that's been causing his diminishing memory. He wonders if there's a need for a locksmith down here, if his neighbors want, as he did, to be extra diligent about safety—gated community or not.

He tries not to think about his friend whose sudden death brought him to this good life. Not that Joan wouldn't want him to have it—she would—and not that he could have done anything to prevent her death—he couldn't. It's just that the whole incident remains incredibly painful and best not thought of too often.

Brad's perfected the art of forgetting, he's become very good at it.

"Came around to bite me in the ass," he chuckles to himself.

Tonya overhears him. "You vant to bite me in the ass?" she asks.

"Maybe later," he says.

CHAPTER TWENTY-SIX

ouie had hoped for a bold color but "Milano Verde" (a.k.a. "pea green") was the only Vespa on the lot. His cousin, the one who is amazing with engines, advised him to choose one with no body damage, he would take care of everything else. His other cousin, the one his mother doesn't like, said he could only buy a black model, the only color suitable for the 'hood. Bad enough it wasn't a *real* motorcycle.

Louie knows he'll take a ribbing when he gets it home. And another at his promotion party Friday (most likely a roast). It's worth it.

He's wanted to own a bike his whole life.

He's also chomping at the bit to get started on a new assignment but there's something he needs to do first, as a favor to Phoebe, find *Relevant* new office space. It's the kind of job he was asked to do as a PPP—Phoebe's Personal Peon, the nickname he was saddled with when he first arrived.

Being PPP happened to be a great introduction to publishing, and as a bonus, he developed a close, respectful relationship with his boss.

But he's ready to move on.

She asked him to narrow the office options to two or three from which she can choose. He's already seen a couple of vacancies but nothing that's exactly right. The real estate broker he's working with lacks a filter, which is why Phoebe asked him to get involved.

Back when he took on the herculean task of 'everything Joan'—when no one else would touch it—he sometimes wondered if he had made a mistake. It was a huge undertaking with tons of redundancy and time spent just verifying data.

He wanted to be a writer! But refusing to get discouraged, he put his head down and kept at it, and the piece turned out brilliantly if he does say so himself.

"Amazing work for a first-timer!" Phoebe said. He proved to her he could think, write, and was fearless about overtime—it helped clinch this promotion.

"You ready for more?" she had asked. "Because I've got something that may rival 'Who Killed The '60s.'"

Phoebe recently received a tip about a physician who took care of Jack Ruby in prison, one of several docs called in once Ruby's cancer was diagnosed. This physician and Jack spoke to each other in Yiddish so the guards couldn't understand their conversation. Joan had learned that Ruby spoke Yiddish growing up, a little-known fact until she exposed it, so Phoebe feels this tip could be valid and significant.

The informant, who refused to give her name, was also a doctor; she acknowledged that this physician would be too old to be practicing but likely teaching at a medical college or university—she didn't know where. She also didn't know what was discussed in those Ruby meetings, whether they were medically-related or just two guys shooting the breeze.

So what if Ruby actually confessed to his doctor-friend—told him what really happened in Dallas that day? If Louie can find him, *when* he finds him, this will be another bombshell exclusive to *Relevant*. It might even lead to that elusive Pulitzer Phoebe's been coveting.

"Joan's smiling down on you, sending you good vibes on this

one," she said to Louie. "Let me know if you need anything, whatever, you got it."

―――――――

"'PTM, Prepare to the Max,'" he announces at his party on Friday. "It's my new nickname."

"Pounds Too Many," someone calls out, alluding to Louie's size.

"Pity That Motorcycle," another yells over peals of laughter.

―――――――

Louie waits outside Phoebe's door, he hears angry voices coming from inside. He worries this could last all morning and put her into a terrible mood. But when she finally waves him in, it's the normal, we-can-handle-it Phoebe.

"So what do *you* think?" or "You know what to do," is how she typically answers his questions; she's about to shoo him out when she remembers to ask about the office move.

"Nothing yet. The broker suggests looking in Culver City, it's super convenient with the Metro but so far there's not much available, just one or two I'm gonna go see."

"We're running out of time, Louie. If we don't nail down something soon I'll be forced to renew this lease!"

"I know, I know, I'm all over it," he says.

―――――――

He decides to stop at Bernie's on his way home, the bar where *Relevant* folks hang out. He doesn't see anyone from the office but gets drawn into a basketball game on the big screen TV. The Celtics are getting clobbered by the Clippers and it's extra satisfying to watch it on a giant screen.

"C'mon ref, call it, call it!" a young man is cursing out the players who are elbowing all over the place, he inadvertently drops his backpack down on Louie's foot.

"You suck!" Louie yells, bending to remove the backpack. "The refs, I mean."

They laugh.

"Joe Capano," the man says, holding out his hand.

"Louie Ruiz."

"My dad likes Boston," Joe grins.

"Too bad, they're gonna lose. We got this in the bag,"

"Dunno what's wrong with the man," Joe says. "I mean, originally he's from Dorchester but that's like a hundred years ago, he should have gotten over it by now."

"Some people just can't adapt," Louie says still joking. "My dad wants to take me to see the Globetrotters—the Harlem Globetrotters—they haven't been good for what? Twenty-five years! I told him to save his money."

Joe's phone rings. "Yello," is how he answers. "Yeah, yeah, I'm on it. On my way," he winks at Louie and puts his cell back in his pocket. "Duty calls. Keep up the good fight." He finishes his beer and nods to the screen. "Hey, do you know the best way to get to Culver City this time of day, I don't want to take the four-oh-five if I can help it."

"Culver City?" Louie says. "I actually do know another way, I've been looking for office space over there. But if I tell you you gotta keep it to yourself."

"What kind of office space? I might know something."

"Nothing special, we just need decent space, parking, good light. Ten thousand feet on one floor, if possible, which is what is making it hard to find."

"Did you look at that new business park? I know the guy who owns it. He just started renting it out but he's very picky about who he rents to. Solid companies with good credentials. None of these fly-by-night guys."

"We've been around for decades," Louie says. "*Relevant* Magazine, maybe you heard of us?"

"Nah, sorry. Decades, huh? Credit score okay?"

"We're in great shape, never better. Outgrew our current space, that's why we're looking, business is booming. But my boss is frugal, she won't pay midtown prices," Louie starts negotiating, just in case.

"Here, take my card, the family's in real estate. Maybe I can hook you up with something. Call me tomorrow—you never know."

———

Louie parks his Vespa in a spot marked for handicapped drivers. *I got no choice,* he argues with his mother in his head. The lot is crowded with construction vehicles and the trucks of the guys who work here. Louie reckons a handicapped person won't be driving into this pandemonium any time soon.

He makes his way carefully toward the high-rise, stepping over detritus and debris and trying to ignore the dust and noise all around him. Joe is waiting by the door, a Dunkin' coffee in one hand and a cell phone wedged against his shoulder in the other. He ends his call.

"Ya made it," he says.

"You were right about Sepulveda," Louie says.

"Only before school lets out. Buses! Don't forget, you also got the train here," Joe brags. "That's a huge plus for your mass-commuter types. C'mon, let me show you around."

Number One Culver City Center is a modern glass and steel structure with electronic elevators ("For security," Joe tells him); a gym in the basement ("For your millennials"); a massive corporate boardroom that's available to rent; a cafe that will one day feature a "famous chef, not at liberty to say who," and ten thousand square feet of open space on the top floor looking out across the city—ready to be built-out for a successful business like *Relevant.*

It's ideal. Absolutely ideal. *Phoebe will love this*, Louie thinks.

The only drawback is the rest of Culver City Center is a dust bowl. By Louie's guestimate, at least a year away from completion. Which means construction noise and dust and dirt, a messy, inconvenient way to start the day.

"Which is why I can get you a *very* good deal," Joe says. "You'll be one of the first tenants, and, look, this construction won't last forever."

"I think I can convince her," Louie says. "Send me the lease, I'll have our lawyer take a look. Might take a couple days 'cause Ralph likes to read the fine print and he looooves to negotiate," Louie says with a smile.

"That's what ya pay him for, right?" Joe says nonplussed. "Tell you what, I'll put a soft hold on it so no one else can grab it. I already put the good word in with Uncle Donny. He likes your kind of classy operation."

"What a coincidence, right? You drop your stuff on my foot one day and here we are the next—like roommates!"

"Not exactly. Already got a roommate, a lot nicer looking than you." Joe pulls out a photo of his family.

"You got a kid too? Wow—he's adorable. And your wife," he looks Joe in the eye. "Man! What does she see in you—you rich or something?"

"She likes me 'cause I'm a go-getter," Joe smiles.

"Want to meet up at Bernie's later? We can celebrate."

"Got a few things to do here, but yeah, I'll text you when I'm on my way."

———

"They're in, I'm sending them the paperwork," Joe calls Uncle Donny once Louie is gone. "But they'll need to move in soon, like eight weeks, their lease is up. If we're not ready, we lose the deal. You think we can be ready by then?"

"You bet we can," Uncle Donny says. "Because you'll make sure of it. Get back here now, so we can work out the details."

"I gotta go have a drink with the kid but I'll stop on my way home later."

"Good work, Joe. You're doing good work here."

CHAPTER TWENTY-SEVEN

rad has become super busy. His hobby suddenly took over his life, snowballing out of control.

"Snowballing in sunny paradise," he laughs to himself.

It all began with Estelle, his next-door neighbor.

She asked him to keep an eye on her place as she was going out of town. He said of course he would, happy to do it.

But after a quick once-over, he told her she really needed to beef up her security system. He suggested that, at a minimum, she should have what he has.

"Could you handle that for me?" Estelle asked.

So he agreed, spent a few days boning up on the latest technology, seeing what was new to the market and would work in Nicaragua. Then another couple of days installing a reliable and easy-to-maintain system at her place.

She paid him handsomely and it was fun to do.

Easy money, he thought.

Seeing that Estelle's house was not nearly as luxurious as his own was also somehow extra satisfying—an added plus.

Before he could put his feet back up, two of Estelle's friends, also widows, also from the neighborhood, called him to request the same service.

Then the guy across the street left a note in his mailbox . . . the sweet couple down the block . . . another one just yesterday. As it turns out, many La Monaca residents worry their homes could be broken into, or more likely, the plumbing or electricity could develop "island fever" while they're away. His "hobby" had turned into a business in no time.

Brad orders the components he needs off the internet and they arrive a few days later, often without tax or delivery charges.

After he installs a system, he monitors it from a flat screen in his den; he's set up to handle a dozen views at once. Then he treks around to his properties to personally check in every few days, staggering these visits for exercise.

And he's picked up some cool design ideas on the way.

Occasionally a system gets tripped, sometimes in the middle of the night, usually by accident, and then Brad must pull himself out of bed to go see. It's an annoyance for sure, but partially mitigated by the hefty incident fee he charges any time it happens.

For neighbors who don't travel often, Brad suggests a less costly monitoring service, one without personal visits, a kind of "Brad Lite." La Monaca is a gated community after all, with its own security people.

But most of his customers, wealthy retirees like Estelle, don't mind paying for the full package—they appreciate having a nice American guy stop by who can change a light bulb or reach up to a high cabinet, even when they are in town.

Which he does happily.

No extra charge.

It's more work than he ever anticipated, but for now, he's enjoying getting to know his neighbors, AND he loves the added income; Brad's become de facto the "Mayor of La Monaca," which annoys Tonya to no end.

This new role has totally recalibrated their relationship.

When she's in town, and not in Paris or Moscow or New York, he's too busy to shower her with the attention she craves, too busy with his customers and his business. Unavailable for "matinees" and too tired to go out at night. They have devolved into being just friends. That suits him just fine.

She thinks what he's doing is "beneath him."

He thinks she means it's beneath her.

Which he isn't very often these days.

He still lets her have a full run of the place when she's around. Occasionally, she'll bring in a local chef to fix them dinner, but mostly she hangs out by the pool and then goes clubbing at night. What's left of their relationship is mainly transactional.

Tonya charges him 5 percent commission for the use of her American Express platinum card—he won't use his own, doesn't want to leave fingerprints—and he's been spending a fortune on it. He jokes she is Amazon's number one customer.

Prime's prima donna.

"Yes, you are so funny," she says as she twirls around in a new fur jacket. "From commission."

Brad doesn't make withdrawals from the closet anymore and he's hardly seen at the restaurants or shops he once so often frequented. Mostly he spends his time working or online.

At first, he needed to research the latest tech products, that's when he discovered social media—reading what others were buying and what to watch out for. Then he found like-minded sports fans and got into some online betting. Then he added blogs and podcasts to replace the silly stuff on local TV.

And now he's totally addicted.

So between work, sports, the political pundits—well, before you know it—another day is gone.

Occasionally he'll search to see if there's anything online about Joan. Anything that might provide some insight or motive into her tragic end. But all he finds are various postings of the same obituary, the official version, an accidental murder of someone in the wrong place at the wrong time.

This morning, he googles to see if *Relevant* is still being published and is pleased to find that it is. On its masthead "Phoebe Barber" is listed as managing editor.

"That's Joan's friend, Phoebe," he says to Tonya at lunch later that day, "Joan was a big fan of that lady."

Brad had spoken to Phoebe once after Joan got shot and everyone was praying she'd be okay. That's when his plan for Nicaragua first took hold.

He decided not to visit the hospital, but rather to wait for Joan's recovery, because, well, she might not recover. That wasn't what he was hoping for—not at all—but locksmiths are nothing but practical. And a bit pessimistic. For even if Joan survived the shooting, she might not recover her full faculties, might not remember about the safe deposit box, about the trip he made to Texas to look for it. Not about any of it.

He had cautioned Joan that it was unlikely to be a fruitful trip because he wanted to manage her expectations in case nothing was found there. He had had several experiences with her where things went askew and he was seeking to avoid a repeat performance.

So, if he had found the right bank, if there'd been something of value inside, then he would have surprised her with good news and they'd have celebrated a fantastic success together.

But . . . *man plans and god laughs*, he says to himself.

Brad subscribes to the e-version of *Relevant*, and adds it to his other regular news sources. He's committed to keeping up with the world, not losing his edge entirely.

Here, in paradise.

CHAPTER TWENTY-EIGHT

U ncle Donny is relaxing in his well-appointed den, talking with Joe.

"That lawyer! I gave him such a deal. I threw in the conference room and gym membership for a year! He thought he was such a good negotiator."

"Nice," Joe says.

"Nice? I'm losing my shirt, this better pay off. So here's what I want you to do. First, get us the best state-of-the-art recording equipment, none of the old stuff, and make sure we install it *before* you paint and put in the finishes. I was thinking you hide it in the ceiling, like in those fancy Bose speakers."

"Nah, it's smoke detectors now," Joe says. "This way something goes wrong, I send in the 'fire department' to fix it. Don't worry, I got this."

"I want them everywhere: offices, hallways, even the bathrooms. Don't cheap out. The more the better."

"Easy," Joe says.

"On second thought, that equipment, that's a lot of dough. I got a favor I could call in. You just handle the installation. And here's the other thing, I want you to keep on with that Mexican kid, what's his name?"

"Louie," Joe says.

"Yeah. He's a kid but he's pretty important over there. Trusting him with the move and all. So you stay buddy-buddy just in case we miss something with the bugs."

"Sure," Joe says.

"And you don't make it obvious, right? I mean, we're still keeping a low profile 'cause we're not out of the woods. I got a real scare last week, heard they found the piece from—"

"No way, that's off the planet! I told you!"

"Turns out it wasn't ours, okay, so relax. I'm just saying be careful is all."

Joe nods. "So what about me, Uncle D, you said you'd *give it a think* the last time."

"It's in the cards, Joe. But not right now. Not while we're still watching our Ps and Qs."

"Oh man," Joe says shaking his head.

"Listen. You're doing good work. What you did in Orange County, how you turned that around . . ."

"And the liquor store guy. *And* his girlfriend. *And* the old broad! All smooth as silk," Joe argues.

"But we're not out of the woods yet, we're still watching our Ps and Qs."

Don gets up to refresh his drink and motions if Joe wants one.

"I'll get the equipment to the site. You install before the paint, that's coming up. Then we keep tabs on what they're up to. Fuckin' reporters."

"Okay."

"We can't have stuff getting out there now, at this late date."

"Okay."

"And you stay close to the kid, Joey. Buddy-buddy. Capiche?"

———————

The staff is packing up, getting ready for the big move. Cartons line the hallway filled with decades of *Relevant* history—old issues, tax files, business records, personnel. Some of it will go off to the archives but a lot is coming along to Culver City.

Louie has lined up a moving/storage company his cousin knows, the good cousin, and received a friends-and-family discount—but it's still costing a small fortune.

The staff trekked over this morning to claim territory—Phoebe has heard nothing but 100 percent positive feedback. The architect George hired built it out specifically for their type of operation. She went from dreading the move to becoming its biggest cheerleader.

"Good work!" she fist-bumps Louie.

Louie mumbles something about being happy she's happy and begins to update her on the Ruby assignment.

"So this informant—she's been on the money, this doc is for real, still alive, no longer practicing. He had been on the faculty of Leaven Medical University, that's in Belgium, and I was just about to fly over there but he fell off the radar. Off the teaching roster for next semester. So maybe we lost him for a bit. But don't worry, we'll pick him up again, I've got Claire searching med schools, she'll find him. So when we do, I'm thinking, how about we turn an entire issue over to this, like before?" he asks.

"Don't get ahead of yourself, let's see how it goes. Find him first, get the interview. Maybe he's back in the States, that'd be convenient. So, you need anything from me, you getting what you need from research?"

"Yup. So far so good."

"Okay, so go home young man, get a good night's sleep, you're going to need it. Tomorrow's a big day."

———————

Twenty-four hours later the movers have come and gone, most of the staff too, but Phoebe's still arranging her new office, second-guessing all her earlier decisions.

The open space is spectacular, with views, views, views. Especially the conference room with floor-to-ceiling windows— she can see over the entire city and it's got room to accommodate the entire staff.

Just fantastic, she thinks for the hundredth time. *A complete 180 from the old dump.* She thanks her lucky stars and just in case it's Joan up there making it happen, thanks her too.

It's late when she finally gets to her inbox and notices a hand-addressed envelope buried in the pile.

Phoebe:

GoodWorks, the charity run by your friends, uses recipients to launder dirty money. I know you don't believe me, but it's true. I've got proof. I'm not sure if Ira is aware that those "donations" are just about getting currency out of the country. Maybe you don't want to go there but if Joan were here she wouldn't turn a blind eye, she'd learn the truth. And run with it.

—Grace

Hmm, she sure knows how to hit a nerve, Phoebe thinks.

"I thought you left already," she says finding Louie leaning on an unopened carton.

"I did, but I'm back. Wait 'til you hear this."

"Come into my new office. I'd offer you a chair to sit in but . . ."

"You were right, he's coming-back to the good ol' USA. The doc. Applied to teach at a bunch of med schools, Claire found several applications. We'll keep on top of that. So that's the good news. But here's the bad: He's going to be very difficult. May not speak with me at all, not even off the record. Claire found some research papers he contributed to, medical journals, he teaches ethics in addition to neurology, that's another specialty, "medical ethics" — anyway, he's big about protecting patient information, keeping everything confidential."

"So, okay, that's normal."

"Yeah, so that's what I thought. But Claire—she's been amazing by the way—she kept digging around and it turns out one of her resources has a friend who is a friend of his from way back, from a school where he was teaching and knew him some. Anyway, she says he's notorious about patient confidentiality, I mean, his colleagues even kid him about it. The "Clam" they call him. The guy was an expert on HIPAA compliance before anyone even knew what that was."

"Okay, so he's a tough nut, but you—"

"And he saw some extraordinary cases, according to this person. And here's the other thing—and this is unbelievable. The man keeps *everything*, including all his patient files. He's a pack rat, he's like the Smithsonian Museum! Can you imagine if he's kept all his Ruby files!"

"Okay. So let me think, this calls for a different strategy, right? Not a straight-on approach because he's going to say no."

"Right. And it's more than just ethics, it's his personality; she said he's like a monk. And that makes sense, think about it—he's had these files for what, fifty years? He never breathed a word about them, no one even knew they existed! There wasn't a thing in Joan's research about a doctor. I mean she knew more about Ruby than anyone but not about this doc, and I read every single word in those files."

"Your gray hair," she laughs.

"My extra forty pounds you mean."

"Okay, Louie, I hear you. Let's sleep on it; maybe one of us will come up with something. Meanwhile, it's a full press to find him. We gotta get to this guy."

CHAPTER TWENTY-NINE

Brad reads about the death of Thane Cesar over breakfast. It surprises him that he is doing this, reading obituaries, he credits it to age and distance. Occasionally, he'll recognize a name of someone famous or someone he knew back in the real world, and he saves it in a file. Tonya finds it worrisome, that just eggs him on.

Cesar's obituary catches his eye because of the accompanying photo—Robert Kennedy in the kitchen of the Ambassador Hotel. He reads the caption:

> **Cesar had been hired by Ace Security to protect Robert Kennedy the night he was murdered and can be seen standing behind him in the kitchen of the Ambassador just minutes before the fatal shot. Cesar's reputation remained under a cloud as conspiracy theorists still insist he was involved in that shooting.**

Ace Security? Why does this sound familiar?
Then he remembers.
Brad rushes to the bedroom closet, dumps the bag on the carpet,

and scrounges around until he finds what he's looking for—Ace Security stock certificates and a membership roster from the Wall Street Club. It's been a while since he looked at these papers, he reads them again and comes to the same conclusion: Jack Ruby, through the Wall Street Club, was an investor in Ace Security. Why else keep the papers in his vault?

Brad walks back to the kitchen to fix himself another coffee, trying to piece the puzzle together, trying to make sense of it all. Tonya walks in, wanting to discuss plans for lunch.

"Not now," he waves her away.

She shoots him a drop-dead look.

"I'm trying to think here," he says by way of an apology. But she's gone.

That afternoon Brad hatches a plan. First, he'll need to connect with Phoebe Barber. He finds *Relevant* headquarters' email address online.

Dear Info: **Can you please forward the following email to Ms. Barber?**

Hi Phoebe, it's Brad, Joan's friend. I'll be in LA next week and thought I'd stop by the magazine. Will you be available to see me?

Her answer returns quickly.

Of course, Brad, stop by anytime.

Brad uses Tonya's card to book the trip. He's about to ask her to accompany him, maybe they'd splurge on a ritzy hotel, make a really fun break for the two of them. But he overhears her flirting on the phone and recalls the drop-dead look.

He's in Phoebe's conference room two days later.

"Jack Ruby and his investor friends owned a company called Ace Security. That's the firm that Thane Cesar worked for. Does that name ring a bell?"

"Jack Ruby, yes. The other guy no."

"Thane Cesar was involved peripherally in the assassination of RFK. He was supposed to be protecting him the night he got killed. He's the guy standing behind Kennedy in the kitchen," he hands her the obituary. "Well, anyway, he died recently. So, here's the thing. I know *for* a *fact* that Jack Ruby was part-owner of Ace Security. And Ace was involved in the RFK assassination. But Ruby—"

"Is involved in the JFK assassination! Yikes!"

"Yikes, exactly," Brad says.

"I just got the chills," she says.

They're both quiet, thinking.

"How do you know 'for a fact'?" she asks.

"I do but I can't say."

But he doesn't need to, she's already figured out how.

"Look, I don't care about anything else you found there, in that safe deposit box. But I will need proof of this—whatever you have establishing this ownership—or I won't be able to do anything with it."

"Yeah, I figured. That I can get you," he says. "But I need your word that you won't reveal how you got this information, where it came from. I'm in a precarious position here. I know Joan would give me her word on this. Will you?"

The mention of Joan makes Phoebe pause.

"I'm not sure, Brad, I need to think this over, maybe talk to legal—don't worry, I won't identify you. But this could be big, very big. Maybe too big for *Relevant*. Give me time to think about it and get some advice."

"Okay, that's fair. You let me know. Here's how you contact me from now on." Brad gives Phoebe Tonya's email address. "Belongs to a friend, I don't want anything that links back to me."

Phoebe lifts an eyebrow. "Okay, give me a couple of days, I'll contact you at: puffyslim22@gmail.com," she reads. "Okay, Puffy?"

Phoebe phones Ralph and learns he's in court all week so she decides to call Ira and lets it ring until he picks up.

"Am I interrupting?" she asks.

Ira is still living in a cottage on his brother's Malibu estate overlooking the Pacific Ocean. He'd been watching one of his and Phoebe's old comedies, laughing out loud even though he knows every joke, every setup. He wrote most of them.

"Yeah, *Mimi* and I were just thinking about you. Free for lunch?"

"It's four o'clock Ira. Listen, want to bounce something off you, I need some astute thinking here. Some advice. Ready? I might have a lead on Jack Ruby's connection with—"

"Jack Ruby! Hello?" he taps the receiver. "Is this Joan? *Relevant* ran that story, remember? Time to move on."

"I don't disagree, but something just fell into my lap. It may be important. It ties Ruby into both the JFK *and* the RFK assassinations. That's new news. And it may be too big to ignore."

"Okay, how about dinner then, we can discuss this over Japanese," he says. "I'll stop by around six and you can give me a tour of the new office, I've been dying to see it. And then we'll find a place to eat nearby, I'm sure my GPS can find Culver City."

———

Over dinner, Phoebe catches Ira up on *Relevant* news, including her staffing problem. She doesn't mention the note from Grace. She's waiting for the right moment and this isn't it.

"I'm relieved you look so good, I was worried with the move and all." Ira slides a slice of tuna onto his chopsticks. "No worse for wear."

"Thanks, I think—that was a compliment? Leave some ahi will you?"

"George told you to hire whoever you need, so what's the problem?"

"The problem is talent, Ira, finding talent. As you know, I am very, very selective."

The waiter brings a platter of shu mai to their table.

"And very, very hungry," he kids as she attacks it.

"There's a ton of competition coming from the studios, and not just them—ad agencies, post-production," she says, devouring a dumpling. "I've tried recruiting from out-of-town, you know, like Austin or Utah, but when they get here and see what it costs to live here, they run right back home."

"Oh, yeah. Sure."

"These are so delicious. This place is a keeper," she says.

"They have a branch in the Canyon, it's like impossible to get in there."

"So USC sent me some entry-levels, and that's a start, they're sharp but they're kids and they need to be trained and that takes time too. Look, it's a quality problem, if we weren't doing so well, I wouldn't be complaining."

"So what I can do to help? Besides the talent problem, I mean. What about that Ruby thing . . ."

"Listen, I'm not sure what to do here. I put a call into Ralph, but he hasn't called me back yet. I need some advice. You'll never guess who popped into my office this week."

"Ruby. He's alive."

"No. Brad!"

"Brad, the locksmith—the friend of Joan's?"

"The very."

"Where has he been—you tried to find him for months."

"In hiding. Some place in Latin America, I think. The guy won't tell me where. Totally paranoid. He shows up at the office with a weird story about Jack Ruby owning the company that . . . I'm not even sure how to explain this."

"Did he tell you why he's been hiding?"

"Not in so many words. But . . . obviously he found something valuable in Ruby's bank that day. Money probably. How could he afford to disappear like that? But maybe also something else, something that links Ruby to other crimes, maybe even RFK's assassination. He wanted to tell me more but first needs me to guarantee his anonymity."

"Well, Phoebe, you obviously need to get that story. That's probably something to work through legal, right?"

"Yeah, but look . . . this is our magazine, right? We're *Relevant* after all. We go after the truth. Right? You know George will back me on this."

"Hmm. Do you have enough resources to handle this? You were just complaining about being short-staffed."

"I was thinking of maybe going outside for help."

"You got someone in mind?"

"I do. You."

"Me?"

"We're a great team, Ira, I'm sure you haven't forgotten. If I roll up my sleeves on this, will you? Roll up your sleeves? Let's do this together. Let's do it for Joan."

"Jeez, how can I say no to that?"

"Oh, and something else . . . you know that data company George acquired? The one with the crazy name, Data doo-doo or something—"

"DataBear, he renamed it."

"So can you connect me? Maybe they can track down someone, my regular sources hit a wall."

"Well, it's George's company so yeah, he'll do whatever he can for you," he smiles. "I'm actually going to New York on Thursday and meeting some of these data folks—I'll bring it up when I see them."

"Perfect!" she smiles back.

———

Louie decides to stop at Bernie's and get some dinner before heading home. The old gang isn't there but he spots Joe sitting on a stool in the corner, nursing a beer.

"How's it going?" Louie asks as he signals for a draft.

"Same old, same old. Wish I had a big-time job like yours, something to sink my teeth into. Real estate can be sooo boring."

"Really? I thought it looked like fun, looked like you were into it when you were showing us around Culver."

"Yeah, sure. When you land a deal, make a sale, that's fun. But escorting looky-loos around all over the planet, knowing they're never gonna pull the trigger?"

"Ah, see your point."

"So what ya working on, something juicy over there?"

"Actually, not at liberty to say."

"Secret, huh?"

"Nah, not a secret, just . . . we don't talk about what we're working on until it's in print."

"Oh sure. So you guys all settled in? Space working out okay?"

"Yeah, it's great. Everyone loves the place. We're still unpacking boxes tho', probably will be for years."

"Ha. Remind me to introduce you to a bar I like over on Higuera, not quite as fine an establishment as this, but the beer's two bucks and they make epic wings."

"Wow, sounds great! Want to go Wednesday? The Lakers will be televised—you could pick me up at the office and show me the way."

"Deal. Want another? I'm buying."

"Wish I could but I gotta get going. See ya Wednesday."

CHAPTER THIRTY

George is sitting in his corner office on the thirty-sixth floor of the Lipstick Building perched high above Third Avenue. It's unusual to find him here, in New York. When he's not in Malibu, he's often flying around to other cities getting to know the businesses he's acquired, getting to know the execs who run them.

It's all part of his master plan to roll up into one of America's biggest media conglomerates, Baxter Media Group. He wants to revolutionize the industry.

The plans for BMG include a vertical integration, subtle and elegant like its chairman. He's managing it carefully, having his executives meet one another on neutral territory, orchestrating social occasions before assigning a project to work on together. The idea is to get them to experience first-hand how knowledgeable, talented, and responsible the other is. George is convinced this is the best way of making disparate companies come together and gel.

He calls Phoebe to tell her he's spoken to Ira about her request and will ask one of DataBear's top executives to help in her search for the elusive doctor.

DataBear (nee Datadoo) was one of the last independent data firms of any significant size when George acquired it; he paid a fortune but is betting it will be worth it in the long run. Data is driving the economy and George can't afford to let *Relevant* or its brethren get left behind. He liked the folks he met there and they knew how to communicate in plain English, so that clinched the deal. He already has several projects lined up for them to tackle besides helping Phoebe find the doctor she's looking for—renaming their company DataBear (which unfortunately means more expense for signage, stationary, public relations, etc.) and identifying the "valuable vulnerables" inside the *Relevant* subscriber base. These are customers unlikely to renew a subscription once their term is up—those planning to jump ship. *Relevant* has already seen three months of subscriber erosion and George wants to stem attrition now, before it significantly impacts his bottom line.

DataBear can also identify newsstand buyers who might be persuaded to become subscribers. *Relevant* will offer them a gift—a tote bag, T-shirt, something cheerful and cheap and see if any work better than the introductory discount they're currently offered.

Then he'll encourage them to bring in their own ideas; DataBear's worked with some of the most successful companies in the country, media and otherwise, and George is always open to stealing good ideas from anyone.

He is smart and ambitious and this is an exciting time for him. After years of being dismissed as just another Hollywood pretty boy, George is finally able to unleash his entrepreneurial talents, build this media empire and stick it to the naysayers.

With *Relevant,* he lucked into a formula that worked, that not only kept the publication in business, but let it really succeed. Now he's hungry for more.

Phoebe was the right choice to head up the magazine, she hired top-tier creatives and gave them full berth to produce stories that matter. It's now become a "must read" periodical with a circulation that reaches far outside Los Angeles city lines.

He just needs to fix this subscription problem.

"It's the millennials, they hate commitment," the CEO of DataBear tells him over lunch. "We might be able to bring them around. Let us take a shot."

This luncheon also marks an important milestone for Ira, although he doesn't know it yet. Ira will eventually run BMG, this is also part of George's master plan. The company's not ready for that appointment—nor is Ira—but George is a strategic thinker who knows it's best to lay the groundwork early. He doesn't like to surprise people with his decisions. That said, he'll deal with his brother's surprise on the plane ride home.

———

Ira is waiting in George's outer office, sipping an espresso while on the phone with his agent. He too is at the top of his game, coming off a box office success that has overwhelmed him with new project offers. Before accepting the next one, he agreed to come to New York and listen to what George had in mind.

And get to know the DataBear people since he'd be around.

The last time George asked him for help was when Phoebe took over the magazine—he wanted him on her advisor board. It's not been heavy lifting. Today he'll charm the pants off the data geeks just to please George.

"No problemo," he said. Ira never turns down a request from his brother.

Later, when he hears what George's thinking, he'll ask to sleep on it. But they both know Ira's going to say yes. It's the perfect opportunity for him at this stage of life and working closely with Phoebe is icing on the cake.

———

Phoebe summons Louie to her office to tell him DataBear will be working to locate the Yiddish-speaking doctor.

"Can you send them his AMA applications—they'll need that. Better yet, send them everything we've got."

"They can find out where he's going, which med school?"

"So they say. I also asked for any other information they can unearth—maybe something that could help guide our approach, something that would encourage him to be forthcoming."

"Brilliant."

"So I might have another interesting assignment coming up, Louie, another deep dive. But I'm saving it for later."

"Well, I got a full plate, but why not tell me . . ."

"Couple of years ago, *Relevant* was researching a story on non-profits, who was doing what, which were stand-outs, which maybe not so. Joan was looking into it herself but then . . . well, you know. Anyway, I have the research and I'd like to pick this up again, got a hunch it could make for a very meaty story."

"You got a hunch, I'm your man," Louie says.

"Once you come up for air."

"Right, I'm flattered. I may also have something in the wings."

"Yeah? Shoot."

"You know my 'friend' in real estate? The guy that turned us onto this office space, Joe. I don't think that's all he's into, I think he may have something to do with organized crime. It's just an instinct, a couple of things he's said to me in passing, but I'm going to see if I can get in a little deeper there, see if it leads to something."

"Well, you know what I say, follow your instincts. But we're keeping our powder dry for now, right?"

"Right."

"Organized crime, huh?" she smiles.

———

Across town, Joe and Uncle Donny are having courgettes and cocktails.

"You heard about Cesar?" Uncle Donny asks.

"Who?"

"Thane Cesar. Don't you read the Times? The guy is working security, has a massive heart attack, and drops dead right there by the entrance to his store. The back entrance, the one from the parking lot. Made it very convenient for the hearse to back in," Uncle Donny says laughing. "You going to the funeral?"

"Uh, no, I'm not," Joe says bewildered.

Ira and George fly back to Malibu together and are about to enjoy a quiet dinner at home.

"So, bro, tell me what this is about 'cause I have a lady friend who wants me to stop by tonight," Ira winks.

"I'll tell Greta to speed things up," George says and heads for the kitchen.

George has been following a paleo diet so Ira isn't sure what's in store, but typically dinners here are spectacular. Nuts and seeds somehow made delicious.

"So is this the BMG thing? 'Cause I really want to sleep on it."

"You were snoring so loud on the plane—" George waits until Greta has dished out her mystery casserole. "No, it's about GoodWorks. If we want to keep expanding we're going to need an infusion of capital. Chad is costing a lot more than anticipated. And we can't throw one of the fundraising dinners, obviously, not after what happened with the last one."

"No, no, god no. We'll think of something else."

"Right. So what could that be, bro? Got any ideas?"

"Hmm, thinking aloud here. What about an evening cruise to Catalina, you know, a couple of hours on a beautiful ship drinking and . . . nah. Too much like the dinner."

"What about a movie night?"

"George, that's what they do during the day. Something to honor Joan?" Ira says, his eyes lighting up.

"Yeah, keep going."

"Um—a scholarship in her name. To a promising young journalist?"

"*Or* a journalist who graduated from one of the schools we support in a third world country!" George offers.

"Yes, yes! I love that!" Ira says. "But has anyone made it that far? Maybe we can't limit it to just the schools we support. It probably needs to be broader."

"Right, you're right. Okay, how about a budding young journalist in the international arena? Or journalists? Maybe we do more than one?" George says.

"Yes! We host an event for young journalists from developing countries. We call it the YJDC or something like that."

"And we award the 'Joan Ross Memorial Scholarship.'"

"Perfect."

"I'll get some folks working on it. Okay, you're free to go. Unless you want dessert. Greta said she's got something special."

"Nah, I'm good. Love you," Ira says as he leaves.

"Be careful out there!" George calls after, like he always does.

———

Louie is making the bar scene at BobbyG's on Higuera, it's become his regular place in Culver City. Some of the *Relevant* folks have adopted it too. He's nursing a beer with a couple of them when Joe arrives.

"Hey, these your magazine compadres?" Joe asks Louie.

"Yeah, stranger—let me introduce you to—"

"It's been nuts—" Joe's cell phone is already vibrating. "Wait a sec—hold your horses," he yells into the phone. "What!!! Okay, okay, I'm on my way."

Joe shoots Louie a look. "This sucks. I hate my job," and leaves.

———

Uncle Donny is pacing the den, chewing on a cigar. "We got a real problem, a real headache," he says when Joe arrives.

"Well, here I am, let's fix it," Joe says.

"I should never have trusted that schmuck. He was supposed to have destroyed those papers, that's what he told me. He burned 'em up." He's working his jaw like something's stuck.

Joe's never seen him so upset.

"That's exactly what he said, 'I burned 'em up' —I can still hear him that idiot. But did he? No, he did not, not if that guy has them! If this falls into the wrong hands, Joe, I can't have that."

"What are we talking about Uncle D?" Joe asks.

"Picked it up on the tap, this guy has Ruby's papers. The tap, you know, the one you handled, Joan's place."

Joan's place. Joan? She's been dead for years. Man, he is losing it.

"What kind of papers?" he asks.

"Some worthless stock for a company out of business. It's nothing, it's just that . . . we got to nip this in the bud," Uncle Donny says.

"Sure, okay. Where do I find it?"

"You got a passport?"

"Um, no I don't, actually. I was gonna get one for the honeymoon, but then we decided on Vegas—"

"Get an emergency passport, takes a day or two, I still need to find the schmuck's address. He keeps the papers in his house," he shakes his head in bewilderment. "Some place in fuckin' South America."

———

Three days later, Joe is on his way to Managua, he's pretty excited to be going. It's his first trip outside the US and just the second time Uncle Donny has awarded him such an important mission. He could have picked from a bunch of guys, but he picked Joe. That's saying something.

He checks into an airport hotel, rents a car, and drives over to Brad's house that same afternoon.

La Monaca reminds him of his own neighborhood—the streets radiate from a roundabout and there's a clubhouse perched on a hill. He doesn't know what he was expecting but it wasn't this.

Brad's house looks like all the other high-end houses on the cul-de-sac—contemporary craftsmanship with lots of green space and a pool in the back. Pretty snazzy.

He finds a parking spot halfway down the block that's in the shade. He's brought along the iPad Tobeye gave him for Christmas, state-of-the-art earbuds, a bottle of water, and two bags of pretzels he took from the plane; he settles in, ready for a watch. He's looking forward to it.

He's still enjoying his quiet time when the neighborhood lights come on for the evening. It's then he realizes he's way under-prepared, this could take a while. The next thing he knows, the sun's coming up and he's in desperate need to relieve himself. He makes a fast run to some bushes and prays no one sees him do it.

Then he realizes he's going to need to replenish supplies—his stomach's growling and he's out of water. He googles to find a nearby convenience store, *What? They don't got Wayz!* when finally, at one o'clock, Brad's front door opens.

Brad leaves the house walking slowly, strolls right across from Joe's car up the hill, turns left, walks out of the cul-de-sac, and out of sight.

Joe rings the doorbell just in case and is surprised when a beautiful young woman appears. He scrambles to readjust his thinking, he had been planning to just toss the place.

"Hi, I'm Richie, a friend of Brad's. He around?" He gives her a big smile.

"Ah, no. You just missed. He left for work."

Richie makes a face. "I'll come back then."

"Oh no, come in. You friend of Brad's, you wait here," she leads him into a large but hardly lived-in living room. "Make yourself comfortable. I'm Tonya," she points to herself. "I was going to have wine. Care to join?"

She says all this graciously, with an accent he can't identify. Not Spanish.

"It's a bit early for me but . . . sure, why not? That's mighty kindly of ya."

He sits down on a sofa that reminds him of his grandmother and she pours him a glass from an open Chablis.

"Cheers!" they both say.

It's astonishing how quickly they hit it off. Tonya is fluent in bad guys and although Joe's a bit out of practice, flirting is like riding a bike.

"So I didn't know Brad had a job down here, thought he was retired. Where's it at?" Richie asks after their second glass of Chablis.

"Oh, not a real job. He just walks around, checks on neighbors, makes sure everything okay there. That's all." She laughs. "He was bored, you know," she stands with her head tilted provocatively. "Let me show you around the place."

She takes him into the beautiful backyard with its pool and sauna, and then shows him the media room with its plush seats and screening area, Joe oohing and aahing in all the right places. She takes him into the kitchen and dining room and a couple of other spaces which are sparsely furnished, he's not even sure what the rooms are for. Then she heads down a long hallway to the 'sleeping quarters' with many bedrooms on either side.

"And this my room, I sleep here," she says, neglecting to say, "when I'm not sleeping with Brad." She looks deep into Joe's eyes.

"Oh! You want to see cabana? Best part."

So they walk back outside and around to the far side of the pool—he sees a cute, small structure that's a replica of the main house and realizes it's a cabana. He thought she said banana.

"You have bathing suit? We go for swim?"

"I didn't bring one, no," he says.

"Too bad. Pool is heated."

She quickly removes her silk blouse before he has a chance to say anything.

"We still get comfy," she says. "Come—don't be shy. Come join me," she makes room for him on the day bed. "Come," she says again, patting the space next to her.

He does come, a bit faster than intended. But she's a piece of work.

Afterward, Tonya offers to make him a snack and they walk back into the main house. She rifles through the refrigerator and finds cheese and what looks like moldy guacamole. He quickly scoffs down all of it with some salty crackers and tells her why he's come.

"Brad's been keeping some papers for me. Just some paperwork, nothing exciting," he explains.

"Oh? I don't know about that," she says, worrying that she might.

She starts looking at her watch. "I think he back soon."

So they move into the living room to wait. The crackers have made him very thirsty, they polish off the wine.

Brad finally returns.

"Well hello," he says wide-eyed as he enters his living room. "Have we met?"

He extends his hand, but Joe pulls out a small curved knife from an inside pocket and stabs him in the stomach; he manages to get his hand over Tonya's mouth stifling a scream as Brad grasps the sofa and slides onto the floor.

"I won't hurt you, hon, I just need those papers."

Tonya takes him into Brad's bedroom. She fumbles with the lock, punching in codes unsuccessfully; Joe goes out to the garage, grabs a garden shovel, and breaks open the closet door.

There's a large bag under a mess of splinters and shoes and he dumps it out all over the bed, finding the papers under a mass of cash.

Tonya's eyes grow wide, she had no idea Brad kept so much money here, he never let her anywhere near the bag.

"Look," Joe says. "I'll make a deal with you. I don't kill you if you do a couple things for me."

He nudges her into a chair.

"One: forget about today. Just forget about it, it never happened. Because if you mention it to anyone, I'm gonna find you and I'll have to kill you. I should be doing that right now but we had a thing, and I got a soft spot for you. Two: I don't want the cash, you keep it. Take it and get out of here. But you can't spend it in the States. So it's better that you never go back there. Leave Nicaragua, go somewhere else, anywhere you want, just not America. Got it? You'll be fine, there must be close to a million bucks here. I'm letting you have it in exchange for keeping your mouth shut."

He stares at her intently.

"I understand," she says.

"Yeah, repeat it."

"I understand," she repeats.

"No, repeat what I told you. How come I'm not killing you now?"

"I never saw you. I leave Nicaragua. Don't go to America."

"These bills are marked," he tosses one in the air. "If you spend it in the States, they're gonna arrest you. And torture you until you tell them how you got it. That leads them to me. That can't happen. You understand?"

"But I don't see anything," she says as she fondles a $100 bill.

"No, you can't see it. They mark it so only they can see it. Do. You. Understand?"

"Yes. I never spend this in America."

"Better you never go there. Just leave the house when it gets dark, he'll have bled out by then," he says. "Unless you want me to try and resuscitate your friend. Do you?"

She shakes her head no.

"Out loud," he demands.

"Don't resusc . . . recus . . . don't help him," she says.

"Okay. So now you're an accessory. My car's down the street. You have wheels?"

"Yes," she nods.

"Okay. I'm leaving now. It was nice knowing you."

CHAPTER THIRTY-ONE

The DataBear team work their magic and locate Dr. Benjamin Dailey at the Mayo Clinic College of Medicine outside Minneapolis, he's listed on their roster for next semester. And, more importantly, they find a valuable data point missed earlier—the good doctor is a lifelong advocate of the euthanasia movement.

Claire in research takes this lead and finds more—how Dailey set up the Hemlock Society when he was at Southwestern Medical back in the '60s; how he later opened its first chapter in Europe; how he was awarded a prize of distinction for debuting euthanasia studies in medical colleges curriculum . . . and so on.

"This is great, Louie, something we can really use," Phoebe says. "So what if you start attending meetings of the Hemlock Society in Minneapolis, for sure he'll show up there, let him see your face, get to know you."

"I already looked into that. But those meetings are spaced every other month. That's a slow, drawn-out process. And then, what if he misses one?"

"Right. Okay. Let's see . . . he won the 'Reimagining Residency Initiative Award' whatever that is—maybe something there? Or why don't we just run a story on euthanasia and you go interview him for that?"

"That's where I was heading. And here's something else—did you know that there's a growing problem of young doctors committing suicide? Maybe we work that in conjunction with his interest in euthanasia, the whole ethics thing."

"If that's supportable with data, this suicide thing, that would be a very interesting piece. I can see it coming together, the pressures new docs are under, the control euthanasia provides, the ethical dilemma. Our readers would flip for this kind of story."

"Absolutely. I'll keep you posted."

———

Phoebe calls Ira to thank him for his help and then finds herself complaining about being short of staff. He's heard it all before but he wisely lets her vent.

"It's taking a toll. Two of my best creatives threatened to walk if I didn't hire an additional art director—tomorrow! It's a never-ending battle, Ira, I can't keep up, the need for talent, it's keeping me up at night."

"If there's anything I can . . ."

"How I wish there was. Oh, I've been meaning to tell you, the Brad thing—*PuffySlim*—so that's not happening. Puffy's emails bounced back. Changed his mind I guess."

"Ah, that's too bad, I was looking forward to working with you on that. Tee me up for the next one."

"Will do. Hey, maybe there is something you can help us with."

She gets him up to speed on Dailey's reluctance to speak about his patients, including Jack Ruby.

"So now that we know where he is, and we know about his involvement with the Hemlock Society, we're going to try and bridge the gap, get him talking about his time in Dallas. Louie and I were discussing a piece about euthanasia, we'll tie it into a problem of young doctors committing suicide . . ."

"I didn't know—doctors and suicide—that wide-spread?"

"DataBear is collecting data as we speak. So assuming it is, or even if it isn't, and we stick to euthanasia, we can connect with him on that and get a good story, but it's still not an opening for Ruby and I see him just shying away from that. Got any better ideas?"

"Let me sleep on it," Ira says. "I do my best thinking around three a.m."

Two minutes later he calls back.

"It's not even three p.m.," she kids.

"What if we sponsor an award to the Hemlock Society because I just remembered George was involved with them with that Kevorkian film back aways."

"What film?"

"*You Don't Know Jack*, remember?"

"Oh, yeah, I didn't know George was involved."

"One of the producers. So what if we invite what's his name—"

"Dr. Dailey."

"—up here to accept this award and receive the donation that goes with it. Since he's been a life-long member, etcetera, etcetera."

"More than a member, he was a founder."

"And while he's here, we put him up in one of George's cottages on the Malibu property, tell him to bring his wife, he's married?"

"I'll ask Louie."

"And have a once-in-a-lifetime Hollywood experience—an exclusive dinner with Mr. Hollywood in his home—etcetera, etcetera. Then we let George loose, get him talking about his early days, starting out, you know how George is, and that leads to working with Ruby, speaking Yiddish. All that."

"God, Ira, you're a genius."

"You should see me at three a.m."

"I have, I like this better."

———

George thinks it's a home run. *Relevant* gets a blockbuster story, one with the potential to deliver them a Pulitzer—or at least a ton of exposure—and it paves the way for him to promote Ira to president of BMG.

His people connect with Dr. Dailey and explain the prestigious award, the presentation luncheon, and the donation to the Hemlock Society. And, as Ira predicted, the invitation to stay with George Baxter at his Malibu estate seals the deal. Dr. Dailey and his wife are thrilled to accept.

Louie arranges for *Relevant's* best photographer to cover their visit. George instructs his staff to ready a guest cottage and asks Greta to prepare a special dinner the night before the award ceremony.

He decides to play it 'elder statesman' with the Dailey's—think Sully Sullenberger or Atticus Finch—competent, calm, and trustworthy. He knows he can come off intimidating, so he'll stay low-key and unassuming, let the good doctor relax into his surroundings, then lead him into telling his whole life's story. From the beginning. Take all the time he needs.

They'll eventually get to Ruby.

Ira has a date that he offers to postpone, but George thinks it might be better to welcome the Dailey's by himself. He dresses carefully, choosing a conservative jacket and tie, hoping it telegraphs legitimacy as well as congeniality.

The annunciator signals they're at the gate, so George heads outside. He watches as Tom circles the fountain with brilliantly sparkling rainbow lights for the occasion and hears an unusual buzzing sound coming from somewhere near its base. He's annoyed thinking the buzzing might spoil the moment, after all he's prepared—

BOOOOOOOOOMMMMM!!!

The sky alights in a thousand shiny metal fragments within a maelstrom of rainbow brightness. The entire estate heaves off the ground. Greta, Tom, Dr. and Mrs. Dailey, and George—George Baxter—are erased from the earth forever.

Smoke and fumes carry down the hills of Malibu, down past the Pacific Coast Highway, past Santa Monica and out to sea. Falling ash and the smell of burnt flesh will linger there for days.

CHAPTER THIRTY-TWO

Lianne McMurphy runs on set in street clothes and little make-up. Her segment producer waves her on, shaking. The news chief has tears in her eyes.

It's a strange scene for these consummate television professionals, one Lianne will never forget.

"We have just learned of an explosion at the Malibu beach home of George Baxter, the billionaire philanthropist and *People's* Man of the Year. Our news crew is heading to the scene right now to make sure this is not a mistake or some awful social media prank," she moves in closer, too close, forcing her cameraman to dolly back. "Several residents reported hearing an explosion at . . . one moment please." She stops speaking and tilts into her headset. "My crew is reporting the area is in lock down with police and fire vehicles at the scene and they cannot"—she pauses to collect herself—"they cannot confirm whether this is the Baxter estate or whether anyone was there at the time of the explosion, if there have been any casualties. We do not know . . ." she gulps hard, tears up . . . "I will interrupt your regular programming the moment we get more details. I promise to keep you informed. As always we are here for you. But, please, please, let this not be George Baxter. Not George Baxter."

CHAPTER THIRTY-THREE

George had become lapsed when the Catholic church's sex abuse scandals came to light; he and Ira had never been very religious to begin with. So there will be no priest officiating the funeral. Yet someone must run the service, a master of ceremonies type, someone who will organize, choose the right people for eulogies and set time limits. That's not something Ira can handle at the moment.

Phoebe asked an actor friend who is also an ordained minister; he's agreed.

The Malibu grounds, George's favorite place, would have made a good venue. It had once been the setting for Ira's wedding—an elegant affair with a short shelf-life—but as it was part of the ongoing investigation, the LAPD refused to allow it. Fortunately, Sony Picture Studios, coincidentally around the corner from *Relevant's* office in Culver City, offered its facility. And with a full security detail already in place, it was ideal, only needing folding chairs to accommodate the 2,500 by-invitation-only mourners.

In exchange, Sony asked to stream the service; Phoebe stipulated all Fox stations were to be excluded. She knew that's how George would have played it.

By the time she gets to Sony this morning, there's a long line waiting for valet, so she parks at her office and walks back to the tent. She spots Ira sitting quietly, lost in a sea of condolences. People come and go around him, they whisper in his ear or put their hand on his shoulder. Some are media associates, some are industry people, others are friends and family. Many have traveled long distances to be here.

George was an important man, critical to many of their careers and their fortunes. They're not sure how to deal with this loss. Some, like Ira, have disassociated from reality, they are numb. Some worry about their own safety, so little is understood about the crime.

Is there a vendetta on the industry? Was George even the target—could it have been someone else, the doctor staying with him—the wife? Who would do such a thing! What is going on with this city!!!

Phoebe notices the LAPD have fanned out along the perimeter, it angers her just to look at them. *You should be out there, looking for the killer, not standing around here collecting over-time. It's weeks and weeks! Who would want George dead!? And how could you suspect Ira because of the inheritance angle, you guys are pathetic!!*

"Amateur hour," George's business manager had said. "They'll wear themselves out chasing dead ends then call in the Feds. Then we'll get an answer. You wait and see."

She notices there are some FBI here too, men in dark suits trying to blend in with the crowd. She'll go over after the service ends and complain about the local cops, maybe they can step in now instead of waiting to see them fail.

What she doesn't know is that the FBI has been on the case for a while. They are somewhat sympathetic to the cops' dilemma— it's not always possible to trace these custom explosive devices. And they too start with family when weeding out suspects.

She takes Ira's cold hand in hers, feels him shuddering. The room grows quiet as the first eulogy begins. She steels herself to be strong.

The minister calls for the next speaker when Ira gasps and falls out of his chair, he begins convulsing on the ground. Phoebe moves down beside him as he loses consciousness—several doctors in the crowd rush to help. An ambulance arrives quickly and takes him to a nearby hospital—the memorial service continues on without them.

Ira remains sedated for several days, recovering from a severe epileptic event; Phoebe spends the first night on a chair beside his bed. Ira never told her he had epilepsy as a child, by the time they had met it was ancient history. The doctors are convinced they'll get it under control, but for now he is heavily medicated and barely awake through her visits. She feels envious of this drugged state. She too would like to forget that George is gone, put this all behind her. But she can't allow herself to surrender to the feeling, not for Ira's sake nor for her own.

"Any news on the Malibu explosion," she asks Louie a few weeks later. "There's hardly anything in the dailies."

"Cops might not want to release details to the press," Louie says.

"They must have figured out who engineered the bomb by now. I read they had been looking at the gardening crew but no longer. So first they think it's Ira in it for the money, and then a disgruntled landscaper blows up Hollywood's most beloved star because, what, he trampled their gardenias?!!"

"I know, it's pure incompetence. After all this time."

"So, okay. Let's put our heads together. Go talk to the cops. Find out where they are in the investigation. I haven't read one word about the doctor and his wife being there—couldn't they have been the intended victims? Stop by the Parker Center and if they won't grant an interview, get loud. Tell them we have our finger on the pulse and the citizenry is outraged that they haven't made more progress."

"I'll find a way to ask without getting deported."

"Huh?"

"Cops think people who look like me are illegals—we should go back to where we came from."

"Oh jeez, Louie, you're from Covina. Okay, find a nice way."

"I will. And speaking of nice, I owe you a beer—tonight?"

"I'll take a rain check, going to visit Ira."

"Is he doing any better?"

"Making progress."

"Send him my regards," Louie says as he leaves.

She rifles through her desk drawer until she finds the clipping she was looking for.

> **Thane Cesar, shown here being questioned at the Parker Center, was employed by Ace Security to protect Robert Kennedy at the Ambassador Hotel the night the senator was shot. More recently, Robert Kennedy Jr. took to social media to tweet that Cesar may have "murdered my father" . . .**

She tries phoning Brad again, hoping his phone is back in service. It's not. "Puffy, where the heck are you?" she asks looking up to the ceiling.

———

Louie hasn't been to BobbyG's for a while so he's surprised to find the place decorated for the holidays. The bar is so crowded he's tempted to leave but then sees Joe waving at him from the corner.

"Hey, Joe, long time no see. How ya been?"

"Good! Real estate's picking up, thank the lord. And I snuck in a short vacation down south. You know what they say about taking time off, it really does recharge your batteries."

"I wouldn't know," Louie says. "I've never had a real vacation in my life."

"Get out, seriously? Wow, you got to learn to live a little. So what's new with you?"

"Same old same old."

"So—take a vacation now since you got nothing going on."

"Oh, no I'm still busy at work, looking into that explosion in Malibu."

"George Baxter's place? What a sad thing that was. Come to think of it, I haven't seen anything about that recently. You know, that's worrisome, what, the cops can't figure out what happened?"

"Whoever planted the bomb knew what he was doing."

"Figures. Hey, there's a table, let's grab it."

Joe orders a beer for himself and one for Louie and two shots to go along. Louie excuses himself for the restroom.

"What's up with the Lakers?' Joe says on his return. "They're sucking wind. Uncle Donny has season tickets that I can use whenever, but I don't want to go to see them lose."

"You got tickets?" Louie drinks his shot to keep up with Joe. "How about we go when they play the Clippers? They're on a roll. You can get those?"

"Probably—they're for the business but he never uses them. When is the Clipper game—lemme look—oh, it's next Thursday."

"That works for me."

"Okay. I'll meet you here, we can leave our cars and Uber over. Say four thirty—he's got a box so we can eat there too—the food's not too terrible."

"Deal! Wow, I'm psyched to see the Clippers play!"

Joe signals for two more shots. "I think something happened to the LA cops, they have all these unsolved cases, this town is going to hell in a handbasket."

"What's a handbasket?"

"You know, an expression. 'Hell in a handbasket.' You never heard that?"

"No. And I don't get it."

"Now that you mention it, I don't get it either. It's an Uncle

Donny special, he's got a lot of these. Like, for example, watch your Ps and Qs," Joe says with a shrug.

"Beats me," Louie says.

"How about a fagala?"

"Never heard that word before."

"It's a fag, a fairie, you know, a homosexual. No offense," Joe smiles.

"I'm not gay. What, do I look gay to you!!!?"

"Gay comes in a lot of shapes and sizes. Hey, it's no big deal."

"Well, I'm not, jeez. But fagala—that's kinda funny, mind if I borrow it? I work in publishing."

They laugh. Joe signals for two more.

"So what happens to your story if the cops never find the guys that set off the bomb—that's a lot of wasted time on your part, right? That must be frustrating."

"It happens," Louie shrugs. "But I think they're getting closer on this."

"Oh yeah—they know who the perpetrator was?"

"No, they got no idea. But wanna hear something amazing? They found a bone."

"A bone? What do ya mean, like a person's bone?"

"Yeah. I got to interview a forensic guy, one of those experts, and he told me—this is wild—that some doctor who lives in Naples, in Long Beach, has this big German shepherd he lets out in his yard . . . so the dog comes back with a bone in his mouth. The doc thinks it looks like a human bone and calls the authorities. And guess what—it is a human bone, and it's from that explosion."

"Get out! That's sick. All the way to Long Beach? From Malibu? That's crazy!" Joe picks up his drink. "To flying bones!" They down them and Joe signals for two more. "You know, they got all kinds of ways now to figure out who that bone belongs to. From DNA. Like maybe it's George Baxter's or his chauffeur. Or the starlet he was gonna bang," Joe says.

"Don't think it was a starlet. Say, where are our wings? Can you get her attention? I'm getting blotto," Louie says.

"I gotta take a leak, I'll find her," Joe heads to the men's room. "So how do you know she wasn't a starlet," Joe asks when he returns.

"You ready for this: 'cause that bone came from an old woman."

"NO! Get out? For real. Mr. Hollywood's banging an old broad. That's disgusting."

"They dated it and it's over seventy years old."

"It's fuckin' amazing what they can do with DNA, right?" Joe says looking at his phone. "Shit, I gotta go. Forget the wings, or you eat them." He signals for the check. "On me, buddy. Hey, you okay to drive?"

"I think I'll get a ride. Booze on an empty stomach."

"I'd drop you but I'm running late."

"No worries."

"Don't forget, Thursday. You sure you're okay? You better put that date in your phone now just in case, you don't wanna miss the game." Joe puts his arm around him. "You sure you're not a fagala, Louie? 'Cause they can't hold their liquor either."

They laugh.

———

Phoebe is packing up for the night. She decides to skip the gym. It's been a crazy day and she's bushed.

"Hello! Is Phoebe Barber here?" someone calls out from the lobby.

She walks toward the voice. "Who wants to know?"

"Brian Wilson, I'm with the FBI, ma'am. I've come to ask Ms. Barber a few questions."

"That's me, Mr. Wilson."

"Is now okay?"

"Do you have some ID you can show me?" she asks. "I was just about to leave but . . . here, step into our conference room, I'll join you in a minute."

She retrieves her bag and some reading materials. Mr. Wilson is busy checking out the place.

"*Pet Sounds* was my favorite," she says, walking back in.

"Never ever heard that one before," he says smiling. "Listen, I'm sorry it's so late, I see you're about to leave. I'll call tomorrow to make an appointment, okay?"

"Um, sure, okay. But I do have a few minutes now if—"

"No, I'll make an appointment. Sorry to have disturbed you, have a nice evening," and he's gone.

———

Joe drives straight from BobbyG's to Uncle Donny's to tell him what he learned from Louie and get tickets for Thursday night's game.

"Good work, Joe, very helpful. This is paying off, worth my investment."

"What, these?" Joe asks, brandishing the tickets.

"No, the lease. I'm losing my shirt on Culver City."

"Yeah, so you said. A couple of hundred times."

"Don't get smart with me," Uncle Donny says pretending he's angry.

"So what's my reward?" Joe asks.

Don motions to the tickets, still smiling.

"No, I'm serious. I've done everything you've asked. And then some."

"You're a broken record, Joe. I told you before you're on the list. When we open the books, you're the first one called."

"I know, I know, so when do the books get open? That's what I'm asking, that's what I need to know," his voice rising. "Because I'm getting the feeling that you're just stringing me along here. This has been going on for a long time, Uncle Donny!"

"Lower your voice. I said you're on the list. This conversation is over, don't bring it up again." He motions to the tickets, "Now go, enjoy yourself."

Joe stomps out, he can't believe he's been dismissed like a child. *What a fool I am.* Back in the car, he starts rehearsing what to say to Tobeye when he gets home. Now that he's made up his mind to quit this fucking family business once and for all.

He's still stewing when he pulls into the driveway, anxious to get the conversation behind him. He climbs the stairs to their bedroom and sees Tobeye in bed reading quietly. He decides to wait for morning, and goes back down to settle in the den with a scotch. He switches on cable news. There's no way he's getting any sleep tonight, feeling like he does.

———————

Phoebe has put a chicken in the oven, not sure she followed the instructions properly. She's trying out a new roasting pan that was a gift from the owner of a popular kitchen store. She had been trying to upsell him to a full-year advertising plan when the roaster caught her eye. He sent it to her with a note rejecting her plan—"too rich for my blood"—but continues to send her gifts from time to time.

She thinks he's sweet.

"Been a long time, kiddo," she says aloud.

The knock on her door is a surprise.

"It's Brian Wilson from the FBI, ma'am, may I come in?"

"Something wrong, Mr. Wilson?" she asks, unlatching the door. "I thought you were going to call to make an appointment."

"I can explain," he says, following her into her living room. "And please, call me Mr. Beach Boy." They laugh. "Brian."

"Phoebe."

"When I was in your office earlier, I noticed something. I needed to double-check and I was right, I thought I'd tell you about it now. It seems you have a very special smoke detector in your conference room."

"Huh? You came to check on our smoke detectors?"

"No, ma'am—"

"Phoebe. Please."

"Okay Phoebe. I'm part of an investigation, looking into a murder. It has nothing to do with the smoke detector. The victim had your business card in his wallet."

"WHAT?!"

"Do you know a man named Bradley Greenfield?"

"No, I don't think so," she answers, suddenly nervous.

"Expat, living in Nicaragua, fifty-five years—"

"Oh, Brad! Oh yes. I know him. Oh, my god, he's dead?"

"I'm sorry to have to tell you, I hope he wasn't someone close."

"No, no. I only met him once."

"Can you tell me about that? Whatever you know about Mr. Greenfield."

"I only met him that one time, when he came to my office. I guess I gave him my card."

"Okay, what else ?"

"Well, hmm, this is a bit of a story. Can I get you something to drink? A soft drink, a Coke maybe?"

Phoebe tells him about her visit from Brad, about Thane Cesar and Jack Ruby, about Brad's suggestion there was a connection between them. And about Joan Ross, her death, and Phoebe's suspicion that Brad found something valuable in the safe deposit box.

Forty minutes later, she says, "And I've been unable to reach him ever since. I guess I now know why."

"That's quite a story."

"Okay, your turn. What's this about?" she asks.

"Here's what I can tell you. Bradley Greenfield was found dead in his home in La Monaca, Nicaragua, a little over three weeks ago. He had already been dead a couple of days when a neighbor found him and called the local police. They futzed around for a while and then finally did the smart thing, called us. It was a stabbing, someone stabbed him and left him to die—and he was an American citizen—not something the locals should handle."

"Puffy Slim," she remembers. "That's his email address, I have it back at the office. He said it was his girlfriend's, he didn't want anything to lead back to him."

"This girlfriend is key to our investigation. Brad's neighbor gave us a pretty good description and it didn't take long for Interpol to pick her up, we're bringing her in from Dubai."

"Wow," Phoebe says. "So, Mr. Beach Boy, how does my smoke detector fit into all of this?"

"It doesn't, that's something else. An off-shore electronics manufacturer makes a sophisticated smoke detector that can camouflage a listening device—originally it was proprietary to us, we actually invented it, but now anyone can get it if you know where to look. That's what you have in your conference room. I needed to check to see if, for some reason, we put it there. We didn't," Brian smiles. "That's good."

"Oh," she says, a bit confused.

"But it means someone else did, Phoebe. Someone planted a listening device in your office. Someone's been bugging you. Did you know about that?"

"No! God, no! Who would do that?"

"We checked your landlord. Culver City REIT, LLC. It's a shell company but when you untangle it, you find Donato Escarolla. Does that name ring a bell?"

She shakes her head. "No, not really."

"He's 'the don's don'—the bureau's been looking into his operation for years. Don keeps a low profile but he's behind a lot of nasty things. So here's the forty thousand dollar question: why is Donato Escarolla bugging your office?"

"The smoke detectors were there when we moved in."

"So maybe they were left from the previous tenant, I can find out—"

"No, there wasn't a previous tenant. We were the first. One of my associates has a friend who was renting out office space—this was a brand new business park in Culver City when we got here."

"Uh-huh," Brian says.

"We got a great deal."

"Uh-huh," he says.

"Wait a minute, let me think. The magazine had an exclusive on a fraud investigation back then, but we kept getting scooped—do you think one of our competitors was in cahoots with the don's don?"

"It's possible," Brian says. "Maybe Donato wanted to learn whether anything had been uncovered that could be incriminating to the family."

"So he bugged us—bugged our conference room?"

"It's possible. But it's probably not just your conference room. You probably have these devices planted around the office, it's why I came here to talk."

"Holy shit."

"Phoebe, something smells delicious, that must be your dinner. I'm going to go now, we can pick this up tomorrow. And let's just keep this between us for now, okay? I'll call you in the morning."

Joe calls Louie bright and early to confirm their date.

"Just wanted to make sure we're still good."

"Are you kidding? The Clippers are favored by nine points now, nine points! If I knew a bookie, I'd be betting big," Louie says.

"I can get that done for you. You serious?"

"Yeah," Louie says although he's not really sure, he's only bet sports with his cousin before.

"How much?"

"Um, fifty?" Louie says after much thought.

"Fifty?" Joe's flabbergasted. "Oh, fifty bucks, right?"

"Yeah," Louie says.

"I'll cover that myself. Listen, I just had another fight with my boss and I'm thinking it's time I found something else to do with my life. Go someplace where I'm appreciated. I wonder if you know anyone looking for a hard-working, smart, college grad."

"I don't know anyone in real estate Joe."

"Don't gotta be that. I majored in civil engineering at UCLA. I'm thinking something along those lines."

"Hmm, let me think about it, we can talk more at the game."

"Sure, meanwhile keep your ears and eyes open, pal, you never know."

Phoebe sticks her face into Louie's office. "Busy for lunch? Want you to meet someone."

She decides to bring Louie to lunch since he negotiated the office lease—had even met Brad briefly the time he stopped by. Brian asked that she not mention anything about their discussion beforehand so she doesn't.

"This is my go-to place," Brian says as they settle into a booth. "Their french dip is killer, you have to try it. It's messy, but they bring you a bib. So," he says to Louie after they order, "Phoebe tells me you've had the pleasure of meeting Mr. Donato Escarolla."

"Who?"

"The gentleman you rent your office from, happens to be the don of a major Mafia family."

"Oh, 'Uncle Donny.' I know his nephew, Joe. He handled the lease, we hang out sometimes. He told me his uncle used to be in the mob but that was a long time ago. Doesn't do that anymore, he's into real estate now. Why, is he in some kind of trouble?"

"Escarolla is the definition of trouble. That's his real business. My business is trying to catch him at it. Hate to admit it, not too successful so far."

"Wow . . . so does this mean Joe's in the Mafia too?" He turns to Phoebe, "I told you I thought these guys were into something more than real estate." He turns back to Brian, "So, is this what I'm doing here, what this meeting is about? I'm seeing Joe at the Staples Center tomorrow, you better not be planning on arresting him before then, we got very good seats," Louie says, only half-joking.

"So, you're good friends with the guy?"

"I'd say we're 'acquaintances.'"

"An acquaintance is taking you to the Staples Center for the best game of the season—with very good seats?"

"Well, I mean, yeah, I guess we're friends. He just confided in me he's looking for a new job."

Brian's eyes grow wide. "Really? Seriously?"

"Yeah. He was pretty upset. He's been getting the run-around on a promotion, been 'in the works' forever he's told me a couple of times. I think he just had enough. We were going to talk more about it at the game. He took civil engineering in college, I think he might be wanting to get into that."

Brian is quiet while Louie and Phoebe trade looks of concern.

"What's going on?" Phoebe asks finally.

"Louie, I'm going to ask you something, and I don't want an immediate answer, okay? I want you to think about it. Did Phoebe mention that Brad, the guy who visited *Relevant* a couple of months back, died? We found him dead in his house in Nicaragua."

Louie makes a face, "Uh, no."

Brian smiles at Phoebe. "We've got his girlfriend and she told us that a young man—his name is Richie, but that's probably not his real name—had been looking for Brad because Brad had something Richie wanted. We don't have the full story yet but we will. There's a chance that Richie is your 'acquaintance' Joe."

"Whoa. When was this?"

"Recently. Like in the past month."

"Joe told me he took a short vacation down south recently."

"Look, we've just started investigating, let's not jump to conclusions. Would you consider wearing a wire when you see him? Don't answer me yet. Here's the thing: If it's him, you're helping to nail a criminal, a murderer, help us put him in jail where he belongs. But if it's not, you're helping to prove that he didn't have anything to do with it, getting him off our radar."

Louie and Phoebe are silent. The waiter arrives with their sandwiches and bibs. No one says anything for a while. Not much eating is taking place either.

Brian finally signals for the check.

"I'll call you tomorrow, let you sleep on it. You're sure to have some questions for me, we can speak about it then."

It doesn't take much soul-searching for Louie to decide to do it, to wear the wire.

It's the right thing to do. And while he suspects Joe may be into something more than real estate, he doesn't believe he's a murderer! No way. Impossible. So, like the FBI guy explained, if he didn't kill Brad then Louie is helping to clear him, clear his name.

He's embarrassed when he mentions that he told Joe about a bone being found at the beach, he knows he probably shouldn't have said anything but he had been under the influence, truthfully, totally inebriated at the time. He remembers how strangely Joe seemed to react, he saw it even through his boozy haze.

Brian tells him that some of his people are on the Malibu case.

"Cops never tell us anything—we offer to trade information but they shut us out, we end up reading about it in the papers," he says shaking his head. "But this time there's been very little evidence. They had no choice but to ask for our help."

Louie is wired up when he meets Joe in BobbyG's parking lot. He's so nervous he's sweating through his jacket, but Joe doesn't notice. He still seems angry about work, he brings it up almost immediately.

"I told Tobeye I'm out of there, I'm done. I need something where there's room for advancement. I'm tired of being a low man on the totem pole. You know what I mean?" he searches Louie's face for understanding.

"Sure, but, I haven't heard anything yet, nothing on that front," he says.

"Hey, no worries pal, I put out some feelers, something's gonna give. Meanwhile, I'm still smiling and nodding, no one suspects a thing. They're all too busy brown-nosing the boss. Speaking of which, I told him your flying bone story. Man, he laughed so hard I thought he'd spit out his dentures."

Louie begins to relax when they settle into their seats.

"Got any more on the flying bones?"

He tells him what Brian said to say. "They think it was from the Malibu explosion, they know it was an old lady. The FBI is sending it to another DNA lab for testing. I didn't know it, but there's like a hierarchy for this kind of thing."

"The Feds are on the case? That's probably a good thing."

"Yeah, got more sophisticated equipment, and they're smart."

"These fucking cops are like the Three Stooges. Can't get out of each others' way."

"Yeah. Hey, I got some really good news. My boss says I'm getting a Christmas bonus after all. The magazine had a good year and they're handing out checks on Monday. So I decided I'm going to take a vacation. A real vacation—finally! So I'm thinking, where did you go that you liked so much? You mentioned a place down south, was that Mexico?"

"Nah, Mexico's not safe, I went to Nicaragua. You got a travel agent? I can hook you up with mine."

"My cousin's married to a travel agent. What was the name of it?"

"La Monaca, very swanky. For rich people, first rate. And plenty of beautiful *muchachas* looking for a good time. You should go, they'll like you. Since you're not a fagala," Joe smiles.

When Brian reaches out to Joe, his timing is perfect, Joe just had another run-in with Uncle Donny. His face is pulsing red when Brian intercepts him getting into his car. He tells him he has something important he needs to discuss, and asks him to take a ride with him to the beach. It's not really a request.

Walking along the water's edge, Brian lays his cards on the table.

"Know a pretty lady named Tonya? She's visiting our office in DC at the moment."

"Tonya? Nope."

"She says she knows you, she told us a lot about you. It's not good, Joe, what she told us. You're in a lot of trouble here. If what she says pans out, you'll be kissing your wife and kid goodbye—forever. This is a forever stretch we're looking at."

"I don't know what you're talking about. And I don't know no Tonya."

"Here's her photo, look familiar? She picked you out from this one, you were a little younger here but it's a positive ID. We got the manifest from the flight to Nicaragua. Your name's on it. You used your real passport? That was pretty sloppy, amateur work. It's only a matter of time before we get all the pieces we need to press charges. And then it's *adios* forever."

Joe sits down on a bench. Brian sits too.

"You killed him and it was premeditated. Murder one. Cut and dry." Brian looks at him intently.

"Not premeditated, I was just looking for something," Joe tries to explain.

"Uh-huh, sure. Save it for the judge. But there may be a way out of this for you, Joe. I want you to think about something. Don't answer me right away. Maybe I can get this reduced down to involuntary manslaughter, you know, or even a lesser charge depending on how it goes. Something that maybe could include a relocation for your family, someplace safe. I can start working on it. But you're going have to give us Donny."

Joe knew as soon as Brian said "a way out" that he would have to flip on somebody if he wanted to beat the rap, if he didn't want to spend the rest of his life in prison. He knew it would probably be Uncle Donny. And he had already decided to do it. It wasn't even a hard call.

"Sign me up," he says.

CHAPTER THIRTY-FOUR

ra walks into Phoebe's office slowly and sits down carefully in the visitor's chair. While his epilepsy is under control, it's obvious how much that plus the loss of his brother has changed his demeanor, changed him. How he's still struggling to deal with losing George.

One of the first things Ira did after leaving the hospital was to create a fund to give away George's fortune. It was cathartic, part of the healing process.

He awarded a few, sizable gifts to charities he knew and now is establishing an advisory board to help guide future giving.

"There are so many worthy ones, it's impossible to know which to support."

Phoebe offers up a couple of names for the board, including the gentleman who owns the kitchen stores.

"Smart, socially attuned, practical, he'd be a good addition."

Ira's also begun the process of selling off George's residences, extremely valuable properties whose proceeds will be deposited in the fund.

"Telluride went in one day—there was a bidding war!"

"I'm not surprised, that place was magnificent. Remember last winter—George invited the whole *Relevant* team out, we spent the day skiing then had that incredible dinner . . . that was special!"

"Oh right, I totally forgot about that. I'm still not operating on all cylinders."

"You're doing fine, don't be so hard on yourself."

"George would rent that place out for the film festival—four days—and it paid for the entire year of maintenance."

"George was very smart."

"That he was. Were you ever at his place in Geneva? Stunning, right on the lake, what a view! He bought it years ago at a great price, but it's been a bear to sell—the Swiss changed their real estate rules about foreigners. Our lawyers are trying to work through it."

"I can only imagine," she says.

"And, oh, listen to this. His Tribeca loft that was sooo cool—it was actually owned by somebody else."

"The city place?"

"So George had taken some money, I think it was when GoodWorks was just getting off the ground, to show that there were other donors on the books besides himself. Anyway, the loft was involved somehow. Like collateral. I'm sure he was planning to clean that up at some point but . . . anyway, right after I get out of the hospital, these two guys walk into BMG with a note claiming ownership of the property. Needless to say, everyone was super skeptical but the lawyers did a deep dive—turns out it was theirs. And it's worth a ton of money."

"What guys? Film guys?"

"No, they were representing somebody else. I really wasn't functioning at the time, Pheebs. You know. But the lawyers said it was kosher."

Phoebe's mind flashes to the note she got from Grace:

. . . charity run by your friends . . . dirty money . . .

"What's happening with Malibu?" she asks instead.

"Here's the thing. You know how he felt about Malibu. How much he loved the place. It's been really hard for me to think about letting it go. It'll need to be something very special, I'm not just selling it off to the highest bidder."

"Of course," she says. After Ira, no one knew George better.

"You should stop by . . . we're cleaning it up now that the cops are gone. The big house is gone, demolished. I spent time digging around the dirt, hoping to find something, maybe some of his personal stuff," he shakes his head sadly. "Then the city came, declared it a hazard, and bulldozed what was left. So . . . But my cottage—can you imagine, Pheebs, the one from *Long Road*—the foundation was good enough to rebuild from. A couple of people tried to talk me out of doing that but the place holds so many good memories."

"I'll have to stop by."

"You have no idea how dealing with this stuff takes up my day—George had so much going on, so many people depending on him. Now they're all over me. Speaking of me, how's the search going?" he smiles his old Ira smile.

"We saw a couple of candidates but nothing yet. I got excited about one, I think I mentioned him, his resume was stellar, decades of experience. But when he came in for an interview," she makes a face. "Hadn't done his homework, thought we were still some rinky-dink operation. Very disappointing."

"Too bad."

"And a young woman the recruiter sent over, she was Ms. Personality. A ton of energy, the right attitude—I thought maybe? But the more time we spent together . . ." Another face. "She lacked real-world experience. It started to worry me, could she manage through the good times *and* the bad? I'd end up having to hold her hand half the time, this place is a roller coaster."

Phoebe doesn't really want to find a replacement for Ira anyway. She thinks there's a fair chance he will change his mind once the dust settles.

They order lunch and Ira walks her through some of the proposals he's received for Malibu. With twenty-four acres facing the Pacific Ocean, it's an extremely rare and incredibly valuable property, an amazing opportunity for the right developer.

"There's one from the David Geffen/UCLA Medical College, they want to build a campus on the property. Lecture halls, bio laboratories, some residential housing, and here's the interesting part—it's going to feature precision medicine—'artificial intelligence and robotic technology.' Different from your traditional med school. They proposed calling it 'UCLA Medical Theranostics.'"

"No David Geffen, that would make George happy," she says.

"Yeah. Maybe even call it Baxter Theranostics."

"Oh boy, even better!"

"I got another one from Eventmo, it's an entertainment company. They want to build a venue for small entertainment attractions, like folk concerts and puppet shows, that kind of thing, geared for families. They erect a dome, a kind of permanent tent that's environmental-friendly and leave space for local artisans—T-shirts, posters, toys, food. Think Woodstock in the twenty-first century. You know how George used to complain about us having only these mammoth facilities with big commercial ventures, so this would be different, fill the gap in the market. They suggested calling it the Baxter Arena."

"Wow, George would like this too."

"I know. That's what makes this so hard. And there's one more. A small boarding school for young people with social, emotional, and behavioral difficulties, like Asperger's, attention deficit, depression. It's a school from back East that wants to expand, they approached me with a fully fleshed-out proposal."

"Thinking about your recent health bout—George would have been all over that trying to help."

"Agreed. So, got a favorite?"

"No, not really, they're all terrific, this is going to be a tough decision."

Agent Wilson meets up with Phoebe later that afternoon.

"Good news. The DA plans to throw the book at Escarolla,

they're asking for five life sentences to be served concurrently, one for each victim in the Baxter explosion."

"So it *was* him, I can't believe it. Our landlord!"

"We subpoenaed the tapes from your office, it's all there Phoebe. Everything. He knew about the doctor from Minneapolis because he heard you and Louie discussing it. He learned about Brad the day he came to your office. Look, we could have gone for more, there's a host of crimes Joe told us about, but we're focused on Malibu because it's so heinous and weighing on everyone's psyche."

"It's terrible to think that *Relevant* was supplying this guy with information, but at least we understand what happened, who was responsible. And a relief to know he'll spend the rest of his life behind bars."

"Well, this next part may not thrill you. Escarolla's lawyers have started lobbying for medical dispensation. They argue at his age, prison is the same as a death sentence, and California repealed the death penalty in 2016."

"What!! No. NO!"

"They've been negotiating for house arrest."

"Brian! That's not punishment for killing all those people! He gets to stay in his mansion in Beverly Hills!"

Brian admits they're seriously considering it.

"The courts have been leaning toward this lately and if we agree to it now, before the trial begins, we can exchange it for more information."

"C'mon—he killed George and four other people. It's not fair!"

"There are a lot of crimes we've never been able to solve, ones we've pursued for years. Look, Phoebe, other victims' families need closure too—it just might be worth it. He's already started 'spewing'—the only word I think to describe it."

"I'm going to be sick thinking about him in his mansion and George in the ground."

"He's already dropped a couple of big names. If we go for this, he's promised to tell us everything, hold nothing back."

The court allows his home arrest. And Don has a very good memory.

Some of his earliest recollections involve Cuba and the casinos his father helped to build there. He talks about vacations spent in the tropics, playing with kids from the other families—and then later, as a young adult, nights full of mischief, at parties, with women.

Things take a more serious tone when Don takes on a bigger role in the family business. He relates stories of partnering with the CIA to take down Castro and win back the casino business. Don even recalls how the same agent used a different name depending on who he was working with.

"Thought he'd confuse us 'stupid goombahs'—that's what they called us behind our back," he smirks.

He drifts into a long-winded tale about a bank executive and colleagues who were customers there. He goes on for an hour then stops speaking abruptly.

"Smart woman, too smart for her own good," he says finally.

He tells them how he got rid of Joan Ross.

"We knew all about the big gala they had planned, the fancy pants, and thought what better place to remind them who's really in charge! So I got rid of that bitch and her scummy liquor store pal and scared the crap out of the rest of them."

He explains it was Joe's first hit.

"I know you gave the kid a break. That's fine by me," Don lies.

He also explains why they planted listening devices in the *Relevant* office.

"Just because Nancy Drew is gone, don't mean those other reporters stop digging up dirt. Paranoia, you know? So when Joe learns that they're looking for new offices, the whole thing falls into place. I had considered investing in an office park over in Culver, it's still menza/menza over there, some streets good, some not so good. But they got a rail system that goes right through the area, that was the real reason I had been interested in the first place, so I put a REIT together and buy the property and offer the magazine an unbelievable deal on a lease. They couldn't say no. Then I had it bugged so I could hear what was going on there every minute of every day. We hire a bunch of kids who do nothing but listen to that shit twenty-four seven—can you imagine? Would drive me crazy. Most of it's just bullshit like where to go to lunch and who's banging who but I got alerted whenever something relevant happened. HA! *Relevant!* Get it? Cost a small fortune but look, it paid off, right? I found out about Ruby's papers and made them disappear. It was just a coincidence that Cesar died when he did—*natural causes in case you're interested*—so when that Nicaragua guy crawls out of his cave, we fix that one, two, three. And I made sure that doctor wasn't gonna be a problem 'cause that stuff couldn't come out. Another piece that could tie the whole fuckin' thing together. Jesus. Can you imagine that? What bad luck."

At this point, one of the younger agents taking notes is forced to ask, "Can you explain that?" and Don looks at her like she has two heads.

"Are you paying attention? When were you born?"

"1990, why?"

"Kennedy. Robert. Was gonna open up the whole assassination thing about his brother—Kennedy. Jack. The whole thing from Cuba to Dallas to Mexico to DC. That could not happen. So that means Bobby isn't getting to the White House for which he was clearly heading. Had to be stopped. So we stop him in LA and that Arab takes the fall, the shmuck still doesn't know what hit him, and now everything is back in the bottle where it belongs. Hunky-dory. Until that doctor starts explaining what Ruby told him and well, you start pulling on that thread and it's—The whole thing unravels, everything gets exposed—us, the Texas fat cats, your favorite president, your guys . . . well, you people know that."

"I'm sorry, what comes unraveled?" she asks again.

"Hey, kid, go ask your boss. He'll fill you in."

––––––––

The October issue of *Relevant* features a tribute to the Malibu victims along with some behind-the-scenes photos which they are permitted to share with the public at this point. The issue sells out quickly.

Ira flies the editorial staff to New York for a special evening to commemorate George. They share their favorite funny and sweet George memories and toast October's success at the newsstand.

It's when Phoebe announces a staff promotion that the evening pivots to gallows humor. Luis Ruiz is now senior editor in charge of special features. And as she knew he would, Louie gets pelted with ribbing and teasing. One of the writers dubs him señor wenses—"the man pulling our strings," another recites a litany of Louie faux pas' from his days as an assistant.

A good time was had by all.

Phoebe and Ira share a cab back to the hotel and she confesses she's been working on resurrecting her personal life.

"I hope that doesn't shock you."

"It does, but in a good way," he says.

Now that she can shoulder Louie with more of the grind of getting a monthly out the door, she can almost see her way to having a regular life again.

"Best of luck with that, I mean that sincerely."

"Already stuck my toe in, went on a date."

"No way!"

"My first in years! It was fun!"

"That's why you look so good."

Although Brian Wilson has two ex-wives, a college-aged son, and a married daughter—plus a full-time, stressful career chasing bad guys—he still finds time to make a nuisance of himself.

"You'd think he'd have his hands full," she says.

"Brian Wilson huh, like the Beach Boys?"

Phoebe laughs. "No, the FBI guy who came to the office, the one I told you about, who broke the case. So, how's Malibu coming . . ."

"Hold on a sec. You're dating an FBI agent? Really? With all the men in California, that's who you pick to date? You better watch your step Pheebs. Those guys are . . ."

"Don't be ridiculous, he's a perfectly regular person, Ira. He's not Eliot Ness, some television character."

"If you say so. Still, I'd keep my guard up."

"Okay, thanks. So tell me about Malibu, how's the project going? Did you settle on one of those proposals?"

"I'm still so conflicted."

He tells her that he hired an engineer to analyze the ecological impact of each proposal, hoping one will stand out. And in the interim, installed a children's playground on the plateau, where the fountain was. He was tired of looking at the empty space.

"A shame to let it sit idle. I put in a few picnic tables and opened the gate and a couple of families drove up! My first customers! I gotta tell you, it was really fun to watch the kids run all over the place."

Halfway across the country, Joe is pushing his four-year-old on the swings in his backyard, keeping an eye on the burgers grilling, their new Sunday ritual.

This neighborhood's not as nice as his old one, there's no pool or tennis court, no chi-chi neighbors Tobeye needs to keep up with.

But there's no Uncle Donny either, snapping his fingers, expecting him to show up at a moment's notice, expecting him to do the dirty work.

His new life is so much better now, he stops to count his blessings. His family's safe, he's not looking over his shoulder every minute, and his new job is satisfying—using skills he trained for more than a decade ago.

The company he works for is converting an old shopping mall and his boss has Joe's next assignment already lined up. He finds the work both challenging and fun—he especially enjoys the collaboration, feeling part of a community.

Best yet, Tobeye is thrilled to be back teaching. She can't wait for the new semester to start.

Witness protection is working out as promised. Turns out that that Fed was good for his word.

———————

A couple of months later, Ira finally makes a decision on what to do with Malibu: he's doing nothing—nothing at all.

"The city approached me. There's so little undeveloped property left, so few public parks, they asked me to consider keeping it like it is. And it's already caught on, Pheebs, people are coming up on weekends. Last Sunday an ice cream truck came by. That clinched it—we're a park! Baxter Park!"

"Good for you," she says, loving the way Ira seemed to sparkle.

"I'm gonna expand it, put in a bunch more swings and slides. Maybe a sandbox and trampoline—the lawyers are looking into liability. And remember George's two tennis courts? I'm having them rebuilt. Better than ever."

"He'd love that."

She's glad she decided to forgo looking into Goodworks.

Brian had mentioned that Uncle Donny "spewed" about involvement in film finance and that one of his "competitors" used Hollywood investments to legitimize their operations.

It was an opening to an investigation that Phoebe had been putting off, the one Grace had said she should look into. She made a gut decision to table it, at least for now.

"It's the kids," Ira says. "I just love having them around, watching them run all over the place, laughing. It's like magic— I . . . I . . ." he sighs. "I probably won't have any of my own."

"Well, you never know, Ira," she says, thinking about herself. "But a park and a playground sound like a good call regardless."

"George would be okay with this, wouldn't he?"

"Of course he would! He'd love it. Baxter Park." She smiles.

"Yeah, that's what I thought."

Ira tells her about another decision he made, to stay on as president of Baxter Media.

"That's certainly what your brother wanted," Phoebe said.

But it didn't come easy. Ira doesn't like the corporate world, and while BMG is not particularly bureaucratic, there are still plenty of company meetings and reports and protocols—it's not his thing and he's never been good at it.

"That's just a small part," Phoebe says. "You'll be surrounded by talented, creative people who bring out the best in you, make you want to give your all. In fact, there's something you can do for us right now—kick off the thing."

"Oh yeah?"

"I'm getting flooded with requests to accept speaking engagements, be on panels—you know, that stuff. Now that we're on everyone's radar. I don't have the time and neither does my executive staff. But this is right up your alley, something you'd be great at."

"So what are you asking?"

"Be our outreach, our public persona. Spread the gospel, sell us to the world."

"I'm not sure . . ."

"You get to speak on college campuses and tell kids how important investigative journalism is to sustaining our democracy, how it makes for a rewarding career. You visit with the business community, tell them why they should spend their ad dollars with us, how they benefit from an association with *Relevant*. Like that."

Ira isn't sure that's the job description for the president of a large media conglomerate, but at least he knows he'd be comfortable doing it.

"For example, I was just asked to be the keynote speaker at the upcoming Writers Guild meeting, here in LA. And I'd like to do it—to get that kind of exposure, we might attract some talent, but I was going to decline because I don't have the time."

"What's the topic?" he asks.

"'Making the transition to online pain-free'—they'll be some other presenters."

He agrees to give it a shot. During Q&A, many questions are directed to him: How did *Relevant* expand circulation beyond city limits; how are they able to keep their top-tier stable of writers and editors from being poached? He answers masterfully, really in his element, and charms the pants off the Writers Guild audience.

Phoebe smiles thinking how pleased George would be, how Ira is making *Relevant* and the whole Baxter Media Group look so good. Cast as their ambassador-at-large seems to be working for Ira as well.

"*Ike*." She smiles to herself, still thinking about George.

While they're packing up, Phoebe is approached by a young attendee who tells her he had worked at *George* magazine before it ceased operation. He had been very close with John Kennedy Jr.—in fact, claimed to be his protégé.

He mentions that *George* had many of the same attributes as *Relevant* and Phoebe gets ready to hear him ask for a job.

But he wants to talk about John's untimely death instead.

"Let's grab a coffee," she says. "I've got a few minutes."

"I never believed the story about John being a brash and inexperienced pilot. That's just not who he was. He was a very conservative guy, if anything, annoyingly detailed-oriented. Always double-checking everything." He shakes his head. "He was pretty nerdy. Drove us crazy with nitpicking. The picture the media painted was of somebody else entirely."

"So—what are you saying, you don't think it was an accident?"

"I don't know, but the investigation into the crash felt rushed to me. Like when you are trying to support a going-in theory, you find the evidence that just reinforces it. I was hoping someone with a strong motivation to find the truth—somebody 'neutral'— would look into it. Like you, like *Relevant*."

———————

She decides to pitch the idea to Ira on the drive back, even though it isn't fully formed; she doesn't often get one-on-one time and she doesn't want to waste it.

"Look, Louie has a lot of the same qualities as Joan—as good a researcher, maybe even better. You can lean on him for everything. And you'll love working with him, I promise. Think about it. This could be a very important story for us, it's right in our zone. And you'll get back to writing again. Besides being our ambassador. Nice job, by the way."

"Okay, give me a second to process."

"Think of the contribution you'd be making. Plus, you'll get to know the *Relevant* folks, really know them, work with them, see their talent. That's a win for everybody. The more I think about it, the more it seems like this could be the piece that catapults us to the next level!"

Or leads to nothing, that's also a real possibility, he thinks. "Okay, you can stop selling 'cause I just bought," is what he says.

***

Louie is everything he's cracked up to be. He jumps into the assignment and, before the week is out, back with Ira discussing his progress.

"There's a lot here so I've been thinking how best to approach it. We could parcel out the research, have Claire's team help us out. I could take one category, you take another, we give Claire the rest."

"What do you mean by category?" Ira asks.

"Okay. So here's what I'm thinking: *Equipment failure.* That's pretty cut-and-dry, but what I'm hoping for is we find a pattern, something that's been overlooked in the past. Like maybe there are certain models—or certain manufacturers—that sustain a greater frequency of failure. I'm sure that's looked at by the industry and the FAA, but what does the public know about it?

Does the average flyer care what make or model of plane he'll be flying in before he books a trip? Should he care?"

"Does Boeing make small planes?" Ira asks only half-joking, "because I hate their 737s."

"They're at the top of the list. Boeing, Cessna, Airbus, Beechcraft . . . we need to look into all of them. You want to take this category? Wait, don't decide yet, here's another one—*Geography.* Plane crashes seem to happen more frequently in some areas of the world than others. So you've heard about the Bermuda Triangle . . ."

"Yeah, but not . . . ?"

"A location where the atmospheric pressure can disturb plane stability, throw it off course. There's been a lot of documentation over the years as well as disagreement about its very existence; it's super controversial. I'm looking forward to learning more about it, maybe I'll take this one? It's connected somewhat to the next category—*Weather.* Inexperienced pilots or those without the proper risk tolerance—or some combination of those things—can be taken down by a sudden change in the weather. The 'unexpected' is the most frequent explanation for small plane crashes. Even seasoned pilots confess to losing equilibrium in fog and bad weather. And this was the official determination of Kennedy's crash, taking him, his wife, Carolyn, and her twin sister, Lauren, into the Atlantic. You remember they had been on their way to Martha's Vineyard for a wedding."

"So tragic for the Kennedys and that other poor family!" Ira says.

"Yeah. So there's one more category, the last one: *Criminal intent.* So I don't know if you know this, but airplanes have been used as weapons since the twentieth century. I already started reading about it, it's been going on for years and I'm not talking about carrying bombs or anything war-related—the plane itself. It never happens here in the States, well, except for 9/11, but in other places, it's not uncommon during a regime change or for other nefarious reasons—used by groups who want to destabilize authority. Even the CIA admits to it—very reluctantly—outside the US, of course. And 'way, way back' in its past. They don't do this anymore. So they say. That guy Phoebe met from *George,* that's what he was alluding to. That was what he thought might have happened. It's a far-out possibility but you know, from what we've learned about investigating JFK's death, well, the Kennedys had a lot of enemies who didn't play by the rules—and John Jr. was part of that dynasty."

"Pretty intriguing stuff, Louie. I think I want to take this one," Ira says.

"I think you should. I'll take Weather and we'll give the other two to Claire."

———

Ira meets up with Phoebe at their status meeting a few days later.

"Has Louie briefed you on the John Jr. project? I'm not sure where we'll end up with this but I wanted to try something out on you, a working title. What do you think of *Flying Blind.*"

"You think pilots have trouble seeing where they're heading?"

"It's a double-entendre, Pheebs. The other meaning of flying blind—not knowing what is really going on—who is really pulling the levers."

"Whoa. Okay. Sure, if we can prove something."

"Well, we may not, like if it turns out to be simple pilot error or bad weather. But if it's something else . . ."

"Yeah, I get it. So tell me now how much you like working with Louie?"

Ira smiles. "Like you said. He's special. We're about to start digging in."

She smiles thinking about Ira and Louie together, huddled over a computer, brainstorming ideas. She's pretty proud of this arrangement. Maybe she even made the next Woodward and Bernstein? Wouldn't that be something!

"Actually. The more I think about it, *Flying Blind* . . . God, Ira, this could be huge. We'll really need to substantiate everything a thousand ways to Sunday. Seriously. Or this could bankrupt our credibility. Everything we've worked so hard to achieve up 'til now. But jeez, it could also get us to that prize that keeps eluding us."

She looks at the covers hanging on her wall. The ones from the Joan era and some from her own tenure. Their best issues to date.

"Wouldn't that be something," she says. "You and Louie write it, I publish it, the world reads it."

"And *Relevant* gets its Pulitzer," he says.

"And Joan was right all along," she says. "The world really does want to know."

"The pit bull," he laughs.

THE END

AUTHOR'S NOTE

Cover Story is fiction but its underlying premises are not. It was *not* a lone nut assassin who killed JFK.

The Warren Report is also fiction but its underlying premise is deceit. It was fabricated to protect the guilty and appease a worried public.

Let me convince you.

In a 1969 interview with Walter Cronkite, LBJ says, *on camera*, that the assassination "may have been a conspiracy." An astonished Cronkite then challenges him about the veracity of the Warren Commission report and Johnson continues to sow doubt on its conclusion: "I can't honestly say it wasn't a conspiracy."

This eye-opening interview can still be found on YouTube—search "Walter Cronkite, Lyndon Johnson, September 1969." The interview is prone to censorship and moves around, but I found it on: https://www.youtube.com/watch?v=h5psrZmT0tY. More astonishing is that CBS taped but never broadcast it.

YouTube has other revealing interviews.

From his hospital bed in Dallas, John Connally tells a reporter he was *"not struck"* by the same bullet that hit JFK and that he heard three rifle shots. This refutes the Warren Commission's one-shot "magic bullet" theory. Try: https://www.youtube.com/watch?v=SsIGlSFB7E4&t=958s.

Years later, the conclusion from the House Select Committee on Assassinations (1979) will also contradict the Warren Commission report; it states: JFK was probably killed as a result of a conspiracy.

Robert Kennedy was also doubtful of the veracity of the Warren Commission report. On the eve of his declaring a run for presidency, he told an aide: "If the American people knew how my brother really died, there'd be blood in the streets."

For some reason, the Warren Commission report is still cited as the definitive account of the assassination.

———

Here's a little-known story about Jack Ruby's preplanning role in Dallas.

The night before the murder of Lee Oswald, District Attorney Henry Wade held a conference to brief the press about his prisoner. He stated that Lee was likely a communist and a member of the Free Cuba Committee. Several voices called out to correct him; Oswald's group was actually called "Fair Play for Cuba." One of those helpful voices came from Jack Ruby, his voice and face are captured on video and in photos of the press briefing. Find it on YouTube: https://www.youtube.com/watch?v=xhckLcuEINg.

Why was Jack Ruby, a nightclub owner, included in a press briefing?

And how did Ruby know the correct name of Fair Play for Cuba—it was relatively obscure with no outpost in Dallas? In fact, the group had only one member outside of New York and that member was Lee Harvey Oswald. Ruby testified that he never met Oswald before shooting him.

———

How to think about JFK's assassination:

Many conspiracy theorists divide the "big event" into three buckets:

- Who planned it?
- Who executed it?
- Who covered it up?

Question #1: Who planned it? Who had a strong enough motive to kill JFK?

Answer: Kennedy had many enemies.

• Big Oil

In October of 1962, JFK altered loopholes in the Oil Depletion Allowance that would have raised taxes on prospectors and producers an additional $300 million a year. Clint Murchison, a millionaire Texas businessman, held a "pow-wow" with some of Texas's biggest oil executives and they decided this change was *unacceptable*. The night before the assassination, the oil men regrouped and LBJ dropped by, and according to his long-term girlfriend, Madeline Brown, Johnson left that night telling her: "After tomorrow, those goddamn Kennedys will never embarrass me again. That's no threat. That's a promise." Worth noting: LBJ revoked the change to the Oil Depletion Allowance after Kennedy's death.

• Federal Reserve Bankers

With Executive Order #11110, JFK had plans to issue a new currency, one that was *not* backed by the Fed Reserve Bank but rather by silver. After his death, LBJ made sure that #11110 was never enacted.

• Intelligence Community

JFK had inherited a Cuba problem. Eisenhower/Nixon initiated "Operation Mongoose" to eliminate Castro and JFK brought it into crisis mode with the Bay of Pigs and Missile Crisis. Kennedy blamed the CIA for trying to maneuver him into war with Cuba/Russia. He famously said he would splinter the CIA into "a thousand pieces and scatter it to the wind."

• The Military Industrial Complex

JFK's National Security Action, NSAM #263, issued October 5, 1963, was going to start bringing home forces from Vietnam. Four days after his assassination, LBJ rescinded the order.

- **The Mafia**

  The Mob had a host of reasons to dislike the Kennedys:
    - o   Jack was unable or unwilling to solve the Castro problem and they were losing a ton of business in Cuba.
    - o   Jack's brother Robert, then attorney general, was working to clean up gambling and put several of them on trial, some in jail.
    - o   And finally, several researches have said the Mafia helped Jack's father, Joe Kennedy, get JFK elected and this was not the payback they were told to expect.

- **LBJ**

  JFK would not be taking LBJ with him on his second run for president. Johnson's aides Billie Sol Estes and Bobby Baker warned Lyndon that he was being dropped from the ticket. Worth noting that both these men later spent time in jail.

  JFK also intended to replace J. Edgar Hoover (Lyndon's closest friend) when he turned seventy—then, the mandatory retirement age. Once president, Lyndon would extend Hoover's tenure to "lifetime."

  As Robert Caro noted: "The crucial thing with Lyndon and the Kennedys was his relationship with Robert. There was real hatred there."

- **Lee Harvey Oswald**

  He had no motive. He anecdotally expressed admiration for the president.

Question #2: Who executed it? Who could pull off a complex assassination?
- Top elements of the US national security apparatus, like the CIA, with experience in assassinating other leaders of nations.
- Top echelon of the military.
- Other intelligence operations: France and Israel have been noted by conspiracy theorists.

- The criminal underworld: the Mafia, the Outfit, and the anti-Castro Cubans.

One theory: There were several sharp-shooter teams on site that day. Organized by the CIA. Lisa Pease's book suggests that Howard Hughes, through surrogates, funded the entire operation.

Question #3: Who covered it up?
- The Warren Commission
- US major media outlets
- The FBI

LBJ needed to convince the American people that the assassination was not a communist-inspired event, and that they were safe.

The Warren Commission quickly concluded that Lee Oswald acted alone, that Jack Ruby acted alone, and that there was no conspiracy and no cover-up. Every major media outlet of the day supported its findings.

Who made up the Warren Commission?

Johnson appointed six men to work alongside Chief Justice Earl Warren, who led the commission. As Warren was busy running the Supreme Court, much of the commission's activity was actually steered by another commissioner, Allen Dulles.

Members of the commission included:
- Lawyer John McCloy
- House Representative Gerald Ford
- Senator Richard Russell
- House Representative Hale Boggs
- Senator John Sherman Cooper
- and Allen Dulles, ex-CIA

Note: Dulles had been fired by JFK after the Bay of Pigs.

Warren, McCloy, Ford, and Dulles all supported the single bullet theory ("magic bullet") while Russell, Boggs, and Cooper were unconvinced it was one lone gunman.

The CIA would later admit they withheld information from the Warren Commission.

Recall John Connally at the hospital? He later recounts his story in order to jibe with the Warren Commission's one bullet theory.

- **Mainstream Media**

Not one major US media outlet challenged the Warren Commission report. This was a few years before the appearance of Woodward/Bernstein—imagine if they had been around to dig into the assassination the way they exposed Watergate?

- **The role of the FBI, led by J. Edgar Hoover**

After a tussle in a hospital hallway, the FBI wrestled Kennedy's dead body out of Parkland Hospital where Dr. McClelland had already begun his autopsy. The body was flown to Bethesda Naval Hospital creating a serious breach of Texas jurisdiction and medical protocol.

McClelland's autopsy report differed significantly from that of Bethesda's—the direction of the killing shot, for example.

The FBI's involvement extends to misplacing or tampering with evidence, intimidating witnesses, and secreting files. They chose to carefully edit what evidence the Commission was able to review:

- o Many eyewitnesses differed on the number of shots heard, and some reported seeing shooters on the grassy knoll and a freeway overpass. Most were ignored.
- o Some evidence that went missing, such as the Zapruder film, would later reappear to support the Commission's conclusions.
- o And despite claims that they were unaware of Oswald before the assassination, both the FBI and the CIA had files on Oswald beginning *before* the shooting:
  - The FBI had assigned him file number S179.
  - The CIA maintained a 201 personnel file on Oswald and family.

- **More about the CIA's involvement**
    - o   E. Howard Hunt, a key player in the Watergate break-in (thirty-three months in prison), was an ex-CIA agent who admitted *on tape* that he was a benchwarmer in the *"Big Event."* He also implicated LBJ. His son, Saint John Hunt, recorded this deathbed confession. You can find it on YouTube.
    - o   Frank Sturgis, another Watergate plumber and ex-CIA agent, told a magazine reporter, "We killed Kennedy." Watch Jack Anderson's 1988 interview with Sturgis and Hunt on their roles in the JFK assassination, in Watergate, and their attempted assassinations of Fidel Castro. It's found on YouTube.

- **Freedom of Information**

The cover-up is still in place. In 2012, the National Archives reversed an earlier decision to declassify all records for the fiftieth anniversary of the assassination, including 1,171 CIA documents from that period. While many have been released under President Biden, some are still delayed.

Stay tuned.

ACKNOWLEDGMENTS

This novel is dedicated to Jane Beale, whose ideas, words, and friendship contributed mightily to this book. *Cover Story* also owes a debt of gratitude to its early readers, some of whom read the manuscript several times, and whose feedback helped fine-tune it: Lori Christensen, Lee Cohen, Michele Aronesty, Lori Golden, Nancy Palley, Robin Schletter.

In 2008, I went down a rabbit hole of research from which I am yet to ascend, beginning with the ten-part documentary, *The Men Who Killed Kennedy* by Nigel Turner; his documentary was instrumental to *Cover Story*'s background as were the insights and learnings from Cyril Wecht, Ed Tatro, David Scheim, Patrick Nolan, Gorden Goldstein, Jefferson Morely, Phil Nelson, and Anthony Summers—experts in their fields.

Special thanks go to Lynn Scherr, Bob Hennelly, Anne Kenny, the team at BookLogix, and to my husband, Larry, whose support and love have always meant the most to me.

ABOUT THE AUTHOR

In 2008, I awoke thinking the fiftieth anniversary of the assassination of JFK was fast approaching and we (or I) still didn't know what happened back then. The *real* story. In particular, how did Jack Ruby walk into a Dallas police station and shoot Lee Harvey Oswald in front of everyone? Who was he? And what was that murder really about?

It ignited something in me that turned into a burning desire to learn the truth and expose it. I am a writer and so I started digging into the extensive—and sometimes conflicting—research on that period and spent several years piecing it together. Then I picked up a pen.

The result was an off-Broadway play titled *Witnessed by the World*, which I wrote with my good friend and co-writer Jane Beale, and a few years after that (and nearly three hundred pages later) this book, *Cover Story: Still Deadly after All These Years*.

If you enjoyed what you've read, you may also enjoy the next book in the series, *Blood in the Street*. That story tells the tale of Sirhan Sirhan, now-dubbed America's first Arab terrorist, and a small, committed legal team's effort to get him released from prison. Was he really just a disgruntled Palestinian who took out his frustration on the likely next president of America? Or was the murder of Robert Kennedy a necessary step by the forces that brought down his brother? Think about it: How could they allow Bobby to ascend to office when he swore he'd get to the bottom of JFK's murder?